Jacob
BLACK INC.

LISA MARIE RICE

OLIVERHEBERBOOKS

Published by Oliver-Heber Books

Cover art by Dar Albert at Wicked Smart Designs

0 9 8 7 6 5 4 3 2 1

 Formatted with Vellum

CHAPTER
One

BEND, OREGON

The rain washed away the tears, but they kept coming. Alex Hethering took a hand off the handlebars of her bike to keep swiping at her face as she pedaled wildly toward the trailer park. She needed to see her best friend, Jake Simpson. Needed to see him like she needed to breathe.

A car passed by her, the left front wheel slipping into a huge pothole and showering her with mud and freezing water. Alex glanced sharply at the driver, a woman. She had wide eyes and a hand clamped over her mouth. Mo Harris, the librarian, who was horrified that she'd splashed water on Alex, today of all days. Mo was slowing down. Probably wanting to pull over, get out and apologize. Offer to drive her home.

No. Alex didn't need apologies and the muddy freezing water didn't make her feel worse than she already did. Nothing could. She'd just buried her parents. The freezing cold water was warm compared to how she felt inside.

And home wasn't home any more, anyway.

Mo had come to a full stop and Alex knew she couldn't deal with Mo's apologies, with that soft look of pity. She'd had nothing but gentle pity, warm hugs and low voices whispering condolences these past two days. None of it helped and she didn't want any more, so she put her head down, long drenched strands of hair hanging in front of her face, and pedaled harder, faster.

Maybe if she pedaled hard enough, she'd leave her sorrows behind.

No, she wouldn't leave her sorrows behind, nothing could do that. But if she pedaled harder, then she could get to Jake faster, so she didn't let up. The trailer park was five miles outside of town. She'd only driven by it in her parents' car, her father pressing on the accelerator a little as they drove by. Everyone did. It had a horrible feel to it, like the air itself was infected. Jake lived there with his father and no mother, and he'd never invited her to his place.

Instead, he spent most afternoons at her house. Except it wasn't going to be her house for very much longer. The day after her parents died in the crash, with the shades drawn and neighbors quietly coming and going, depositing vast amounts of food on the kitchen counters that she could never eat, not in a million years, Mr. McKenzie from the bank stopped by. He'd been one of those vague adult figures that she'd seen around all her life but had never given a moment's thought to.

He sat her down with an open laptop, opened her parents' current account and started talking. She couldn't understand a word he said. Something about mortgages and foreclosures. She wasn't too sure what a foreclosure was. Her dad had once talked about it when talking about a colleague and a shudder had gone through him. Alex got the feeling it was something horrible but far off, something that could never affect them. Something like those tropical diseases you got when you went to the Congo and puked your guts out, but you were okay if you didn't go to the Congo.

Certainly a foreclosure wasn't anything that could happen to the Hetherings. Her parents were special. Alex knew she should have considered her folks boring and reject them because a lot of her friends rejected their own parents. But her folks were great, really great. Her mom taught English in middle school and her dad taught high school biology and they were fun and understanding and kind. Good people.

Jake told her over and over what good people they were. Jake's father wasn't a good person. That much she got.

So yeah, her folks were fantastic, smart and good and solid. So 'foreclosure' wasn't a word that could ever apply to her family.

Except, well, it could.

Because—crazily, it turned out they didn't own their own home. That had completely escaped her. She knew every inch of her house, of the back yard. She knew the window that got stuck, the doors that creaked, the little damp spot on the ceiling of the living room that never got bigger or smaller. It was her *home*. Only, apparently not. It didn't belong to Mom and Dad, it belonged to the bank.

And the bank wanted it back.

Mom and Dad were gone. She still couldn't wrap her head around that. They were... gone. She'd buried them not an hour ago, both of them. No open casket because they'd been burned alive. So Alex didn't see them. It kept occurring to her that the two caskets with the flowers on top, side by side in the funeral home—whatever was inside them had nothing to do with her. Those weren't her folks inside. Couldn't be. Any minute now her mom would peep through the window and laugh. Her dad would tap her on the shoulder and say *come on hon, let's split. This place gives me the creeps.*

And they'd all leave because, yeah, the place gave her the creeps, too.

Only, her mom didn't peep through the window and her dad didn't tap her on the shoulder. Some guy was droning on and on, and Alex couldn't figure out what he was saying. Then it was over, and people were crowding around her, saying it was okay for her to cry only she couldn't, and then someone drove her to the cemetery where two holes waited in the ground and the caskets were lowered in. A colleague of her mom's told her to throw dirt over the casket and she obediently knelt and scrabbled with her hand. But there was only mud. She threw fistfuls of mud into the two holes and ran.

Ran all the way home. People called after her and she saw one of her mom's friends driving around looking for her, but Alex knew the town like the back of her hand. She ran home through back streets, grabbed her bike and lit out.

The cold rain beat on her head and shoulders and she shivered. Her teeth were chattering. She wanted Mom or Dad but they weren't there, and the next best thing was Jake.

Jake. Always there. He'd stopped Dean Morris from bullying her by knocking him out. Dean's father was a big shot and Jake had been suspended for a week. Alex and her folks had gone to the principal, but he said there was nothing he could do. It was unfair, but then Jake was a lost cause, he said. He'd failed two years and was two years older than the rest of the class. Later, Alex found out that he'd simply stopped going to school the year his mom died and he'd been held back another year.

So she'd made Jake her crusade, coaching him in math and chemistry and English, only he didn't really need coaching. He understood everything just fine the first time. What he needed was some decent food and a home.

He'd become like a brother to her, only not. She loved him like a brother, counted on him, needed him, but not really like a brother. She couldn't explain it. She only knew that the one person she had left in the world was him. That she was holding off on breaking down completely until she could be with him because she knew, deep down, that she could let her pain and grief go while she was with him. She could fall because he would catch her. She felt safe with him.

There it was, FAIRFIELD TRAILER PARK. A sad sign in faded letters, half askew, attached to two poles and a cross pole that acted like a gate. The striped bar of wood was permanently up, the gate forever open.

Alex braked just inside the trailer park. There was a dirt road, muddy and pot-holed, right in front of her. Further down the road she could see another road crossing it. Trailers were parked haphazardly, not respecting the lines of stones staking out lots.

Alex had no idea where Jake lived.

Every second of the funeral, she'd been expecting him. The day before, with all the people pouring into her house, she'd expected him. She'd looked up every time the door opened, sure that it would be him, but it never was.

The only thing she could think of was that he was sick. But it was hard to think of Jake as sick. He was so big and strong and tireless. Jake being sick just did not compute. Or that he hadn't heard about her folks.

That seemed impossible. The whole town was talking about it.

If he somehow was sick, she'd take care of him. She was good with sick people. She wanted to study medicine. If he hadn't heard about her folks, she'd tell him and then they'd cry together.

He loved her folks, too.

She rode her bike over the muddy track. The rain was like a waterfall now, coming down so hard it bounced off the ground, and it was hard to see. There weren't that many trailers. Inside of twenty minutes she'd seen them all. Some were boarded up and looked abandoned. Some looked abandoned even though there were signs of human habitation. Those were sadder than the empty ones.

Jake had never described his place, ever. Never spoke about his father. She didn't have a clue how to find him, which trailer was Jake's. They all looked equally awful. Finally, she put down the kick stand on the bike right in the middle of the forlorn, muddy intersection and got off.

"Jake!" she called. Her voice was hoarse and low. Probably no one could hear her over the drumming of the rain. She made a megaphone of her hands and yelled "Jake!" at the top of her lungs.

She turned around, yelling, in a full circle.

God, what would she do if Jake wasn't here? And if he wasn't here, where was he?

Her heart thumped painfully in her chest. He wasn't —? No, he couldn't be. God couldn't be that cruel, to take her parents *and* Jake away from her. Besides, Jake was so tough. Tall and big. Death wasn't going to get him any time soon.

That was her grief talking.

"Jake!"

It was pouring down now, soaking her to the skin. She was shivering uncontrollably. She hadn't eaten and hadn't slept in two days, and she could feel it now. Feel the effects of the shock, of the funeral.

"Jake!" Her voice broke on a sob and she stood under the rain, head bowed, rain soaking her to the skin.

"Shut the fuck up, bitch!"

She lifted her head, wiping the rain and tears from her eyes, looking around. It couldn't be someone talking to her. No one had ever called her bitch before. But it was the first sign of life in the trailer park. However rude the man was, maybe he knew Jake. Knew where he was.

She walked around until she saw a man standing on a ramshackle porch made of badly poured concrete with splintered wooden handrails attached to a rusted trailer home. It wasn't even on the road. She walked over, hand on her forehead, shielding her eyes from the rain.

He was dressed in filthy, torn jeans and a stained tank top. What she'd read once was called a 'wife beater'. He looked like a wife beater. He looked mean, mouth twisted in a nasty sneer. He was tall and big, including a big belly, and held a half-empty bottle of beer by the neck. There was dried blood on the side of his face.

"The fuck you want, girl?" he said, swaying.

Alex stopped well away from him. Even through her pain she recognized this was a man you didn't want physically near you. That was instinct talking because she'd never seen anyone like him in her life. "I'm looking for Jake Simpson. Do you know where he lives?"

He snorted. "That pussy? What you want with him,

girl? To fuck him?" Horribly, he clutched his crotch. "You need a man, not a no-good kid. Useless little snot."

A sudden chill shuddered through her. She stepped back and swallowed heavily because this was... this was Jake's father. Once you saw it, it was unmistakable. Jake was lean, his features sharp and this man was a blob, features hidden beneath blubber covered by black stubble, but he was definitely Jake's father. He was an awful and creepy and drunk version of Jake.

Oh Jake, she thought, her own sorrows forgotten for a moment. No wonder he never spoke of home or his father. The door to the trailer house was open, banging against the aluminum siding, and she could see inside. Could see filth and disorder in the few feet visible from the outside. A gust of wind brought a stench of beer and feces. She stepped back again. Just being here, just seeing this man made her feel even sadder.

But awful as the man was, maybe he knew where she could find Jake. She had to try. She needed Jake.

"Do you know where he is?"

"Gone." The man's face closed up like a fist, pinched and cruel, eyes squinting. "Fucker's gone. Leaving, he said. Good riddance to the little shit." He swayed forward and for a horrible second Alex thought he would step down the porch stairs and come after her, but he didn't. He turned around and slammed the door behind him. The door bounced back open, and she saw him inside, in profile, fat belly protruding over his belt, opening another beer. With the bottle to his mouth, watching her, he reached out and pulled the door closed.

Alex stood in the rain, looking at the door as if it could tell her where Jake was. She was weary beyond belief, exhausted, brought so low she had to stiffen her knees to remain upright. The temptation to drop where she was and howl her sorrow to the winds was enormous.

But she didn't. The torn cloth covering a grimy window twitched to the side and the man eyed her. He seemed to enjoy watching her in the rain. She'd never come across anyone like him in her life but something deep inside her, as old as humanity, told her he was the kind of man who enjoyed other people's pain. She'd rather die than give him pleasure.

Fucker's gone. Little shit. It had shocked her down to her bones to hear a man describe his son like that. Nobody in her life would be remotely capable of describing their child in those terms.

She'd barely taken in his words when he spoke them, but as she rode back into town, she thought about them. Gone. Leaving. He'd said Jake was leaving. She was so tired she could barely think straight. But leaving could only mean one thing for Jake—a bus. The bus station was on the other side of town and buses left all the time. Chances were she'd never get there in time if he were catching a bus.

But she had to try, *had* to. There was a lump in her throat, something huge and hard and dangerous and she had to see Jake, had to see if he could help her cry her way past it. Otherwise she'd choke to death on it.

Determined, she put her head down and pedaled wildly toward the bus station, thankful when she got back onto decent asphalt and didn't have to avoid rain-filled potholes. She was drenched when she slid off her bike at the bus station. A drumbeat of panic had started in her, as if she were in a race to the death. She let her bike drop to the ground in a clatter and ran to the covered area where buses took off. It smelled of fuel and exhaust fumes. Two buses were boarding and she ran to the lines, looking for Jake. He was distinctive. Very few men were as tall and broad-shouldered as Jake but there was no one even vaguely like him in either line. A nearby bus closed its doors with a hydraulic hiss.

Alex ran to the bus, frantically scanning the windows for his familiar face and oh my God! *There he was!*

"Jake!" she screamed, pounding on the side of the bus right under his window. "Jake!"

He was looking straight ahead, long black hair hiding a chunk of his face, but she'd know his profile anywhere. He had to hear her. Though his face stayed stubbornly facing forward, she thought she saw his eyes slide to the right, to her.

"Jake, look at me!" Her voice broke as she continued pounding. Why wasn't he responding? What was *wrong?* *"Look at me!"*

Jake's face was like stone.

Later, much later, years later, when she was able to

think of that moment without a sharp stab of pain to the heart, she could look back on herself as she must have seemed to Jake. A drowned rat, dripping water, tears tracking down her face. Mad with grief. Just beginning to understand his betrayal, but refusing to accept it.

She was beating on the bus with the side of her fist as if she could break through the sheet metal. Up high, the passengers were starting to turn their heads to look at her, the crazy girl. The bus started up and she could feel the vibrations of the engine through her fist. She beat harder, crying, screaming. With a tired sigh, the bus rolled forward, going slow as it pulled out of the lot. Alex stayed with it as long as she could, right up to where it stopped at the exit of the depot for a second, in the driving rain, while the driver checked for oncoming traffic. Alex was beating the side of the bus frantically by then, jumping up to reach the window right by Jake when she could. He didn't even blink.

Another soft exhausted sigh of brakes being released and the bus pulled out. She put her splayed hand on the filthy side of the bus, her last connection with Jake, and felt the steel moving beneath her palm as the bus moved forward onto the main road, gathering speed.

She stood by the side of the road until the bus disappeared from sight, hugging herself, ice filling her. She cried until she had no more tears left, until her voice left her, until her stomach hurt and knees gave out and she sagged to the ground, head bent over her knees so the rain fell on the back of her head. She cried until she could barely breathe, then cried some more.

It felt like she stayed there forever, on her knees in the mud. Finally, finally, she could cry no more. No one had approached her, somehow understanding that her grief and pain could not be relieved. No one helped her, no one spoke to her. When she stood, it had turned dark. She biked slowly back to her home, which was no longer her home, and where no one waited for her.

CHAPTER
Two

ATLANTA, GEORGIA—EIGHTEEN YEARS LATER

D r. Alexandra Hethering stopped at the two-story entrance to the black cube of a building on manicured grounds like an alien artefact, and looked at the black marble slab to the side of the sliding doors. It was plain, with only four words etched in gold. *Black Inc. Security. Worldwide.*

Yes, this was the place, no question. She'd heard that though the building was black on the outside, inside it was filled with light. Some groundbreaking technology that was almost magic. But walking through the huge glass doors was more than taking a step inside a building. It would cut her life in two. It could ruin her career. It could ruin a colleague's career. It could save millions of lives.

There was no way to know which it would be and only one way to go—forward.

She put out a hand but the right-hand glass pane slid automatically to one side and she walked through... into bright light. Alex looked around at the immense lobby. It was true. Who knew how it worked, but the impenetrable black glass covering the cube did indeed let light through, exactly as if the panes were transparent.

She'd been told that Black Inc. was super high tech. Well, yes. Two seconds into the building and she was already impressed and she worked in cutting edge science. This was good because if she was right in her fears, if what was terrifying her was actually true, she was going to need all the high-tech smarts the company could bring to bear.

She'd marshalled all her facts so she shouldn't be nervous, but she was. There was something so imposing about this space—immense, pristine, orderly and powerful. Everyone walked with purpose. Of course, she herself worked for an organization that was immense, pristine, orderly and very powerful. And where everyone walked with purpose. The Centers for Disease Control. The world's foremost public health institute and she was an integral, respected part of it. But at the CDC she knew exactly what she was doing. Here, she was going to detail data points that might or might not have anything to do with each other and, in the mix, there was a missing man who might not be missing and the potential for vast devastation on an unprecedented scale.

Or not.

Alex hated not knowing things. Her scientific reports were perfect, each fact proven over and over again. That was how science worked. Here she was on such murky ground and she felt it shake beneath her feet.

But—her colleague Elias Field was missing. And Elias was working on something that, in the wrong hands, could be a powerful bioterror weapon.

If she was wrong, though, she'd blow her career up and smear a good man's name.

She stood just past the huge, impressive glass doors and took in a deep, calming breath. Black Inc. even smelled good—clean and fresh with hints of lemon and mint. She checked her watch. The appointment was in ten minutes' time and she didn't want to be late.

There were five receptionists behind a Perspex and black marble horseshoe counter that looked like a free form sculpture, three women and two men. Attractive, well-dressed, efficient-looking. She approached the first free receptionist. One of the men. He looked up and smiled. The smile actually looked genuine, which surprised her.

In her job, she'd been to plenty of important companies and the bigger the company, in her experience, the snootier the receptionists. Black Inc. was one of the most successful security companies in the world, so she should be looking at the top of the guy's head as he continued working at his computer, but no. His head shot up and he smiled at her.

"May I help you?"

Alex nodded. "Yes. Dr. Alexandra Hethering for Mr. Dylan Gardner. I have a ten o'clock appointment." She'd only made the appointment half an hour ago and had been surprised that someone from BI could see her so soon.

The receptionist briefly checked his computer screen and smiled again. "Yes indeed, Dr. Hethering. Mr.

Gardner is expecting you. Here, put this on your jacket, it will get you through security. Just walk through the gates, take one of the elevators and go up to the 8th floor. There the badge will guide you."

He handed her a credit card sized badge with her photograph—taken as she walked through the door a minute ago—and name written in gold script on the black badge. There was no lanyard. She held it in her hand for a moment, wondering what to do with it. The receptionist smiled. "Just hold it against your jacket."

She did. To her amazement the badge stuck.

"It won't harm the material of your suit, don't worry, Dr. Hethering."

Her hand opened and closed on the handle of her briefcase, trying to offload some anxiety. The fate of the world might just hang in the balance of what she did in the next hour. Millions of lives could be saved or lost. A mussed suit jacket was the least of her worries. "No problem. Thank you."

He nodded and indicated security.

She walked straight through the metal detector with no issues and rode the elevator to the 8th floor. The elevator was as sumptuous as the rest of the building—reflective, polished steel plates with black marble inserts. She watched herself in the steel plates which might as well have been mirrors. There was no sign of her inner turmoil. She looked neat and pulled together. Except for the fact that she wasn't wearing her lab coat, she could be on her way to a routine day in the lab.

Good.

Maybe some of the confidence she felt on the job could translate into what she was doing here, because she was skating on thin ice. The last time she'd felt so shaky and lost had been the day she buried her parents and her best friend—the boy she'd loved—abandoned her. She flashed for a second on her last image of Jake—face stonily turned forward, refusing even to acknowledge her. She'd had no idea why he was rejecting her.

She still didn't.

A familiar jab to the heart accompanied that thought. *Stop that!* she told herself sharply, as she'd done a billion times before. Her parents were dead and buried and wherever they were, they were at peace. Jake was who knew where, and a dim memory. Well, he wasn't a dim memory, but he should be. God knew enough time had gone by. She'd done well, worked hard, was a respected scientist. She was no longer a grief-stricken girl aching for her boyfriend in her hour of need.

The sharp pain in her heart eased immediately. It had taken years to get to this point. Now the thought of him was like a small burr that couldn't be dislodged but did no damage. No biggie.

She was unsettled. That was why she was channeling her 16-year-old self. Something strange, potentially very dangerous, was happening and she didn't have the tools to handle it herself. Which was why she was here, in this sumptuous black building. She worked with the best of the best in her field and now when she was out of her depth, she was turning to the best of the best in this field.

The metallic sound of a drop of water falling and the elevator doors opened. She faced another black marble wall with *8th floor* etched in gold italic script.

"Turn right, four doors down, Room 84, Dylan Gardner," a voice said from her chest. The badge. Four doors down she stopped, raised her fist and a small speaker with superb sound clicked on.

"Please come in, Dr. Hethering," a pleasant male baritone said, and the door slid open.

A tall, broad-shouldered man stood up, walked around his desk and met her halfway across the enormous room. "Please sit, Doctor." He led her to a comfortable chair and sat down again behind his desk. "So, Dr. Hethering, how can we help you?"

Alex forced herself to breath normally. "It's—it's a complex situation, Mr. Gardner—"

"Dylan," he said.

She nodded. "Dylan. Please call me Alex. As I was saying, what has brought me here is very complex, and I must be assured of the confidentiality of what I tell you."

He placed two big hands in front of him on the shiny desktop. "You can rest assured, Alex. This is a security company, and we don't use that term lightly. I'm assuming you want to keep this confidential even from the CDC."

Very clever of them and of him to know who she worked for. She'd only called half an hour ago, giving only her name and they probably had a complete dossier on her, including her college grades. "Yes, even from the CDC, though it is a work-related issue."

"We have experience working with the CDC. But we guarantee absolute confidentiality in all our dealings with clients."

Yes, they had experience with the CDC, that was why she was here. Black Inc. was the go-to company of choice when CDC teams had to operate in difficult places. Last month ten BI men had led a CDC team into Sierra Leone where there were reports of a mutated form of Marburg. In the area, two rebel armies and government forces who were as cruel and ferocious as the rebels, were fighting each other. And the CDC team had to operate in bulky hazmat suits. Her friend Karen Morris had led the team and she told Alex that the BI men had been outstanding, getting them in and out safely. "In and out, slicker'n shit through a goose," Karen, who had grown up in Texas, had said admiringly. "Not even a spider bite."

Black Inc. had been in the city for as long as she had worked at the CDC. As a matter of fact, the day she started her job, the company had broken ground on this building, which had gone up in record time.

Alex swallowed. "The, um, issue revolves around a colleague, Elias Field. If you looked me up, you know that I work in the Office of Infectious Diseases, the OID, and Dr. Field does, too."

Dylan nodded. "And you two are friends? Enemies?"

"Friends," she answered quickly. "Not enemies." She looked him in the eyes. "Colleagues."

He nodded slightly and she knew he'd received the message loud and clear. This was not a jealous mistress asking a topflight security company to skulk around corners to find out if her lover was cheating on her.

Though Elias *had* made it abundantly clear that he wouldn't mind upgrading their relationship to friends with benefits. Alex didn't do casual sex. Actually, she didn't do much sex at all, she thought with an inward sigh.

"Pickier'n hell," was the way Karen put it. *Trust issues*, was the way the psychotherapist she'd once consulted put it. Either way, her love life was pathetic, and since she wasn't ugly or nasty and she showered daily, she could only assume that she was indeed picky and had deep trust issues.

She'd trusted one person with her heart and that was Jake. And then he'd run away, and she'd never given her heart again. God, that sounded so pathetic. She was tired and stressed, that was why Jake re-emerged in her head, like a dragon that slept until it felt the princess was vulnerable. Then it flew up, scaly wings unfurling, ready to attack.

Focus.

Dylan Gardner cocked his head, eyes steady. "So, Alex. Tell me your problem and Black Inc. will do its best to find a solution."

It would, too. She only hoped she had enough money. The mission to Sierra Leone had cost the CDC a cool five million dollars. Of course, what she needed wouldn't cost that much, but whatever it cost, it would be worth it to establish the truth. She didn't trust any other company and if hiring them wiped out her savings, so be it. She could always earn more.

She bent to retrieve a flash drive from her briefcase and placed it on the desktop. "In there are some files that I downloaded from Elias's work computer. He had secondary security and he gave me his password, so I felt justified in downloading his hard disk. He's been missing for three days ,and I fear that something has happened to him. And above and beyond that, I fear that there might be some national security issues, given what he was working on."

Dylan frowned and picked up the flash drive. He was about to fit it to his own computer when his cell sounded. The opening bars of the *Game of Thrones* music. "I would ordinarily ignore that when with a client, but that's top brass calling and I have to take it," he apologized.

Alex nodded. When the top brass called, you answered. "Sure."

He tapped his ear and said, "What is it? I'm with a—" and stopped abruptly. He sat up straight in his chair as if an invisible general had entered the room. She wouldn't be surprised if under the desk he clicked his heels. "Yes," he said and nodded. And then, to her surprise, his eyes shot to her, as if someone at the top levels of Black Inc. were talking about *her*. "Yes," Dylan said. "Yes. Right away. Understood."

Oh *God*. Was she already in trouble at the CDC? She hadn't even done anything yet. All her suspicions were firmly locked in her head. She hadn't talked with anyone. The only person she could possibly tell was Karen, and she was attending a seminar on Viral Epidemiology in Kyoto. As far as Alex knew, the CDC couldn't read minds. Yet.

Dylan tapped his ear again and stood. Startled, Alex rose too. Was the interview already over? Was something wrong? Was she going to be escorted out by security? And if so, what was she going to do then? Because Elias was still missing and her suspicions—which had robbed her of sleep these past three nights—were still there, too.

"Dr. Hethering. Alex. I am going to have to ask you to come with me." Dylan picked up her briefcase with one hand and took her elbow with another. He allowed her to pick up the flash drive, then started walking. He didn't hurt her in any way, but it was clear that she was either going to go with him or leave her elbow behind. They walked in silence out into the hallway where he took an elevator at the end of the hall that required a security pass to access. She stared at their reflections in the mirror-like steel panels as the elevator took them *up*. She looked frozen and he looked tense. He checked the time on his expensive wristwatch. They were on a schedule?

"Am I being kidnapped?" Alex asked politely.

He shot her a glance out of the corner of his eyes. "No ma'am. Alex. If anything, you are getting the white glove treatment. *Super* white glove treatment." He lifted his eyes to the steel panel set in the roof of the elevator cabin. "Orders from on high."

There was no chance to ask questions because the

elevator opened out onto the roof where a luxury heli-copter was waiting, its rotors already slowly spinning. Dylan hurried her to the helicopter, helped her up the steps and secured her seat belt himself. The noise was deafening until he fit a helmet over her head and Muzak Mozart filled her ears. Probably chosen by an algorithm and polled by a focus group to soothe helicopter passen-gers, bring their heart rates down. The pilot looked back at Dylan, who'd pulled on his own helmet. Dylan raised his thumb and the pilot immediately lifted off the roof and banked steeply. She sank in her seat a little. The seat was luxurious, buttery dark-brown leather, immensely comfortable.

Alex tapped on Dylan's shoulder, pointed to her helmet and mouthed *turn on the microphone*. She needed to speak with him, *right now*. He sketched a smile and shrugged his broad shoulders. He was trying to convey that he didn't understand, or that there were no mics. Which was nonsense. Alex had ridden in plenty of helicopters, though none as luxurious as this one—and they all had an on-board comms system.

Her tap was harder this time, on any other person borderline painful, but she knew he wouldn't be feeling any pain. The shoulder she tapped was iron hard, incon-gruous under that expensive suit. She narrowed her eyes and he gave a sigh which she couldn't hear but which was clear nonetheless. The Muzak stopped and she heard, "Yes, Dr. Hethering?"

So we were back to formality, were we?

She was feeling a touch of panic, but she would rather die than let that show. "I repeat—am I being kidnapped, *Mister* Gardner? And I will tell you right now I do not appreciate being shanghaied and strong-armed into a helicopter."

This time she could hear the sigh. "No, doctor. You are not being kidnapped or shanghaied and I certainly haven't strong-armed you. I was given strict instructions to take you to the very top of the company and to make sure that you were very comfortable every step of the way. And it was also made abundantly clear that my job depends on your being comfortable and well cared for until we arrive."

"Arrive where?"

"Sorry," he said and gave an apologetic shrug.

"*What?*"

"I have my orders, doctor. You are to be given the white glove treatment, as I said. You will have the full attention of the top brass and every resource that this company has will be brought to bear on your problem."

"You don't even know what my problem is." Alex refrained from shouting only by immense self-control.

"No, doctor, I do not. And right now, it would be pointless for you to tell me your issues because I won't be dealing with them. My job right now is to get you to headquarters safely and in as much comfort as I can marshal for you." He reached to the side, opening a cupboard. Turning around, he held a flute half filled with bubbly liquid. "Champagne? It's excellent. Bollinger 2022."

Alex opened her mouth and shut it. Screaming and

railing at the man would do no good. He was looking at her with an open, resigned expression and something told her that if she slapped him, he'd take it silently. So, venting her anger and frustration on him wasn't worth it. Would be cruel, even. She herself operated under a strict hierarchy and she knew how that worked. You did what you were told. And if you didn't, you paid the consequences. She was willing to pay the consequences for herself, but she had no reason to cause this man harm. He was just following orders.

So she folded her arms and looked out the window at the scenery flying by beneath them and ignored him. Out of the corner of her eyes she saw him gulping the champagne down as if it were a fortifying medicine.

There was silence until they reached their destination, a small airfield she'd never seen before. The pilot set the helicopter down near a sleek private jet that had the steps down and a smiling pilot waiting at the top of them.

A jet. Unease returned. It was a corporate jet. She didn't recognize the make, but she recognized the type. The top officers of the CDC flew around in them and they had a considerable range. At the end of her flight, she could find herself in Miami or Chicago or Seattle—or even out of the country—with no say in any of it.

Dylan stood, took off his helmet, and held a big hand out to her. She hesitated.

"Nothing will happen to you, Alex," he said gently. "You have my word." So we were back to Alex, were we? She looked into his light-brown eyes and saw nothing but a steady kindness. Sighing, she took off her helmet, unbuckled the belt and stood with his help. He carried her briefcase for her. When they were on the tarmac, she turned to him.

"If wherever we're going requires an overnight stay, I have nothing with me."

His gaze was sober, steady. "Don't worry about it. You'll get whatever you need, no question. My advice? Don't worry about anything. Whatever your problem is, it's over now."

Well, what an odd thing to say.

The pilot at the top of the stairs greeted her with a smile, took her briefcase from Dylan's hands, and ushered her to another buttery-soft leather seat. The jet sat twelve people and it had a level of luxury that made the helicopter look like a covered wagon.

"Dr. Hethering, my name is Sam Lawrence and I will be your pilot today. Is there anything I can do to make you comfortable? Drinks are in the cabinet over there and if you want tea or coffee there are thermoses in the galley, together with turkey and veggie wraps and fresh fruit. Our estimated flying time is just under four hours."

"Flying time to *where*, Mr. Lawrence?" she asked.

He opened his mouth, looked at Dylan who shook his head almost imperceptibly, then simply smiled and nodded at her and went back to the cockpit.

She turned angrily to Dylan, who held his big hands up. "Headquarters. That's where we're going."

"Headquarters of *what*?" Alex nearly shouted the words.

"Black Inc. And that's all I can say, sorry. So sit back and enjoy the ride. I'd suggest a cup of tea if you don't want alcohol. We have a blend of Indian chai that comes in fresh from Mumbai every week. It's absolutely delicious."

Headquarters of Black Inc. Alex realized she had no idea where headquarters was. She knew they had offices in several US cities and offices abroad. For all she knew, headquarters was in London or Paris, though London and Paris were much more than four hours' flying time away.

She could of course take out her cell or open her laptop and Google it. But it would be clear what she was doing, and she didn't want to give Dylan the satisfaction.

And wherever headquarters was, there was nothing she could do now. They had started taxiing and the pilot announced take off in the next three minutes. She obviously wasn't going to get Dylan to tell her anything more, she couldn't throw herself out of the plane, she might as well relax. Or at least go over the details of the problem once more in her head so that, wherever she was being taken, she could give the best possible account of her troubles.

The small plane leaped into the air and the suburbs of Atlanta soon gave way to green hills and lush farmland. Alex leaned her head against the window and ordered her thoughts, went over the mental bullet points, once more reviewed the explanations of the abstruse technical issues for a layman. And wondered who she'd be explaining them to.

Man was she tired. The past three nights had been sleepless as she worried about Elias being missing and then began to worry about the implications of a missing Elias, as worst-case scenarios danced in her head. She'd gone over and over everything and, until there was new information or until she'd consulted with someone outside the CDC, it was pointless obsessing. Her eye lids grew heavy as she watched the almost hypnotic flow of fields beneath the plane.

For years, whenever she travelled somewhere, whenever she flew, she wondered if she was close to where Jake was. It angered her and saddened her that he was always so close to her thoughts, but there wasn't much she could do about it. Though nowadays, at times, whole days went by without her thinking about him, thoughts of Jake were still a constant in her life. She knew the physiology of the brain and knew that thinking the same thoughts over and over actually caused a change in the morphology of the brain. It tunneled permanent neural pathways. Somewhere inside her head was a sulcus named Jake and it was probably permanent by now.

She watched the roads, towns, and farms slide by. Did he live down there? Was she flying over his house without knowing it? Was he—was he *right there* and she didn't know? Was he married, with a family? Was he a good husband, a good father to someone?

Usually, thoughts of Jake were accompanied by a shot

of white-hot anger, but right now, she was too tired to be angry. And what was always beneath the anger was a vast lake of melancholy. The sadness of not knowing what had happened to him. It was almost more painful than the thought of her parents.

She'd come to terms with their deaths. They'd lived good lives that had been cut short. They'd been great parents, they'd loved each other and they'd loved her and they were dead. But Jake? Where was he? Was he sick? Homeless? Jake had had the worst possible start to life. When he disappeared, he hadn't even finished high school. What kind of jobs were available to men like that? Almost zero, or the kind where you could barely survive. One thing she knew, he wouldn't end up on drugs. He hated drugs and never drank. Having seen his father, she understood why.

Oh Jake, she thought. He'd been such an important part of her life. She'd seen him every day. He'd given her her first kiss and instead of a tentative shy first-kiss meeting of lips it had been overwhelming. Every hormone in her body had been kick-started and surged into life.

It was, hands down, looking back, the best kiss she'd ever had, even eighteen years later.

She had built him up into a myth in her head, she knew that. Her best friend told her that, her therapist had told her that. Endless self-help books told her that. But somehow the space he occupied in her head had never been filled by anyone, ever again.

She was so tired. Her eyes closed as she thought—

Where are you, Jake? A tear seeped out from beneath her closed eyelids, and she wiped it away angrily. A silk cushion had been placed in the seat next to her and without opening her eyes, she placed it between the seat back and the window, settled her head more comfortably and let her thoughts drift...

A gentle hand nudged her shoulder and she sat up, disoriented. She followed the hand up to a face, but the name eluded her.

"Wake up, Sleeping Beauty, we've landed."

Dylan. Dylan Gardner. He handed her a glass of water with a slice of lemon in it. The glass was cut crystal. Of course. She shook her head no. At this point it was a principle not to accept anything. The pilot came out of the cockpit and opened the plane's door, letting in heat and the smell of aviation fuel. Rollup steps were already there.

"Okay." Dylan picked up her briefcase and gestured with his hand to the door. "Last stage of our journey."

He clearly wasn't going to say journey to where and, out of stubbornness, Alex refused to ask again. He wasn't going to answer her anyway and she'd just make a fool of herself. She hesitated at the top of the stairs. At the bottom, waiting for her, was a limo. The real deal. The limo came with a driver in livery, down to the cap, holding the back door open for her. She descended slowly, Dylan right behind her. The limo driver seated her in the luxurious back as if she were the Queen of England, closing the door with that vault-like whump only insanely expensive cars had, then slid behind the wheel.

"Just a few minutes, ma'am," he said cheerfully over his shoulder, sounding exactly like Michael Caine. "I'll have you at the helo in no time."

Dylan held up his big hand again. *Don't ask.* No, she wasn't going to ask. And if she was being kidnapped it was in the most lavish, luxurious style possible. The limo glided forward with an almost inaudible purr and Dylan's hand hovered over an array of crystal decanters. "Would you like anything to drink?"

She sighed. "No." Then, remembering her manners, "Thank you."

He sighed too, reluctantly removing his hand from the decanters. "Remember, I have strict orders to make sure you are comfortable and treated well. I wish you'd drink something, anything. Even water. At least I could report that you accepted a drink. There are probably sandwiches somewhere in the limo."

Michael Caine's voice sounded from a speaker. "Indeed ma'am. Not just sandwiches. There is fresh fruit and a cheese platter in the mini fridge. But with all due respect, we have arrived."

The limo slid to a smooth stop and Alex saw another helicopter. Again, the driver helped her out of the limo as if she were a queen and she walked up the stairs of the helo, looking around. Again, it was an airfield, one she'd never seen before and there was no signage to show where they were. The sun was high in the sky and it was hot, almost hotter than Atlanta. Were they in Texas? Arizona? Southern Florida? How many hot places were there four hours from Atlanta? No, they were out west. Her watch said three, but the sun was at noon. At least three hours west, in another time zone. Wherever she was, she was many hours away from home. Wherever she was, she was probably going to have to stay the night.

Wherever she was, only a handful of people knew her location. But whoever was guiding this whole thing seemed to mean her no harm. She certainly couldn't complain about her treatment. Clearly the police were not going to find her headless body by the roadside.

Maybe.

She didn't even try talking to Dylan through the headset as the luxury helicopter took off. After fifteen minutes of anonymous small houses and rundown industrial lots, water was visible on the horizon, to the west, and then it was clear where she was.

San Diego.

The helicopter swung out over the ocean then swung east, and she saw San Diego's beautiful skyline on the horizon.

The helicopter was fast. They crossed toward land and soon she could see the landmark buildings so close to the water they were reflected upside down in the ocean. A black cube with a distinctive profile came up and the helicopter swung around, hovered for a moment, then settled gently on the roof.

Two men and a woman stood to one side on the roof, watching the helicopter as it landed. They shielded their eyes against the rotor wash but otherwise stood at attention as if they were soldiers. The two men were at the steps the instant the skids touched the surface of the roof. The pilot didn't cut the engines. One man stood sentry at the bottom of the steps, one leaped into the helicopter, looking as if he were prepared to carry her down. They were her age, maybe mid-thirties, very fit and, though dressed casually in sports jackets and chinos, they looked hard and tough.

"We'll take it from here, mate," the man who'd entered the helicopter shouted in pure Aussie to Dylan. The man took her briefcase in one hand and with the other guided her down the three stairs as if she would trip at any moment. On the rooftop, Alex turned and saw Dylan give her a two-fingered salute off his forehead and mouthed *good luck* as the helicopter rose. She bowed her head, then turned again at the feel of a hand at her back. The two men flanked her as they approached the woman standing near an elevator door.

"Dr. Hethering," the woman said, shouting over the noise of the helicopter taking off. She held out her hand. "It's a pleasure to meet you. My name is Catherine Macy. I am Mr. Black's personal assistant."

Whoa. Personal assistant to the big man himself. Jacob Black, reclusive genius billionaire founder of Black Inc. Good God. Was she here to meet *him?* Could that possibly be good? He was immensely powerful. In turning to Black Inc. for help, she'd wanted to keep the lowest possible profile. Jacob Black spoke with presidents and heads of state. A prickle of unease went down her back, but she kept her face calm. No sense giving anything away.

Alex shook the woman's hand firmly. "Pleased to meet you, Ms. Macy."

"Catherine is fine. This way please."

She was in her forties, tall and elegant, looking efficient and no nonsense. Well, Jacob Black wouldn't have an idiot as his personal assistant. Catherine Macy pointed at the open doors of the elevator and they all walked in, the two men flanking her. Alex, Catherine and the two men who looked very much the way bodyguards looked in movies. They acted that way, too, keeping close to her, attention diffuse but still focused on her. They moved together as a unit, with her in the middle.

It occurred to her that maybe they weren't bodyguards after all but... guards. She shifted her weight on her heels and they instantly turned to her. For just a split second, but still. There was no doubt that if she changed her mind and wanted to cancel the upcoming meeting and simply walk away... she couldn't. Certainly not if they had orders to stop her.

So.

She was in an elevator with two hard men who looked and acted like guards. True, there was another woman here. Presumably Catherine Macy meant her no harm, but she was an employee of Black Inc. and if Black Inc. meant Alex harm, Catherine would not come riding to her rescue.

Alex had come to Black Inc. because it had experience with the CDC. But what if—what if her most horrid, darkest suspicions were true? And the CDC was involved? What if someone at the CDC was involved in bioterrorism? What if that person thought she knew more than she did? What if that someone wanted to simply... get rid of her? Wipe out a problem before it even began? More than fifteen thousand people worked in the CDC and everyone she knew who worked there was smart and hard-working and dedicated to making the world a safer place. But if even one or two were bad apples, that was enough to present an enormous risk, given what they knew.

And what had Alex done? She'd run right into the arms of a tough, secretive security company, famous for getting the job done no matter what. A company that made tens of millions of dollars a year from the CDC.

Right now, right this instant, no one in the world outside Black Inc. knew where she was. The two men in the elevator with her looked perfectly capable of violence. They were lean and hard, and both were unmistakably armed, slight bulges under their jackets. Both faces were set and hard. Their hands were open and loose and the way they stood, balanced lightly on their feet, showed that they could spring into action at any second. Both men were much taller and much bigger than she was. The six-week self-defense course she'd taken five years ago would be no use to her against them.

If they meant her harm, she was as good as dead. If they had been given orders to somehow contain her, dispose of her, well then she was lost.

Catherine was looking up with that bored thousand-yard stare of someone in an elevator, closed off entirely. No help from that quarter.

A musical note sounded and the elevator doors opened.

The two men and Catherine stepped immediately to the side and looked at her. Only one way to go—forward. They were in a large corridor with travertine floors and white walls with a few pieces of very good art on the walls. They turned a corner onto a two-story reception area so large you could have planted corn there. Sleek, modern, elegant. Almost extravagant in its use of office space.

Alex moved forward slowly, very aware that she might have made a huge and deadly mistake. Every nerve tingled and she felt her shoulder muscles tensing at the thought of the two armed men behind her, watching her back.

At the end of the space was an enormous glass wall with an inset door and beyond that a large metal door with black marble around it.

Catherine Macy had kept pace with her for a few steps, but then she halted, tilting her head toward Alex and pointing with a manicured nail. "Walk through the glass doors to the door beyond. It will open automatically. He's waiting for you."

Alex swallowed. "Who's waiting for me?"

"Mr. Black."

Oh God. The big man himself. This was either very good or... very bad. She ran through what she knew about Jacob Black in her head. It wasn't much. His company was famous, but he kept to the shadows. He was never personally in the news. He was never profiled. She knew nothing of the man himself beyond the fact that he was ex-military and very rich and powerful.

She found it hard to continue. Her feet felt nailed to the travertine floor. As long as she was out here, she felt—well, not safe. Not really. But Catherine and the two guards would find it hard to hurt her out here. Wouldn't they? Walking through those doors into Jacob Black's office felt dangerous. Felt like something she shouldn't do.

"Dr. Hethering?" Catherine asked as Alex hesitated. She took in a deep breath. There were no good options here. The two men had taken what looked like sentry stations at either side the elevator, standing with legs apart, hands loose at their sides, watching her carefully.

A flash of fierce regret shot through her. What had she been thinking, going to Black Inc.? Maybe she wasn't saving Elias, herself, the CDC, the world. Maybe she had stepped into a nest of scorpions, boiling up from a hole she hadn't seen. All of a sudden, she fiercely wanted to escape. To get back into that elevator, go down to what was surely another amazing lobby, catch a cab to the airport, take the first flight out of San Diego and make her way home again. Get back to her calm, pretty apartment and...

And then what?

Nothing had changed. Elias was still missing and her fears were still there, sharp and dark and fanged. She was still desperate. She was still worried sick.

There was no going back, not really.

Alex swallowed, sketched a smile and walked forward. She could feel Catherine and the two men staring at her back. She forced herself to walk steadily onward, through the glass door and to the big metal door. At the last minute, it slid open and she walked through without breaking her stride. The door slid closed at her back.

She was in the largest office she'd ever seen. Not even the Director of the CDC had an office like this. She'd been in the offices of the CEOs of huge pharmaceutical corporations and she'd never seen anything like this.

Here, too, like everything else in Black Inc., everything was sleek and modern and high-tech. One wall was covered in thin monitors, there was a conference table bigger than the conference table in the Situation Room of the White House, which she'd been in, a fully equipped kitchen and a living room suite for informal talks. One thing was missing. Though she knew, because she'd read it somewhere, that Jacob Black had been a highly decorated soldier, there was no glory wall. No citations, no photos of him with important politicians or generals, no medals. Nothing. Not one of those items that so fed the egos of important men. It could have been any man's office, if that man ran one of the largest security corporations in the world and was one of the richest men in the world.

The office faced west and it was the moment when the setting sun's lambent rays hit the eyes full on. The moment she hated when driving west at sunset. The ocean reflected the sunlight and was mirror-bright.

Alex held up a hand to shield her eyes. The man sitting behind the desk touched something and the window instantly polarized.

She dropped her hand as he stood up. Though the sun didn't hurt her eyes anymore, he was hard to see as anything more than an outline. He was very tall and had extremely broad shoulders. His suit was expensive but it looked like a costume on a man built like that. A rich man's costume over a fighter's body.

"Alex," he said. His voice was deep, rich.

Shock immobilized her. It was a voice she didn't know but it reverberated through her, scaring her. What was wrong with her? It felt like a hand was squeezing her heart so hard it would burst. Her knees shook. She couldn't breathe.

"Alex," that dark voice said again, and all the breath rushed out of her body. She gasped for air, the sound loud in the huge silent room. Every muscle was frozen.

She didn't know the man, how could she react like that to his voice? It was as if his voice had cast a dark spell over her that paralyzed her. Turned her to stone.

He moved out from behind the desk, walked toward her. His face came into the light and she was so unsettled that at first she couldn't make sense of his features. His face was made of dark, hard slabs. Dark hair. Dark eyes, deeply tanned skin. One side of his face was badly scarred, both knife and burn scars. He wasn't good-looking—no man who was as scarred as he was, who looked as dangerous as he did, could be considered good-looking—but he was compelling, fiercely focused on her. His dark eyes burned and he moved to her, coming right into her personal space.

Her limbs wouldn't work. She didn't have the strength to take a step back.

He was so close she had to tilt her head back to see his face. He reached out a huge hand, cupped the back of her neck and she was shocked at the reaction her skin had to his touch. Heat shimmered over her, like she was burning up. She still couldn't breathe.

Who was he? She didn't know him, so why was she reacting so strongly to him?

"Alex," he said again, and it was as if the spell he held her under shattered.

"*You!*" she gasped.

CHAPTER
Three

"You!" Alex gasped, face suddenly ice-white.

A shudder ran through her. And then, horribly, her knees buckled. Jacob Black reached out and caught Alex before she could fall. The idea of Alex falling, hurting herself... he couldn't go there. Alex would never fall if he was anywhere near her. He'd catch her, always.

He'd had time to get used to the idea of Alex with him, in his office. She'd flown halfway across the country to get to him and in these past hours waiting for her, that was all he could think of. Alex. Coming to him. At last.

He had two big contracts to go over, one with the Pentagon. He had after-reports to read, particularly one of a dangerous mission to Kazakhstan. It had ended well because Black Inc. only hired the best, but it had been a close thing.

Jacob was a highly focused man. Focus had taken him from a trailer park in Central Oregon where he lived with a violent and crazy drunk, into the Navy, into Special Forces and then to the creation of a big, powerful company. Focus was the very bedrock of his personality.

But, oh God, right now, that focus was lost, gone up in smoke.

When he'd realized that Alex had walked through the doors of the Atlanta building, he'd set things in motion immediately and then hadn't been able to think of anything all day except for the fact that Alex was being brought to him. Every minute brought her closer to him. He'd been in a fever of anticipation. He couldn't even go over what he was going to say to her because his mind slid right off that shiny central thought. That *Alex was coming*. He couldn't think of anything else.

Unable to get beyond the thought of being with her again after eighteen years, it hadn't occurred to him what a shock it would be for her.

It had crossed his mind that she wouldn't recognize him. Would barely remember him. In that scenario, he was a guy she knew in high school who had disappeared out of her life when she was still a kid and she hadn't spared him a thought since.

That seemed possible. Likely, even. Why not?

So much had happened to her. She'd gone east to live with a great-aunt, excelled in the last year of high school there and went to Harvard on a full scholarship. Did a two-year stint in Geneva at the WHO. Worked for a big biotech corporation before being head hunted for the CDC. Eighteen years was a long time. They were both different people. He'd been prepared to remind her who he was when they met again.

He hadn't calculated that meeting him would knock her out.

Hell no.

She was in mild shock, there was no mistaking it. God knows he'd seen men and women in shock before. He'd seen people fucking die of shock.

Not him and not his teammates, though. No way. SEAL training beat shock right out of you. The only way he'd ever go into shock would be to lose upward of two liters of blood. Their training prepared them to deal with more or less anything life could throw at them, even if it was thrown at warp speed. Hell, the SERE course alone was based on delivering nonstop shocks to the trainees.

But Alex was trained in science, not soldiering.

Alex's pupils were dilated. Her fair skin had lost every trace of color as the blood rushed to her core. It was the animal response of someone who thought she was in mortal danger. Shock was the body's response to what it perceived as danger.

Jake was definitely dangerous, though not to her. Not in any way. God no. Shit, he'd die to keep her safe. But she couldn't know that. Her mind had simply blanked from overload.

Jake carried her to the couch, carefully laid her down. He sometimes slept over in his office. The closet held five suits, ten shirts, underwear, shoes, boots, several changes of combat gear, workout clothes. And a blanket.

"Be right back," he murmured and two seconds later he draped a blanket around her, tucking in the sides.

Alex was trembling. Kneeling next to her, Jake wrapped his arms around her, transferring his body heat. His head dropped next to hers as he tightened his hold, drawing in a deep breath, nose next to her cheek. He'd never smelled anything as good as her skin.

She smelled different. Jake had always been sensitive to smell. His father's trailer had nauseated him, reeking of shit and sweat and beer. He'd spent as little time there as possible. He'd stayed over at the Hethering's for as long as they would put up with him.

Alex had always smelled good, like a young girl. She used a strawberry shampoo and soap and she always smelled of strawberries and freshness.

Now she smelled like a woman. Something elusive and rich that bypassed his brain entirely and went straight to his groin. He hardened in a rush, absolutely unstoppable.

She was moving slowly, the way you do in shock. She was trying to sit up, awkwardly. Her hands on his shoulders trembled.

Jake pulled away, placed one hand between her shoulders and pushed her upright. He was still kneeling, face on a par with hers. Her pupils were dilated and she shuddered when she took in a breath.

No. No. These were the physical reactions of pain. Deep and devastating pain.

It hurt him to see her like this, so lost and wounded. He was a hardass, always had been to everyone, with the exception of Alex and her folks, who had somehow reached beyond the hard face he showed the rest of the world. But seeing Alex like this hurt him, physically. There was a sharp thudding pain right behind his breastbone where his heart would be if he had one.

He knew the basics of her life since they'd parted. He'd kept tabs on her as much as he could when he was Stateside, which wasn't often. From an innocent, shy, smart young girl, she'd become a well-known and respected scientist, a woman of substance, whose papers were often the keynote lectures at international conferences.

So, yeah, the young girl was gone.

But one thing couldn't have changed—her heart. She'd had the kindest heart of anyone he'd ever met. Her parents had been good people, too, but he didn't know them the way he knew Alex. His entire childhood and adolescence had been among the cruel and the brutal and the crazy, his father at the top of the miserable heap. Meeting Alex had been like meeting a member of another species, a better one than his.

The idea of her suffering because of him was... he couldn't even go there. He folded himself around her to try to control her shivering.

His heart was thudding so hard he was surprised it didn't knock its way out of his chest. He couldn't remember the last time his heart raced. Certainly it never raced in battle. He was cool, even cold, under fire. Now? Now sweat was trickling down his back and he had to work to keep his hands steady.

"Jake," she whispered hoarsely. She fought to free her hand and laid it against his cheek. Her eyes searched his, seeking something. Fuck yes. Whatever she wanted, he wanted to give it to her.

"It's me, honey." The words came out scratchy. His mouth was dry as dust.

"Jake. How—"

He kissed her.

It came out of nowhere, like a desert storm, overwhelming and unstoppable. He'd spent the entire day rehearsing what he was going to say to her. How to explain his absence, how to show her he hadn't stopped thinking of her for eighteen long years. And most importantly, how whatever problem she had was now his. He'd gone over the words in his head, gamed his body language, thought through possible scenarios.

He'd been prepared for everything. For anger, bewilderment, distrust. Indifference, even. But nothing had prepared him for his reaction to being an inch from her, holding her, his heart thudding in his chest at her nearness. He couldn't have known that the world would disappear, with only Alex left in it.

She was so freaking beautiful she nearly burned his eyes.

There was nothing in him that could resist her. He couldn't speak. He had no words for her, only a flash of heat so intense it burned him up as he held her head and kissed her.

A hot wind was in his head and it caught fire when his

lips touched hers. He held her head in his hands, cradling it. Her skin was cold to the touch but her mouth was hot and her taste was rich. Not a girl anymore. A woman. She tasted like hot spice and sex and he was going to stay here, kissing her, forever.

He dove straight into the deep kiss, fusing his mouth with hers, tongue tasting hers, so close he was breathing through her. He lifted just enough to take in a deep breath for both of them, then slanted his head to kiss her from another angle, tongue stroking deeply.

He couldn't get close enough, fast enough.

All that soft, pale skin. He wanted to touch every inch of it, every inch of *her*. Something in the way...

The buttons of her blouse opened like magic under his fingers. The buttons were small and his hands were large, but there was no force on earth that could stop him from touching her. The blouse gaped open and he smoothed his hand over her breasts, the skin as silky as the bra. He cupped her breast and she was just as perfect as he'd imagined she'd be. More.

He slid his fingers under the silk bra and ran his thumb over her nipple. They both shivered and Alex cried out, his mouth muffling the noise.

"Alex," he whispered and she jolted.

Jake lifted his head, surprised. It felt like she'd received an electric shock and not in a good way. Wrenching her shoulders from his grasp, she sat up straight on the couch, ramming her fingers into her hair as if trying to keep her head from exploding.

"Alex," Jake said again, voice low. He could see her pulse pounding along her throat.

She shoved him, hard, and scrambled up, awkward, as if her limbs wouldn't obey her. For a moment, her legs were tangled in the blanket he'd used to cover her and he reached out a hand to steady her.

She stiffened. "Don't touch me!" she cried, voice unsteady.

He withdrew his hand and waited, still on one knee, looking up at her. Alex was standing, staring down at him in horror.

Jake understood body language very well, particularly the language of dominance. It was a language he'd spoken forever. He'd always been tall and muscular. Strong. He could overwhelm almost all civilians by height and body stance alone. No question he could intimidate a slender woman.

But he didn't want to do that. He didn't want to dominate Alex, so he stayed down on one knee. It was the position a gunman took when setting up a shot, but she wouldn't know that. All she'd know was that he was kneeling before her, almost like a subject.

He stayed down and met her eyes.

Electricity crackled between them. He had to remind himself to breathe.

"It's okay, Alex," he murmured.

"Okay? *Okay?*" Her voice rose, shaky and breathless. "How can you say it's okay? Do you—do you know where we are?"

Yes, he knew where they were. He remained silent. She was really smart. She'd figure it out once the clouds cleared in her head.

"We're in Jacob Black's office! I don't know how you got here—I don't even know how *I* got here, but you…" her voice trailed off as she took a couple of steps back.

He watched her as she put it together.

"Oh my God." She covered her mouth with a hand and reached out with another to grab a chair for balance. Jake rose slowly, staying a couple of feet away. He was much taller than she was and he didn't want to intimidate her. "You," she breathed.

He dipped his head once. "Yes. Me."

Her eyes went round and she stared without blinking for a minute, two.

"You're… Jacob Black." The words were low, hesitant. As if she expected him to contradict her.

He didn't move.

She blinked, baffled. "How can you be Jacob Black?"

Fair enough. Start from the easiest question. "I changed my name legally when I joined the navy. I didn't want to share a name with my father. If I could have changed my DNA I would have. I couldn't. But at least I could get rid of his name. Black was my mother's maiden name."

Her beautiful eyes turned shiny, then welled with tears. Jake moved forward, instinctively, and she backed up a sharp step, hands out to ward him off. "No! Don't come closer!"

A tear rolled down her cheek. Jake gritted his teeth, clenched his hands. Alex crying and him not taking her in his arms seemed alien, unnatural. It didn't compute in his head. And it was fucking hard keeping his distance. The only thing that allowed him to do it was the panic in her voice and the pain in her face.

She drew in a sharp breath, breath wheezing in her lungs. Her shoulders slumped. She hastily buttoned up her blouse.

"I looked for you," she said simply. "Everywhere. Every city I was in, I checked for Jake Simpson. Found a few, too, only they weren't you. I checked on the internet, constantly. I couldn't help myself and hated myself for doing it, but it was a compulsion. Over the years, with every single new social media site, I'd check for your name. Facebook, LinkedIn, Meetup, GooglePlus, Skype, Tik Tok, Twitter then X. All of them. I even tried the dating sites, until I had to get off, for my sanity. For years and years. Until about ten years ago, any city I travelled to, I looked your name up in the phone book, first thing on entering the hotel room. Half the time I didn't even take my coat off until I'd looked for you in the white pages, while they existed. Thought I was looking for Jake Simpson. Stupid me." She gave a harsh laugh and wiped at her eyes. "All this time I was looking for the wrong person. It was my guilty secret, no one knew except for a shrink I once saw, to see if I could get rid of the compulsion."

Jake's heart turned over in his chest. *She'd been thinking of him!* She hadn't forgotten him! Yes!

Her face tightened with anger, eyes narrowed until only sky blue glints were visible. "Is that a *smile* on your face, Jake? Or should I call you Jacob? Is this a *joke* to you? Does it amuse you that I kept looking for you all these years?"

"God no!" He stepped forward, not wanting her to think that for one second, but stopped when she scrambled backward. As if she were afraid of him.

She was wounded, he could see that. As if she'd taken a bullet to a vital organ. He couldn't stand it, knowing she was hurting, but he didn't know what to do. If he could, he'd fast forward to when all this was over, after he'd explained, after she'd understood, when it was all okay.

He had no idea how he'd get from here to there, but he would. It was the most important mission of his life. He and his SEAL team had stopped two coups, rescued a kidnapped ambassador, taken down an ISIS cell. There'd been an old saying about SEALs dating back to DEVGRU days in Vietnam. That few SEALs lived past thirty. Jake had. He'd done hard, nearly impossible things since he walked through the recruitment office door eighteen years ago. So there was no question that he would get Alex to trust him and then share her life with him. He didn't know how, but he would get there.

That might be far in the future, but it was coming. It had to. Because she was never leaving his side again.

Right now, though, she was in pain and she was angry. Worse—she was in trouble. Nobody came to Black Inc. because things were fucking fantastic. They came to him because they were in deep shit, because something dangerous and nasty was going down. The kind of things Black Inc. saw on a daily basis often led to death and destruction.

Alex. In trouble. It made his bones weak, just the thought of it. Instinctively he held out his hand for her. She flinched and shuddered.

"Don't touch me, Jake. Or rather, *Jacob*." The slight hysteria in her voice was gone. She stood straighter, face blank, voice calm and remote. Completely in control. "I don't want you to touch me."

Jake was a problem solver, but he didn't see a way out of this. Not now, at any rate.

He let his hands drop to his sides, kept perfectly still. "You came to me, hon..."

He swallowed the word. *Honey*. He'd been about to say honey. He wanted to be free to say it all. Honey, sweetheart, darling. Love.

That wasn't love he was seeing in her eyes, however. He'd have to take this one hard step at a time.

"You came to me because you have a problem and I'm good at problem solving. My company is good at problem solving. So why don't we set all of this to one side and deal with whatever it is that's wrong?"

"Wait a minute." Alex's eyes narrowed. "Are you handling me?"

"No." He looked her straight in the eyes. He was a brilliant liar and could pass any polygraph. Any SEAL could, but he was particularly good at lying. It was why he'd been able to stay undercover for so long.

He wasn't lying now. He wasn't handling her, he wasn't trying to diffuse her anger. She had every reason to be mad at him, to distrust him. She'd learn to trust him again, though. He'd spend the rest of his life working on it if he had to. But right now, she had a problem and he wanted to help her. Had to help her. Everything else he was working on suddenly became secondary in importance. Alex's problem was top priority.

She stood still, searching his eyes. She could look all she wanted but all she'd see was his resolve.

A sigh. "If I didn't have this... issue. If I weren't so worried... I'd walk right out of here and you would never see me again. Trust me on this."

She meant every word. He bowed his head, keeping his eyes on hers. "Understood."

Silence. She was still studying him openly.

It didn't make him uncomfortable. She had every right.

He knew what she was seeing. She was seeing a man far removed from the tall, too-thin, rawboned youngster she'd watched pull out of a bus station a lifetime ago. The Navy had given him the tools to dominate the physical world and his business had given him so much money he dominated the social world.

The boy she knew dressed in rags he could never keep clean, no matter how hard he tried. Now he was wearing about twenty thousand bucks' worth of clothes and five-hundred-dollar boots. He knew he was well dressed not because he knew how to pick clothes, or because he had a fashion sense, but because he had a tailor with an unlimited budget to make suits and shirts for him. The tailor's only instructions were: nothing trendy, top quality. The tailor knew what he was doing because any time Jake walked into a room, he knew he was the best dressed man there. He himself didn't give a shit, but dressing well was a metric in the world he lived in now, so just as he aced Hell Week, he aced this, too.

He wasn't the kid she'd known. Every line of his body should have told her that. He'd changed in every way there was, except one. She couldn't know what was in his heart, that a corner of it hadn't changed. Every single thing about him was different except for that—the part of him that belonged and would always belong to Alex.

Finally, she sighed and he understood that whatever problem she had trumped her anger. It must be a very serious problem and fuck, that worried him.

"Do you want to sit down and tell me what's wrong?" Jake indicated the couch. He never used the couch and armchairs for clients, only friends and employees. But sitting behind his big desk when talking to Alex seemed obscene. He wanted her within touching distance even if he couldn't touch her.

Yet.

With a sharp glance at him, she sat in one of the armchairs and he sat down on the couch, at right angles.

She was still pale. He pressed a button on the small marble-topped side table and when the intercom light blinked on, he turned to Alex. "Coffee? Tea?" Though he knew the answer.

"Tea." She hesitated then huffed out a breath. "Thank you."

Bingo. She was still the best-mannered person he had ever met. She was angry at him, but it went against her grain not to thank him.

"Tea," he said, knowing Catherine would arrange it. "Earl Gray, milk, sugar. The usual for me." He'd helped a Colombian businessman get back his daughter who'd been kidnapped by one of the cartels. Besides doubling Jake's fee, the businessman vowed to send shipments of the finest coffee on earth for the rest of Jake's natural life. So, it would be coffee for him.

She said nothing but glanced at him sharply. Earl Gray had always been her favorite tea and she took it with milk and sugar. What? Did she think he'd forget? No way. He remembered everything about her. He remembered every conversation they'd ever had. Every moment spent with her.

Every time he had sex with a woman, he had to forcibly eject Alex out of his head.

So, yeah. He knew what kind of tea she liked.

She was sitting stiffly in the chair, back ramrod straight, looking everywhere but at him. She was biting her lips not to ask him how he'd gone from Bend to this. It had been a long hard road and he'd answer anything she asked, but she wasn't asking.

Patience. Patience was the hidden virtue of the warrior

and Jake had it in spades. They were going to have the rest of their lives to talk about it. For now, he wanted her to be at ease and he wanted to hear about a problem so bad she had to come to Black Inc.

Nobody came to him unless they had big, big trouble.

A discreet knock and Kevin from reception came in with a large tray, put it down on the coffee table and quietly left.

Alex seemed to barely notice. She was fixated on the floor, deep in thought.

Jake cleared his throat, gestured at the tray. There was a teapot, coffee pot, a cup and saucer and a mug. Milk and sugar doohickies, cubes, whatever they were called. "Do you want me to pour?" he asked, hoping she'd say no.

Alex gave a slight start as she came to herself. She looked up at him briefly, light blue eyes flashing almost silver. "No, of course not. I can pour my own tea."

Thank you, God. Jake was sure he'd do something wrong. He wasn't afraid of spilling boiling liquid on her. He could never do that. No, his hands were steady. It was just that it seemed tea people had all these fucking rules and he never understood them. Coffee people just wanted their coffee and didn't have a ritual. He poured himself a cup, black, and sipped as she fussed.

Milk first. Then she checked inside the tea pot and seemed to be satisfied that there wasn't a bag but loose leaves, poured herself a cup, gently stirred in some sugar. He'd finished his cup by the time she took her first sip.

Luckily, tea people were calmed by their tea. Alex sat

back in the chair holding the cup and looked him full in the face for the first time in several minutes.

"Do you want to tell me about it?" he asked quietly.

"No," she replied. "I don't want to tell you about it at all, but I have to. I've gone around this over and over in my head and I need to put this in someone's hands. I wouldn't have chosen you, but here you are."

He nodded. Yes, here he was.

She took another sip then leaned forward to place the cup on the table. Jake leaned forward, too. He knew he wasn't showing any signs of impatience, but they both knew it was time.

Alex's eyes searched his. For a second, Jake was distracted. God, she was still so fucking beautiful. More than before. He drank in all the details—the curve of her cheek, those incredibly thick eyelashes, the long white neck...

But the whites of her eyes were bloodshot and the skin under her eyes looked bruised. She hadn't been sleeping well and it showed.

She drew in a deep breath. "First of all, I need to know whether any contract we sign contains a confidentiality clause. What I have to talk about is serious. If I am wrong, a good man's name and reputation will be shot. But there are also national security implications as well. I need to know that what we discuss will be confidential."

There was no question of signing a contract. Every resource of Black Inc. was at her disposal and would be forevermore. He met her searching gaze. "Not one word of what is said in here will be repeated to anyone you don't want knowing." He meant every word and she saw that.

Alex nodded. "Okay. I've tried to put together a cohesive narration of my concerns and I think the best thing to do is to tell you things in chronological order."

"Start at the beginning. Always a wise choice," he said and she glanced at him sharply, to see whether he was being ironic. He wasn't. He'd given hundreds of debriefs and it always worked best when you started at the beginning and went on from there.

"Okay." She clenched her hands together so tightly the knuckles whitened. Jake would have given anything for the right to put his hand over hers. His hand itched to cover hers. But she wouldn't allow it. "At the beginning. A colleague of mine is missing. He's been missing for three days. I'm really worried."

Fuck. Colleague. What the hell did *colleague* mean? Jake kept his face still, but inside he was boiling.

"A colleague," Jake repeated, voice neutral.

Her face tightened. "Your man Dylan asked what the colleague was to me. You don't have the right to ask that."

He did. He absolutely did have the right. It was vital information to the case because... because. But Jake knew when to step down.

"By colleague, you mean he works at the CDC?"

Alex nodded. "Yes. In the Office of Infectious Diseases."

"Your office. There are about thirty people in that office,

right?" He shrugged at her sharp glance. He'd made a special study of the CDC since Alex started working there. As a matter of fact, he'd set up the Atlanta office of BI when he heard that Alex had been recruited to work there. The fact that he'd made a lot of money from CDC business was a bonus. "We work with the CDC. I know the structure pretty well."

"OK. There are thirty-two of us. But people are seconded to our department all the time for special projects. And at any given moment people from our department are out in the field."

"This colleague—has he been in the field a lot lately?" He'd probe around the edges of this.

"Some. Not any more or any less than any of us. But he did go to a conference in Budapest a few months ago and came back... changed."

"Changed how?"

Alex kept silent, breathing quietly, eyes probing his. Finally, she spoke. "This is the thing. My colleague is, like me, in mid-career. Like me, he has worked hard to get where he is. We both work in highly specialized fields. Apart from the private sector, there are very few government jobs in our area of expertise and we both hold the best job possible, given our talents and education." She stopped, hands clasped tightly in her lap. "I—I don't know if I can do this."

"Okay." Jake leaned forward until his elbows rested on his knees, hands clasped. Relaxed, non threatening. He watched her face carefully. "Let me see if I can guess. That way you haven't told me anything. Your conscience will be clear."

She nodded jerkily.

"Your colleague went to this conference in Budapest and came back a different man. I'm guessing he came back... emotionally different?"

"How—how do you mean?"

"Maybe a little euphoric, like he'd discovered a wonderful new world. Or else a little paranoid. Maybe frightened. Which one was it?"

Alex blinked. "Euphoric."

Uh-huh. Jake knew exactly what had happened. "And his lifestyle changed, too, didn't it?"

"Lifestyle?"

"Or standard of living. Let's call it standard of living. Did he buy a new car? Have better quality vacations? Better clothes? Eat out often in fancy restaurants?"

Alex's hands were shaking. "Yes. To everything. I didn't notice at first. We all earn excellent salaries. You'd have to run your own lab to make more, but most of us don't want to do that. It would be more admin than science. We certainly earn enough to live well. To tell the truth, many of us don't even have time to spend the money we do earn, like me. But Elias—my colleague, Dr. Elias Field—he started going crazy. He bought two new cars. One a BMW and the other an SUV. This, for a single man who basically lives in the lab. He usually wore the CDC outfit, the one all the men wear. Khakis, cotton shirt, cotton sweater in the summer, wool sweater in the winter. In all shades of beige, from ecru to taupe. And then after Budapest, Elias bought himself several Ermenegildo Zegna suits."

Jake must have looked blank because she sketched a smile.

"An Italian brand of menswear. An expensive one. The suits go for about eight thousand a pop. Ordinarily I wouldn't have noticed except he started wearing colors, which he never had before. Salmon and canary yellow shirts."

New car, new clothes. Yep. Good old Elias—and what the fuck kind of name was Elias anyway?—was ticking all the boxes. "Vacations? Restaurants?"

"Yes. He went to Vail over the Christmas season and to Aruba in March. Any of us can do that, of course, except none of us actually do because we rarely have the time. And he's been on a quest to eat at the top twenty restaurants in Atlanta in a month. He actually said that in our rec room."

Stupid fuck. He might as well have taken out an ad. *Just sold my country out.*

She shrugged. "I never really thought about that much, except in hindsight."

"Because he disappeared," Jake said.

She bit her lips. "Because it looks like he disappeared."

Jake leaned forward. "Tell me about it. It's only a couple of days but you're worried. There must be a reason for that." *And I hope to God it's not because you love the fuck.*

She hesitated. "This has national security implications." It was the second time she'd said that. Considering where she worked, this could be very dangerous shit.

Jake didn't smile and didn't frown. He kept his voice even. "I spent eight years on classified missions. BI works for Homeland Security on a continuous basis. Hell, we work for the CDC. No one's going to talk."

"I know you work with the CDC," she confessed. "It's one of the reasons I chose to—to approach Black Inc. However, for a moment there, while I was being shanghaied and flown halfway across the country, it occurred to me that BI was very closely tied to the CDC and that maybe I'd made a mistake. That maybe I'd walked into the lion's den and you would try to... to shut me up."

Jake kept quiet. There was nothing to say to that. He would see the CDC burn to the ground rather than see her hurt in any way.

She sipped her tea and leaned forward to place the cup on the coffee table. "Elias was working on something that has profound public health consequences, and that in the wrong hands..." She drew in a deep breath, puffed it out. "But what if Elias isn't missing? What if he had a family emergency and hasn't had a chance to tell anyone? What if he is sick with the flu and simply refusing to answer any of his phones? What if—"

"You think he's missing," Jake said. "That's good enough for me."

She closed her eyes. "Thank you. The thing is that we

are working on a project together in the BSL-4 lab. That's—"

"I know what that is," Jake said quietly. A BioSafety Level 4 lab was terrifying. It was used for the hottest of hot agents. A BSL-4 lab followed the strictest possible protocols to ensure that the diseases could never escape. They were under protective negative pressure and the scientists who worked in a BSL-4 lab worked in space suits as tightly insulated as those astronauts wore. There was an hour of decontamination after working in a BSL-4 lab. There were something like only 50 in the world. There were 12 of them in the US and only scientists who were tops in the fields ever worked there.

Jake's blood ran cold at the thought of Alex in a BSL-4 lab. The suits were overengineered to be safe, but sooner or later everything failed. One tiny hole, a second's breakdown in the air supply, a tiny slip of the hand and Alex would die an agonizing death behind steel vault doors that would never open again.

Jacob had lost two of his operators—excellent men—because of tears in their suits at a ricin factory in Syria. They had died horrible deaths and there was nothing he or his teammates could do.

She nodded. "Okay. So I don't have to explain that. You get it that once a team has begun a trial, no member of that team can be replaced. Something people don't always realize is how—how *physical* our job can get. We're scientists, yes, but a lot of what we do requires a great deal of manual expertise under difficult conditions. Few people can physically do what we do. And most trials require constant surveillance, otherwise the data can be lost or rendered null and void. Nobody disappears in the middle of a trial, no one. Elias has his issues, but I cannot imagine him just... disappearing like this. Without telling anyone. And yet, there it is. For this section of the experiment, it's just Elias and me and Elias being missing has brought everything to a grinding halt." Alex's beautiful face looked distressed. "We're alone during this stage of the trial. If I report that he has abandoned the experiment halfway through, that he is AWOL—his career is over. He'd be on a blacklist and would never work in a legitimate lab again. On the other hand, if something has happened to him, if he's been kidnapped or if—" That long white throat bobbed as she swallowed.

"If he defected," Jake finished for her.

Alex nodded. "Yes. If he defected. If he did, then I would be in very deep trouble for not reporting it right away." She turned, reached down into her briefcase and pulled out her cell.

"And then yesterday I got this." She tapped the screen and held it out to him. Jake took it and listened to a screeching warbly series of sounds that lasted two minutes.

"Scrambled," Jake said.

"Yes." Alex left the phone with him. "I'm not good enough to unscramble it. As you can see, the number is blocked."

"Not for long." Black Inc. had developed an app for this. Inside of a minute, Jake had a number. He turned

Alex's phone around so she could see it. "The message is scrambled beyond reconstruction, but I've unblocked the number. This is the number that called you."

"Oh." She stared at her screen then raised her eyes to his. "That number, + 380. What country does that correspond to?"

"Vostokova," Jake answered. He was already planning his phone call to Nick. Nikolai Garin, Ukrainian-American with a feel for Eastern European countries. A real badass, former SEAL. He and Nick went way back and Nick was one of his VPs. Plus, he could be counted on to do everything in his power to fuck with anyone who was fucking with a country in that part of the world. Especially Russia.

"Oh, no," Alex whispered. She'd turned ice white again. Jake shot out a hand to steady her. She was trembling and didn't pull away, which scared him.

"Alex?"

"Vostokova." She swallowed convulsively. "What part of Vostokova?"

Jake pulled out his cell and Googled the prefix, frowning at his display. "Says here a place called Zalny." He watched her face as it turned even whiter. "Where is Zalny?"

"Not where," she answered. "What. What is Zalny. A tiny town of no importance outside the capital, but it was the site of an old Soviet lab, decommissioned after the fall of the Soviet Union. There was a strong suspicion the Soviets were working on bioweaponry during the Soviet period. I read the reports of our guys who went over to check on former Soviet bioweapons labs, because stockpiles were disappearing. The CIA was more worried about the bioweapons than nuclear weapons. This is—this is awful, Jake. Particularly considering Elias's specialty."

He knew he wasn't going to like this. "Which is?"

"The deadliest disease in human history. Mankind's most vicious enemy. Smallpox," Alex whispered. "And his sub-specialty is blackpox—hemorrhagic smallpox. Think smallpox crossed with Ebola."

CHAPTER
Four

S ilence.

Alex was used to this when discussing her field of expertise. Civilians had a primordial terror of viral and bacterial diseases. Those invisible killers. Certain diseases were supposed to stay in the past, and the idea of them was terrifying, as if countless ancestors reached out to touch them with cold, dead, bony hands to drag them back into the horrors of the past.

Smallpox was the worst.

Jake's jaw muscles bunched as he worked to repress a shudder. "I thought smallpox has been eradicated."

She sighed. "It has. And hasn't. Let me give you a quick history. Smallpox is humanity's oldest enemy. There are signs that some Egyptian mummies died of smallpox. It can be devastating in populations that haven't been exposed. They say that when the Spanish landed in South America, spreading smallpox, it killed most of the infected because they had no immunity at all. Smallpox ranks among the most devastating illnesses ever suffered by humankind. It dramatically altered the course of human history, even contributing to the decline of civilizations. Officially the deadly virus no longer exists. It was eradicated in 1977, in a massive worldwide effort by the World Health Organization. Vaccinations stopped in 1972."

She watched his face. He was frowning.

"But?" Jake asked. "There's definitely a 'but' in there."

Alex sighed. "Yes. There are two small stocks kept under maximum security, frozen, in BSL-4 labs. One is at the CDC itself, in a separate facility. The other is in the State Center of Virology and Biotechnology, known as VECTOR, in Kotsovo, Russia, under close supervision."

"Except, oops, every once in a while, someone finds a couple of vials, right?" Jake said.

She sighed again. "Yes. Sometimes more than a couple of vials. And the CIA is certain four countries have stocks, particularly Russia. The Soviet Union produced tons of the virus as a biological weapon. They say they destroyed them all, but—" she shrugged.

"Jesus." Jake shook his head. "And here I was worrying about cyberattacks and suitcase nukes and runaway AI. Now I have another nightmare to add to it."

Alex met his eyes. "That's not the nightmare. Smallpox is bad, but mankind survived epidemics of smallpox for thousands of years. It's what Elias could theoretically do that is the real nightmare."

Jacob put his hand over hers. "Tell me," he said simply.

Alex looked down at his hand over hers, torn. He knew he shouldn't be touching her. She hadn't given him permission to touch her. He'd disappeared from her life at her absolute lowest point, abandoning her in the most cruel way possible, scarring her for life. It was totally unforgiveable, she'd never forgive him, and he didn't have the right to touch her.

Absolutely. No touching, certainly no kissing.

But...

Oh my God. The warmth, the comfort, the reassurance. That hand was strong. Not a pampered successful businessman's hand. No. Broad, long-fingered, with the raised veins of an athlete along the back. White scars against his dark skin. Nails short and clean, but not buffed and manicured. Hands that weren't pampered, hands that were used a lot.

The skin of his palm was heavily callused. Though he wasn't exerting pressure, just resting his big hand over hers, she could feel power pulsing from his hand. Infusing her with warmth.

Alex was still angry at him. He was responsible for unrelenting unhappiness and sadness lodged deep in her soul, lasting so long her sadness had become a part of her. He'd abandoned her, in her time of greatest need.

But... that was in the past.

He was here now. And everything pointed to him not abandoning her now. She remembered the aching sorrow, and the fear of being alone in the world at 16. As horrible as that had been though, it was nothing compared to what she was feeling now. The weight of responsibility that felt like a boulder on her chest. Knowing if she was right, people would die, in the millions. Civilization could end. If she was wrong, she and Elias were still in a world of hurt. She needed someone, someone strong and smart, by her side. And she had someone. Someone strong and smart. Right there, by her side.

The Jake she'd known had been rawboned, painfully thin. Two classes behind everyone else, looked down on by everyone, welcomed nowhere except in the Hethering household. An outcast, shunned. As low on the totem pole as you could get.

The Jacob she had before her was immensely powerful in all ways, including physically. Though he was as far from a pampered tech bro billionaire as it was possible to be, his name was always prefaced by the term billionaire.

But that wasn't his power. Money wasn't his power. *He* was his power. Power emanated from every cell in his body and not just physical. Alex had never been so close to someone like him, someone who looked like he could bend space and time to his will. All her life since Jake left her, she'd been around science students and scientists and though they mastered the world through intelligence, none of them had this powerful charisma Jacob had.

The horrible leaden weight of what she was dealing with lifted from her and moved to Jacob. She could breathe for the first time in days. Heat emanating from his hand on hers filled her for the first time in days. She'd been frozen and terrified and now... she wasn't. Or at least she wasn't paralyzed from fear.

It was as if he'd surrounded her with a force field. Her troubles were still there but the worst thoughts bounced off the force field Jake created, letting anxiety in, but shattering that frozen wilderness of terror she'd been living in.

Jake—Jacob—had done that. He was dressed in an immaculate suit that looked very much like light-weight cashmere, dark gray, very elegant. But beneath that suit were massive shoulders built to pile on troubles. She was still mad at him, she might stay mad at him for the rest of her life, but right now, she was so grateful he was here with her, letting her breathe, shouldering her burdens.

Even though he didn't understand them yet. Almost reluctantly, Alex slid her hand from his. He exerted this magnetic pull on her and it was worse when he touched her. She needed to be fully in herself, marshalling all her resources, to explain this to him.

Jacob wasn't a virologist, wasn't a biologist or even a scientist and you had to have some grounding in science to understand. It was up to her to make him see the danger.

The instant she tugged at her hand, he let it go and not by a flicker of an eyelash did Alex show that... she missed his hand. The heat and the strength.

"Okay," she said, looking at Jacob. "I'm going to have to go into professorial mode."

He nodded his head, never taking his gaze from hers. "I'll try to keep up."

She looked at him sharply, but there was no sarcasm or

irony. Just that simple statement. He wasn't an expert, but he'd do his best to keep up.

"Smallpox," she said and stopped. Even the word gave her goosebumps. "One of mankind's deadliest enemies. We have accounts from ancient Egypt, three thousand years ago, of epidemics. As I said, when European colonists landed in South America, where there was no immunity, smallpox killed up to 90% of the native population. It is estimated that smallpox has taken upwards of a billion lives. Where it hasn't killed, it has disfigured and left people blind. The fatality rate is about 30%."

"But now we have vaccinations," he said quietly.

"We do." Alex dipped her head. "But we stopped vaccinating. You and I, for example, are not vaccinated. You might be, because we continued vaccinating members of the military. You're probably inoculated against small-pox, but also against typhoid fever, tetanus, influenza, meningococcal disease, adenovirus, yellow fever, pneumo-coccal disease, anthrax."

Jacob nodded.

"But the rest of us are not inoculated against smallpox. We would end up like the native population of South America in the 1500s if smallpox were to break out again. But that's not the worst-case scenario."

Jacob's eyes widened slightly. "Jesus. It's not?"

Alex had a sharp pain in her chest. It hurt to think about it let alone say it. "No. Because there is a lot of improvement possible from the point of view of the variola virus, the one that causes smallpox."

74

Jacob's face froze. "Improvement?"

"In its killing power, yes. Elias is an expert at gene splicing, very talented, so if he somehow got his hands on the vials we have at the CDC or if some... non-state actor got their hands on the smallpox virus, he could, in theory, change it. If he wanted to, or if someone directed him to make it more potent. R_0 is the measure of contagion of a disease. The number of people an individual can infect. The R_0 of smallpox is from 3 to 6 right now, with very little herd immunity.

"Bioengineering could increase that exponentially. A good bioengineer could make it easily contagious airborne, could make it asymptomatic, so that someone could walk around and be infectious even though there are no symptoms, which is not the case with naturally occurring smallpox.

"Smallpox is already scary as hell. Smallpox has a mortality rate of 30%. It could be brought to 90%. Maybe even 100%. Engineered to be a bioweapon, it could..." Alex's throat tightened, as if someone were throttling her. A tear slipped down her cheek. Jacob wiped it away with his thumb, then took her hand. When she felt her voice could work again, she finished the sentence. "Engineered as a bioweapon, it could wipe out the world."

* * *

HOLY. *Shit*. Jacob could feel Alex's cold hand trembling. Yeah. What she'd just told him was horrifying, would make anyone tremble. Jacob's own hand didn't tremble. He'd been a sniper in the military, among other things, and his hand never trembled. But if ever there was a moment to shake, this was it.

And Alex had been living with this, alone, unable to talk to anyone about it.

Jacob had a team that was the best in the world and he trusted them. When there were plans to be made, no matter how bad the situation, he could troubleshoot with them. He was never alone if he didn't want to be, and particularly when there was a hard problem to face. He had teams at his back.

But Alex... Alex was alone. She didn't seem to have a partner. Jacob tried and failed to imagine someone who was Alex's partner abandoning her in a situation like this. He wouldn't be able to, that's for sure.

"Fuck," he breathed, covering her hand again.

Alex took in a deep breath, let it out. The primal stress reliever. Her hand, which had been stiff under his, relaxed a little. It was still cold as ice, though.

"Yeah. You can see why I've been so... worried."

"Worried isn't even the right word. Panicking."

She dipped her head. "That, too."

Alex slipped her cold hand from under his and spread her hands. "What do I do?" she asked, voice tight.

"We put together a team and go hunting for your colleague."

"And hope my fears are exaggerated."

Jacob took her hand again. He felt like he was

unplugged when she withdrew her hand, not a good feeling. He chose his next words carefully. "Hope is not the force that moves the world, Alex," he said gently.

She winced. "No." Her voice was the merest breath.

"We need to proceed as if your fears are reality. Anything else would be insane, given what's at stake."

Alex nodded her head jerkily. "So... what's our first step?"

"My first step. I'll debrief you and you'll stay here, where you'll be protected 24/7 and I'll fly to Zalny. I can have a team ready and waiting there. We will coordinate with you here via secure comms."

"Nice try, but not a chance." Alex straightened. A little color had come into her face. "I'm coming, too. Don't even try talking me out of it."

The funniest thing. Jacob's heart suddenly gave a huge pulse in his chest, a hard knock that hurt, like his heart had come unmoored and was trying to escape his chest. That had never happened before. His heart was always strong and reliable. His heart rate had been measured under live fire and it had never deviated from 60 beats per minute. It had never even occurred to him that it could do anything else but beat steadily and calmly.

And yet, here it was, one fast hard beat, whump! So hard it felt like the walls of his chest shook. Complete rejection of the idea of Alex coming with him. Alex, walking into danger.

That beat knocked him completely off his stride. He was pretty good at convincing people of his plan, whatever it was. He wasn't above using his size and strength to intimidate but that didn't really work in the military, and it didn't work much in private enterprise, or at least not in his company, since he made a point of hiring strong-headed men and women.

So just as he'd learned military discipline, marksmanship, close quarters combat, he'd learned leadership, which was essentially the art of persuading people to do what you wanted. No matter what.

But this?

Nope. He had no words to express his horror at the idea of Alex walking into danger, of Alex anywhere near danger. He knew the basics of her life, knew she'd lived in Boston while going to college, had lived in Geneva while working under temporary contract with the WHO, and now lived in Atlanta. As far as he knew, she'd never faced violence, had never faced danger, unless you counted working with nightmare diseases. But that was different from the kind of danger violent people could wage. You could overcome the dangers posed by diseases by using science, but not the dangers of people. Certainly, she couldn't fight back if someone attacked her. There was nothing in her body language that told him she could counter the violent fucks of the world.

He'd met and worked with women warriors and respected them. But they'd been trained and everything about them screamed *don't fuck with me or I will tear your fucking head off and stick it up your fucking ass.*

Not Alex. Every line of her body spoke of gentility and

grace. The violent fucks of the world would just roll right over her with spikes and he couldn't even stay in the same space with that thought.

No," he said. Thinking it was a miracle that his voice sounded normal. That he didn't scream it.

Alex opened her eyes wide, head cocked to one side. "No?"

Jacob gave a short sharp nod. "No."

"No, as a general principle? Or no on me coming with you?"

"No, you are not coming with me. With us. I have a good friend in that part of the world. He's a Vice President of Black Inc., in fact, with responsibility for a spin-off. Really smart, with a team onsite that knows the terrain."

Alex regarded him, unblinking, for a few moments. Did she think that staring at him would unnerve him? It took more than a beautiful pair of eyes to unnerve him.

"Okay, let's see."

She crossed her arms under her breasts. They were magnificent breasts but they weren't going to sway him. Nope. He kept his eyes firmly fixed on hers.

"Describe an ELISA reader."

Jacob's lips pinched together.

"And how do you turn off an ultrasonic homogenizer?"

His eyes narrowed.

"I thought so. And tell me, what's the difference between a filovirus and a bunyavirus?"

"Don't know." His jaws flexed as he bit on something

bitter. "But we're dealing with bad guys. I have a lot of experience there. Much more than you."

"Uh-huh." She looked him straight in the eyes. "Have you ever spent time in a MOPP4 suit?"

Jacob refrained from wincing at the memory. At least he could answer this.

"Yeah. Spent time in Syria in an abandoned factory where they were manufacturing ricin."

"Uncomfortable, isn't it? The MOPP4."

"God yeah."

"They're bulky."

"And they smell." As if a skunk had farted in there. And the smell never went away.

"Yes. And they overheat. The suits don't breathe very well, and there's a lot of heat buildup. How much time at a stretch did you spend in your MOPP4?"

Jacob had no idea where she was going with this. "Maybe two hours at a time. This was Syria."

"Mm-hmm. And the visor clouds up and it's hard to manipulate things with the clumsy gloves."

"Yeah."

Alex leaned forward and tapped him on the knee. "We work every day, sometimes eight hours a day, in PPPS in the BSL-4 labs. A Positive Pressure Personnel Suit that makes the MOPP4 look like rompers. While doing delicate lab work. Every day."

Jacob kept his mouth shut. If he opened his mouth, he'd start yelling and he didn't want to yell, not at Alex. He didn't want to yell. He was known for keeping his cool, always, but he didn't feel cool right now, not at all.

Alex tapped him on the knee again. "I know Elias and he knows me. He doesn't know you at all, except by reputation, and you aren't known for being a sweet and gentle man. If we go to wherever we think he is, and he is open to talking, who do you think he will listen to. You? Or me?"

Jacob huffed out a breath. Another. Tried to unloose his throat enough to speak. "Wherever this Elias is, he is in deepest shit and possibly—probably—surrounded by terrorists. Whether he is completely in with them, or whether he regrets being bought, they will not give him up easily. This feels like a massive conspiracy of bad guys. Maybe even state-sponsored bad guys, planning on using a deadly weapon. Is that what you want to walk into? Yes, you know viruses, better than anyone, certainly better than anyone in my company or my teammate's company and for sure better than me. But you haven't spent the better part of two decades dealing with these kinds of people, Alex. You think in scientific terms, not in strategic terms. The danger comes from what you think might have happened, that Dr. Field has weaponized smallpox, which might or might not be true, and if it is true, you are the expert. But what is absolutely true is that we're dealing with very dangerous people, and I'm the expert. I've dealt with the scum of the earth all my life."

Alex met his eyes. "If Elias worked up a modified smallpox virus, he did so under my watch, so to speak. We have worked together every day for the past year and a half and I suspected absolutely nothing. If this game changer was created in the past year and a half, I bear some responsibility. I couldn't live with myself if I didn't try to deal with the danger."

Responsibility. Shit. She'd pushed the wrong button. Jacob was nothing but responsibility. It was in his bones. He knew exactly where she was coming from. It hurt, but he did it. He threw up his hands. "I can't let you win this."

"It's not a contest, Jake. Nothing to win."

"No, it's not a contest. But I just can't wrap my head around you walking into danger. Messes with my head."

Alex sat up straight. "You're getting all protective now? Where have you been? When I was with the WHO, we travelled to the Democratic Republic of Congo and to Chechnya. I haven't been living in a bubble, as you seem to think."

Jacob set his teeth. She was not going to like this. "You were travelling with an official UN delegation on a diplomatic passport, both times, to conferences. The delegations were surrounded by local police and were afforded every diplomatic courtesy and both times you never went outside Lagos or Grozny."

Alex drew back, pale blue eyes wide. "What the hell? Have you been stalking me? How do you know so much about my life?"

"Not stalking, no." Jacob treaded carefully here. It was like walking on a floor where grenades had been thrown, the pins pulled. This could go south very badly, very fast. "I kept informed about what you were doing. And since

Black Inc. works closely with the CDC, we have access to personnel files."

Alex stood abruptly, standing ramrod straight. She looked furious. He'd never seen her furious before, or even sad or mad. As a young girl she'd always been even tempered, sunny, happy. This was new. It made her even more beautiful, like some Greek goddess ready to hurl arrows down on the mortals from Mount Olympus.

"You've been stalking me since before the CDC? I worked for the WHO before accepting the job at the CDC."

Jacob fudged. "Like I said, our contract with the CDC includes access to all personnel files," he repeated. Though the truth was he'd been following her since forever.

Alex was blinking rapidly, eyes shiny with unshed tears. Her fists were clenched and she was trembling from head to toe. Not in fear. In rage. "Oh my God. You've known where I was this whole time." She shifted her weight from foot to foot as if getting ready to take off. Not even in the sense of running but of a rocket shooting through the ceiling. "I can't believe it. You could have gotten in touch at any time."

Jacob said nothing.

Alex swallowed heavily. "I missed you so goddamned much. And I had no way to know if you were okay or not. If you were even alive." Her eyes swept him from head to foot, then looked around his office, and he knew she was taking in the expensive clothes and the huge office. "I imagined it all. You homeless, sleeping under a bridge. You hurt, because you never hesitated to take on bullies. You sick, because you never took care of yourself. I worried myself sick and I missed you terribly, all at the same time. Aunt Emily took me in, but she wasn't happy about it. She was cold. I didn't know any of the kids in the local high school in Boston, so I did the only thing I could do, which was study like crazy.

"But I was so... so fucking lonely. Missed you so much. You could have gotten in touch at any moment, and yet you never did."

"I did," he said quietly.

"What?" Alex wiped under her eyes with a finger.

"I did come visit you."

Her eyes widened with shock. "You came—when?"

"During basic training, the Navy realized that I was a natural and that soldiering was something I was really good at. So I did a kind of accelerated training, but didn't— couldn't—take any time off. Then I was deployed for a year. Abroad. I literally couldn't come back to the States. It would have been desertion. I applied for SEAL training and was admitted and was given a week off before BUDS began. I headed straight to Cambridge."

He'd come from deployment in an FOB and had been filthy and exhausted, with an unkempt beard, long hair and unwashed BDUs. Twenty-four hours before, he'd been under fire, living in bare bones barracks.

Their FOB had been particularly primitive. They slept on cots in converted shipping containers, had been allowed two-minute showers. There were dust storms almost every day. They burned their own shit because there was no sewage system.

They took mortar rounds constantly.

Jacob was so used to the living conditions that it hadn't even occurred to him to clean up, buy some decent civilian clothing, get a haircut, hell, take a shower.

All he knew was that there was a drumbeat in his head, so loud it drowned out everything else, to get to Alex. He'd been offered a ride in a C-130 and he grabbed it. C-130s were freight flights, noisy, with sling seats strapped to the bulkhead. You pissed in bottles.

He didn't care. He had a free week, and he was going to see Alex. Two hitched military flights and he was in Boston. The cab driver who let him off in Cambridge wouldn't take any money from him, thanked him for his service, and kindly suggested he take a shower.

He found himself on manicured grounds, among old, beautifully kept brick buildings. It was a bright fall day and students filled the paths and were sitting on the lawn and on low walls.

Every single kid there was good looking.

Jacob knew that they were his age, but he looked years older. He'd had thousands of bullets shot at him and he'd shot thousands of bullets back. He'd killed five men. He could field strip all his weapons blindfolded but wasn't always sure which fork to use. He was as different from these kids as it was possible to be.

They were like another species. A more evolved one.

He'd downloaded a map and was heading for the

student information office, noticing the strange looks he was receiving. He might as well have come from Mars.

"I walked around, wondering how I could find you, and then I saw you. You were deep in conversation with three other people. Two peeled off and you were left with one guy. Tall, handsome, blond. Elegantly dressed. I hated him on sight. You put your arm through his and walked right by me, the two of you laughing. You were turned toward Mr. Rich and Blond and didn't even register my existence. I felt like a mangy dog in a fancy restaurant."

He'd stood there, stunned, for maybe half an hour. Alex had walked right by him and hadn't recognized him. Though, to tell the truth, she hadn't looked away for one second from the handsome, patrician face of Rich and Blond.

Alex set her jaw. "I can't know what day that was, but it was my sophomore year. I graduated early from high school. I do know who you are talking about. Charlton Fitzweiler."

What the fuck kind of name was Charlton Fitzweiler? Jacob had spent the past fourteen years hating the guy and he hated him even more now.

"We met our first day at a mixer and became really good friends. I was younger than most of the other students and didn't come from a privileged background and I was feeling really lost. Charlton did come from the right background. He was a legacy, back when those were still possible. He came from a rich, very religious family in the deep South and spent years in therapy. He was an incredible friend, a major support in that first difficult year. I loved him, but not in the way you think. He was gay and his family made him struggle with that."

"Was? Was a good friend? You're not friends anymore?"

"He committed suicide four years ago."

Well.

Jacob kept his mouth firmly shut. There wasn't anything he could say that wouldn't dig him deeper in the hole he was already in.

He trusted his judgment, always had. He never second guessed himself. But now he realized he'd fucked up badly, all those years ago. He'd have forgiven himself because he was young, but that wasn't it. He sometimes thought he was born a hundred years old. He'd never felt young.

No, what it proved was that Alex was his weakness, his melting point. The one thing that could bring him down.

He'd made the wrong call all those years ago and he'd wasted precious time. What might have been a chance to reconnect had been tossed away out of hurt pride.

Alex crossed her arms. The tears had disappeared from her eyes and her features were tight. She'd gone back to anger after the hurt. Those seemed to be her major emotions regarding him. Anger, and pain. "Are we done here? Done digging up the past? Because I have a big problem, right now."

They weren't done here, not by a long shot. But Jacob recognized when to retreat.

"You've got a big problem, yeah. And it just so happens

that my company is specialized in big problems. Gnarly, dangerous ones, where things can go wrong. I told you I know just the guy to call. Nikolai Garin. He knows that part of the world well. He can put together a good team."

"That team will include me," she said steadily.

Jacob hung his head. "Look, Alex," he began.

"Don't you 'look Alex' me," she said. "We've gone over this. There's no way you can access the expertise to deal with this, if technical problems come up. Elias and I work in highly specialized fields. Our knowledge wouldn't be available to you. There wouldn't be anyone you can call up."

Jacob said nothing.

Alex's face softened, just a little. "Look. I understand you don't want a civilian, a non-security expert along. You think I'll hamper your movements. But I promise to stay out of your way. I just want—need—to be there because I can advise you and your team in real time, on the ground. This is serious stuff and you need an expert along. And no, hiring someone to moonlight from the CDC won't do it."

That was exactly what he was thinking. "No?"

"No. I know Elias better than anyone else. I know how he thinks and, above all, I know his fields of expertise. Virology is a very big field. You're not going to find someone better than me to help."

Jacob opened his hands, almost a symbol of helpless-ness, for a man who was never helpless. "The idea of putting you in danger makes me a little crazy," he confessed, words he had never said before.

"I understand." Alex's face was no longer stiff with anger, but she was clearly stressed. "Look. I am not a thrill seeker, not an adrenaline junkie. I don't rock climb, I don't surf, I don't hang glide for fun. I don't even run. Most days I am too tired to work out, and the most exercise I get is going for long walks on the weekend, when it's not raining. I took a self-defense course once and I've forgotten everything. I only took it because two of my female colleagues had been assaulted. I always meant to start up again, but it never seemed to be the right time and I have no idea where to start. I've never held a gun, I've never hit anyone in my life." She side-eyed him. "Though I was tempted today."

He bowed his head, eyes never leaving hers. Yeah. If she were the violent temper type of person, she'd have definitely slapped him. But that wasn't Alexandra Hethering. Alex was a gentle person and that hadn't changed. He, on the other hand, had never been a gentle person. He'd have definitely punched himself, right in the face.

"So, I'm not going to be of any use from the security point of view. But you have my word that I will follow instructions to the letter and will not knowingly put myself in danger. But by the same token, I will be invaluable when it comes to dealing with Elias and whatever he has gotten himself into." She shrugged her shoulders. "I'm coming and that's it."

Like any good soldier, Jacob knew when to retreat. He wasn't going to win this battle because he wasn't prepared to restrain her, which was the only way to stop her. The only thing he could do was make sure she stayed far, far away from any danger and acted only as a consultant.

Which made this not only a mission but a close protection job, harder and with more variables. Well, he'd done hard before. Hard didn't scare him, but the idea of Alex hurt did. Right down to his bones.

None of that showed on his face, he knew.

"Okay," he said.

Her eyes rounded. "Okay? Just like that? You're not going back on that decision?"

Jacob sketched a smile, stretching unused muscles. "You're not giving up, are you?"

"No." Alex's shoulders straightened.

"So either you come with me or I tie you up or stash you somewhere with guards, against your will. I'm not willing to do that, so..." He shrugged his shoulders.

They looked at each other for a long moment. It wasn't a hardship. She was just so beautiful. She'd been an uncommonly pretty girl, but part of that was, he knew, genetics and money for orthodontics and good food on a regular basis. But now she had a beauty that was all her own. Her face had slimmed down, cheekbones prominent. She had lines in her face that denoted character. She looked powerful. Not the kind of power he was used to. Not dominance, which was his kind of power, but rather the power of holding deep specialized knowledge and using it always for good.

The power of good, which he knew, from decades wading through the filth of evil, had its own allure. The way she held herself, the way she spoke, was the fruit of years and years of self-discipline and hard work and made her a natural aristocrat. A woman of substance, who automatically inspired respect.

A woman in a million, and he'd lost her.

"Okay." He stood and she tilted her head back to watch him.

"Okay, what?"

"We need to get started. Make travel arrangements, I need to put together a team, brief my teammate Nikolai. Or rather maybe you should."

She gestured at her briefcase. "I'm also going to have to order some clothes. I had no idea I was going to be shanghaied and flown across the country."

"You weren't—" he began heatedly, when he saw her watching him for his reaction. "You're baiting me."

She gave the tiniest of smiles. "A little. Apparently, it's not hard to do. I would have thought the great Jacob Black was tougher than that. But no."

Jacob bit his back teeth. No sense rising again to the bait. She couldn't know that he was unbaitable. Tough as they come. Except when it came to her.

"Here." Jacob held out a black credit card. "Buy anything you want, from the skin out. Anything you think you might need." He leaned forward and tapped on a built-in tablet. "Looks like we'll have bad weather in Vostokova. Maybe a storm front, some snow. Buy warm clothes. I have plenty of suitcases but buy yourself any kind you like."

She didn't take the card, just looked at him.

"I have money of my own, thank you."

Jacob stifled a sigh. "Of course you do. This isn't me playing big man. But a Black Inc. card is guaranteed to get you the best service. We need priority delivery, and the card will guarantee it. We need to be ready to go soon and everything will have to have been delivered."

"I'll pay you back," she said and his jaws clenched so hard it was a miracle shards of enamel didn't shoot out his ass. "And I will pay you back for all your expenses. I imagine you won't have me pay your fee, which I'm sure is high. But we're talking private plane, a team of operators... that's expensive. I wasn't really thinking it through when I turned to Black Inc. I was thinking more of a consultation. I had no idea it would require international travel and..."

"Stop it." Jacob held up his hand, then pinched the bridge of his nose. He couldn't stand this anymore. "Just... stop. And none of this is important, anyway. What's important is to get to your colleague and stop whatever it is he is planning."

Jacob couldn't even talk about it. He and every resource of his company was at her complete disposal. And would be forever. She was resisting the idea, but it was a fact.

She sat silently, watching him. Then let out her breath, destressing. "This isn't over, but you're right. We have things more important than money to deal with."

Jacob didn't let his relief that she'd dropped the topic of money show.

"I am going to contact my teammate, who is in Belgium at the moment. But you're going to have to explain the situation. Can you do that?"

Her eyes widened in surprise. "Of course."

"You're not too tired?"

She gave him the side eye. "I'm not a soldier but we've been known to work 24 even 48 hours straight if we have a deadline. I'm tired, yes, but functional."

Yes, she was functional, but she looked exhausted. "Okay, you're going to explain the situation, or the facts you have, to Nikolai. And then while I get dinner together, you order everything you need, and I mean everything. Order solid gold underwear, I don't care." She side eyed him again and he shrugged. "It's all tax deductible."

"Did you book a hotel room for me?"

Every cell in his body rejected the notion, but he didn't let that show either. "The top floor is my home."

"One of your homes."

He nodded. "One of my homes." He had four of them, in the major cities, bland decorator-styled residences so he didn't have to sleep in hotels. But his real home, the one he loved, was a cabin in the Sierra Nevada that had zero creature comforts, an outhouse and was heated by a wood stove. He loved it and could feel stress sloughing off him every time he hiked there.

"I'm not sleeping with you, Jake. Jacob. Not tonight, not tomorrow, not ever."

We'll see about that. Jacob kept that thought way off his face.

"No worries. You'll have your own bedroom. Your own suite. With a door that locks."

"I imagine you're pretty good at picking locks," she said. "But I trust your sense of honor. So—"

There was a beep and Jacob turned to the wall screen with relief. "That's my colleague," he said, as Nikolai's face, bigger than life, appeared.

He was in some kind of comms center, tech-filled and unadorned. "Got your message, Jacob. What's up?" he said.

"Alex, meet Nikolai Garin, my second in command, and now head of a spinoff of Black Inc., we co-own Go Solutions. Nikolai, meet Dr. Alexandra Hethering. She has a very serious problem."

Not by a flicker of eyelash did Nick betray that he knew exactly who Alex was. One night, after a bitter fire-fight where they lost three teammates, Jacob got shit-faced drunk and told Nick the whole sorry story.

"Dr. Hethering," Nick said solemnly.

"Mr. Garin," Alex said.

"Nick."

"Okay, Nick. Then, Alex."

"Okay, Alex, can you tell me your problem?"

"First of all, I'm not a medical doctor. The Dr. is a PhD in virology and I have a masters in epidemiology. I work at the CDC in Atlanta. Or, worked. I might have lost my job by now," she shot a glance at Jacob, "since to them I have gone AWOL."

"So the problem is a biohazard," Nick said soberly.

"The worst kind. I work for the CDC, as I said. At the moment, I am engaged in a project aimed at developing a universal kill switch for viruses. You can imagine the utility of being able to turn viruses off. We are a very, very long way from achieving our goals but we are close to a working model in theory. My colleague in this project, which will run to the end of the year, is Dr. Elias Field. He is an expert in gene splicing and is working on a computer model of the genome of the smallpox virus."

Silence.

Nick looked briefly pained, then schooled his face to passivity again. "Smallpox, eh?"

Alex nodded her head.

"I thought we had eradicated smallpox. Wiped it off the face of the earth. My great grandfather died of smallpox. I'm not even vaccinated against it."

"None of us are."

"But it's gone, right? Over. Extinct. Whatever it is that happens to germs."

"Viruses," Alex said. "Not germs. And, yes, in theory smallpox has been eradicated. But of course, there are still samples available, kept very securely, both at the CDC and VEKTOR in the Russian Federation."

Nick cocked his head. "But? And I wouldn't trust anything the Russian Federation says."

Alex sighed. "There are rumors. There are always rumors. I can personally attest to the fact that the live smallpox kept at the CDC is kept under very secure conditions. And colleagues who have been to VEKTOR say the same about the samples in Russia. But in 2014, six vials were found, mislabeled, in an FDA lab. The CIA believes Russia has illegal, undeclared stocks. They wrote a report in 2002."

"What?" Jacob leaned forward. "How come we haven't heard this?"

"I think, ahm, the CIA keeps its secrets pretty well," Alex said, voice dry.

The CIA was a sieve. Jacob was angry that something like this hadn't been reported.

"So, Alex, your colleague?" Nick was frowning.

She sighed, looked at her hands, took a beat. Two. "Well, this is where it gets tricky. Because my colleague has been missing for three days, going on four. He is not answering his phone, he is not answering on our Whatsapp group, he is not answering his emails, either personal or work email. We are in the middle of a delicate project in a Level 4 Biolab and I cannot continue on my own. But if I report him missing, his career is over. Yet I can't ignore that he is AWOL. I spoke about this to... to Jake—Jacob..." she stumbled over his name. "Elias had been acting strangely and has been throwing money around. I hadn't actually put two and two together until Jacob made me. And—and I guess I just have to accept the possibility, the very real possibility, that Elias has defected. If that's the word I want."

Alex looked over to Jacob, as if to ask if the debriefing was okay. She was clearly rattled.

Jacob faced the huge screen. Nick was looking serious.

They'd faced a lot of bad situations before, but this one had the potential to be devastating.

"Alex received a call, but the number was blocked. We unblocked it. There was no message because it was scrambled. It came from Zalny." Jacob halted. Nick's mouth tightened. Like Jacob, he rarely showed emotions, but his reaction was unmistakable. "You know what it is, Nick?"

"I know what it was," Nick responded. "It was a secret bioweapons lab under the Soviet Union but was shut down in 1994, subsequent to the Treaty."

"It might not be so shut down," Alex said. "There were rumors, but then in my business there are always rumors. We deal with very bad things."

"Wait." Jacob ran requests through his system. Black Inc. had a proprietary AI that would have been worth millions of dollars on the open market. But he kept it in house, where it was used for good. It was insanely useful. "Ah. Here we go. I ran coordinates through a system that checks historical satellite footage and—fuck. Look at that."

The footage showed high speed recordings of the area over the past two years. Far from being a disused lab, in the past two years, there were numerous truck deliveries and unmistakable signs of underground construction. The last image showed an innocuous terrain looking abandoned, with a small shack.

The footage was running for Nick, too. His face tightened. "Goddamn. That's Russian. Got to be. Vostokova doesn't have that kind of money. And Russia probably paid the Vostokovan authorities off to look the other way. The local authorities wouldn't care. They are all venal and corrupt. Except for one Minister."

"There is a good likelihood that there is now a world-class virologist in that complex. Who is an expert on small-pox." Jacob looked at Alex. "With maybe a sample?"

She nodded, sadness in her features. "It is not beyond the realm of possibility. Either a forgotten vial in some lab here in the States, or he is with people who have access to smallpox. There's an urban legend that the Russian mob has kilos of the stuff."

Jesus. Jacob tried to wrap his head around someone having kilos of smallpox.

"But, that's not the bad news," Alex said.

Nick blinked, which for him was a sign of extreme surprise. "It isn't?" he said.

"It isn't?" Jacob echoed.

"No." Alex looked down a moment. "No, the real bad news is that Elias is very, very good at using CRISPR. I'm really good, too, but he is a master."

At their blank looks, she sighed. "CRISPR is a genetic engineering tool that uses a sequence of DNA and its associated protein to edit the base pairs of a gene.

"CRISPR-Cas9 is a scissors-like chemical tool that can precisely cut and customize stretches of genetic material, such as human DNA. It can cut out the gene for lung cancer or hereditary blindness. It can manipulate the gene for, say, sickle-cell anemia and cure the person of the disease. It could theoretically also edit viruses to make them more contagious, more lethal. Like smallpox.

Smallpox is lethal in 30% of the cases in humans. You could edit the virus to make it 99% or 100% lethal."

Jacob and Nick were silent. Jacob was running through horrific scenarios in his head.

"But that's not all," Alex said.

"There's more?" Jacob asked. His voice was hoarse and he cleared it.

"There's more. Elias and I were doing groundbreaking research into kill switches. Which could be hugely beneficial, of course. We're perfecting a technique Elias developed. If he perfects it, he would be eligible for the Nobel. As I said before, imagine being able to switch viruses off, at all. Each virus would have its own switch of course, which makes it hellaciously complex, but still..."

"Be good, right?" Jacob hoped that was the case. But Alex's face did not hold hope.

"In theory, yes. Very good. But in the case of a deadly bioweapon... Do you know why there hasn't been a war using bioweapons? There have been occasional cases of terrorism, like the use of anthrax right after 9/11. But state actors haven't used bioterrorism. For basically the same reason we haven't had nuclear warfare, even though at times we have come close. The reason is MAD—Mutually Assured Destruction. Something like weaponized smallpox, which would be incredibly lethal and spread incredibly fast, would spread throughout the world really quickly, a huge blowback for the country of origin of the attack. You could, in theory, engineer a vaccine for the engineered virus, but not in quantities that would save a nation. Just save at most a terror group. Anyone attempting a weaponized virus could reduce the world to ashes."

"But?" Nick asked.

Alex nodded her head sharply. "But. There's definitely a but. A very clever bioengineer, someone who can edit genes, could take it in several directions. And believe me when I say Dr. Elias Fielding is as smart as they come. You could, for example, engineer smallpox for a very short latency. Natural smallpox has a latency period—the period between infection and disease—of about 48 hours. Long enough for infected people to make their way around the world twice. But you could edit for a very short latency—an hour, say. An hour from the moment of contagion, you're infected, with no known cure. It would spread like wildfire. But, of course a few people could escape or fly out, unknowingly. The whole world could become infected. It would bring down civilization and very few groups want that, really. A person who would want that is usually too insane, mind too disorderly, to plan something so intricate."

"Not all evil bastards are insane," Nick growled.

Alex sighed. "True. And there is a way around Mutually Assured Destruction. Build in an extinction factor. Construct a fast-acting, massively lethal, super-contagious virus, kill off an entire population in a restricted geographical area, then switch the virus off. Within these parameters—a genetically engineered virus, say smallpox, that spreads fast, is lethal, kills the local population quickly but is no longer contagious after a very short set period, and you could conquer, say, Taiwan in less than a week. But this is all conjecture. I have no idea how close anyone is to a genetically engineered small pox virus, or any other kind of virus."

Jacob and Nick said nothing. There was nothing to say.

Nick spoke first. "I'll put together a team."

"Make sure every member has a biohazard suit," Alex said quickly. "And not that MOPP nonsense. HAMMER suits. With HEPA filters, Bioclass five, in compliance with EN1073-1 and ISO 16603-ISO 16 604. One for each member of your team and at least one extra suit for each."

"Yes, ma'am," Nick said. "Doctor."

Alex sketched a smile. "Like I said, Alex will do."

"Alex."

Jacob shook off the dread he felt as Alex described a situation that was as dangerous as it gets. He could barely wrap his head around the idea of her walking into that. But she was also a world-class expert and their best chance of coming out of it alive. One thing he decided—they were leaving as soon as they could. No having dinner and sleeping here. They had to leave, stat.

"Nick, we'll be wheels up in a couple of hours. Text me the coordinates of an airfield and meet me there with your team."

"Will do. I think we should keep the team small until we know our facts."

"Agreed. I'll depend on you for manpower. I'll come with gear."

Nick clicked off and Jacob turned to face Alex. She was sitting composed, hands linked on her lap. But she was pale, white lines of stress bracketing her mouth. She understood exactly what she was getting into—the danger, the potential for catastrophe—but wasn't wavering, not for a second.

He admired her composure.

He himself was going crazy with anxiety, facing the kind of fear he'd never felt before. Had only seen in others. You went on a mission with teammates. Men—almost always men—as well trained as you. Good with guns, with knives, with their fists, hell—with a rock. He never had to worry about them because they knew what they were doing, knew what the odds were, were very well-trained, willing to face mortal danger and usually came out on top, leaving dead bodies behind.

He'd never gone on a mission with a woman he cared about, a lot. Never happened, never thought it would happen. Alex was smart, yeah, but smarts don't tell you to zig when you are supposed to zig and zag when you are supposed to zag. Smarts don't make your weapon aim true. Smarts don't protect you against bullets or grenades or missiles.

Alex was ridiculously unsuited for the mission. She'd never been athletic, not even as a girl. She was a straight A student all the way and her extracurricular activities were band and the Science Club. Editor of the school newspaper. She had always been sunny and tender-hearted. The absolute worst possible teammate. All of Jacob's operators were mean sons of bitches, paranoid and tough. The complete opposite of Alex.

And yet, and yet... a small part of him thrilled to the idea that Alex was here, with him. After all these years. True, they were probably walking into danger and she was really mad at him. Those were downers but not enough to make him down. Nope. He was going to be with *Alex*. The last time he'd felt something even approaching happiness, it had been with her. Something deep inside, something that he didn't know had been dead all these years, sparked to life.

All joy in the world, all softness and gentleness and kindness, all beauty was concentrated in her, and he was going to be with her, with that.

Even now, planning a dangerous mission, with her mad at him, he felt his chest inflate with happiness, a feeling so unusual he didn't even recognize it at first.

It was fucking dangerous.

Terrifying. Happiness could get him killed.

He was going on a dangerous mission with the one person in the world he wanted—needed—to protect and he was doing it in an altered state of mind. It was as if he'd taken a drug, some kind of upper. Mind-altering drugs were absolutely forbidden at Black Inc. The only thing allowed was alcohol and, like pilots, not within 48 hours of going on mission. The one thing combat was, it was fucking *real*. You had to see what *was*, in real life, not what your heart wanted there to be.

He practically was seeing unicorns and smelling roses.

Time to get back into the real world, stat.

"Ok." Jacob stood up suddenly and Alex tilted her head back. Oh, God. That neck. Long, pale, perfect.

Jacob had recently come back from a recon in a country where all the men were bearded and the women weren't allowed on the streets so he'd spent ten days looking at bearded male throats.

God, this was something else.

He glanced away for a second to distract himself and put on his expressionless face when he turned back to Alex. It was his default face, what his face muscles did without him thinking about it. He'd been told it was scary, which suited him. Now he had to think about putting on a face that wasn't scary but was also serious. Because what he wanted to do was smile at Alex. Take her hand, smile in her face, bring her hand to his lips...

No.

"I think we should be leaving tonight, get there fast and do recon. I'll take you up to my place, show you where you can shower. Then you order clothes and whatever you need. Like I said, order anything you want, in quantity because we have no idea what we're walking into. I don't know what kind of shops there will be where we're going, so make sure you have a supply of everything. At this point, send all your orders to my assistant, Catherine. She'll make sure everything is delivered within the hour. I'll have some food sent up, too. We're leaving in three hours."

Reflexively, Alex glanced at her watch. "It's 7 pm now, so... 10? Is that possible?"

"Yeah. The plane's on the tarmac, waiting for us."

"Okay, I..." She stared up at him. Swallowed, that long pale neck bobbing.

Jacob was keeping himself still by sheer will power, though stillness was a gift he had. One of many. A sniper was born with the ability to stay still for long periods of time. Snipers were never agitated. But here he was, looking at her, fists clenched, wanting with everything in him to hold out his arms and have her walk into them.

"Go," he said.

She went.

CHAPTER
Five

FEDERAL SECURITY BUREAU, LUBYANKA SQUARE,
MOSCOW

Colonel Ilya Topolev had never accepted the fall of the Soviet Union, and never would. He remembered very clearly the day it happened. He'd been a brand-new recruit, two days into his dream job as an officer of the KGB. His lifelong dream. He'd graduated top of his class from the Red Banner Institute north of Chelebityevo.

At the time, the school trained over 300 students in espionage, the best and brightest of the empire, eager to defend the empire. Two years later, there were only 50 students studying how to protect the rump state known as the Russian Federation and the Soviet Union was no more.

That traitor Gorbachev should never have allowed the Berlin wall to fall. Just a little show of balls, *chert poberi*, and history would have gone differently. The Soviet Union would still exist, protected by the officers of the KGB.

Topolev had been a brand-new recruit to the KGB then and now he was a senior member of its successor, the

FSB. He'd watched his beloved country humiliated over and over since the fall of the USSR.

For years, he'd watched Russia grapple with its new identity, watched mobsters rise and corrupt everything, watched as a grotesque form of slavish imitations of Western culture permeated the country. Oligarchs stripped his country of its resources while ordinary citizens were left in the dust.

His once-proud nation, a colossus feared and respected, staggered and stumbled instead of standing tall on the global stage. This was not the Russia he knew. This was absolutely not the Russia he'd sworn as a new cadet of the KGB to serve and protect.

The disintegration of the mighty Soviet Empire into crappy little statelets still burned. It had been a disastrous collapse.

It still stung.

And yet, Topolev was convinced that the United States and the West were weaker than when they toppled the Soviet Union.

The humiliation he felt for his country was personal, too. He'd dedicated his life to the Soviet cause, pouring his heart and soul into his training at the Red Banner Institute. Working hard to serve a nation that no longer existed by the time he'd begun his service. And he was forced to adapt to a new system which was incredibly inferior. Many of his colleagues saw him as a relic of the past, beholden to a Soviet Union that was no more, in a country that had moved on.

He was bitter and resentful, but he had plans. Big plans. He worked tirelessly on a way to restore Russia's preeminence in the world and its dignity.

Over the decades, he had watched world events like a chess grandmaster watches the board. He dedicated himself to understanding the new world order. He studied the strengths and weaknesses of the West, its alliances and rivalries, ever-changing. He studied threats and opportunities. He studied all aspects of nuclear power, the possibility of cyber warfare, biological warfare, commercial warfare and built a network of contacts and allies inside the FSB and other security organizations, always just under the radar. A hidden network of like-minded patriots. People who understood, the way he understood, that the world had taken a wrong turn when the Wall fell. He bided his time until the circumstances were just right.

It was time.

The West was faltering, together with the United States. Economic situations worsening for most people, political divisions and strife. Yet Russia was growing stronger, its military well-structured, well-trained. He saw a Russia the outside world did not. It was time the world perceived its strength and resolve.

The US was a paper tiger, hollowed out. One strong blow and it would fall.

Russia would rise. The Soviet spirit—strength and resolve—would return. Russia would become a global superpower to be reckoned with once more. His country had been wronged, humiliated, betrayed.

No longer.

Finally, after years of searching, he had the key.

Topolev never believed in nuclear weapons—expensive to make and to maintain, requiring a vast infrastructure, cumbersome and dangerous to handle. And even if you win, you reign over ashes. Rather, his plan would leverage tiny, minute particles, invisible unless seen through an electron microscope. That was what would bring America down.

He'd seen whole villages destroyed in Iraq and Syria, thanks to chemical weapons. No one had had the courage to use chemical or biowarfare on a mass basis for fear of blowback. Viruses and bacteria do not respect borders.

He'd been funding an expert who had found a way around the dilemma, who was creating a key for him, a kill switch. Dr. Obolensky. But then he'd gone and killed himself.

Topolev had had to put his plans on ice until there was a breakthrough.

A man working at the CDC, in his pay, Elias Field, had perhaps developed a kill switch of his own.

This wasn't a sanctioned operation. Mother Russia had lost its nerve. The FSB had lost its operational horizon. They were busy putting out fires close by and had lost sight of who the real enemy was. The United States. America had always been the enemy and always would be.

Topolev was running a rogue operation working surreptitiously in the FSB with men who had been dreaming of victory since the Fall of the Wall. The former

Soviet Union had fallen. But something strong and united would take its place.

There were too many in the FSB who were time-servers. Cowardly men and now women who just wanted a job and a paycheck. They would all be on the lookout for anything that could shatter their careers and pensions. He and his fellow planners had to be careful, keep the preparations low key. When it happened, it would happen fast and it was entirely possible that it would look like one of those geopolitical actions that came out of nowhere to change history.

This plan could be run on a relatively tight budget that would be easy to hide, with a tightly controlled group dialed in. A few corrupt scientists in the US, one secret BSL-4 lab staffed by a handful of well-paid scientists—the whole thing would cost less than the hidden funds for the mistresses of the members of the Council of Ministers. Done right, the plan could bring the United States to its knees, and with it, the West, all on a shoestring.

Further, he had oligarch friends who would guide his investments on I-Day, Infection Day. He would become rich and powerful beyond the dreams of Stalin.

Da.

It was time to start.

A few days ago, he lured the CDC doctor in his pay to a Georgia airfield outside Atlanta, where he was abducted and flown to Vostokova. It was clear Dr. Field had a taste for fast cars, high-end fashion and lavish vacations and had closed his eyes to what the information he sold meant.

Now there was a glitch.

His men told Topolev that, in custody in Zalny, the good doctor had grown a conscience.

Well, a conscience was a luxury. Topolev was slowly breaking Dr. Field down in a pharmaceutical factory in Zelenograd. Nothing too harsh, because Dr. Field would have to do the physical bioengineering work.

They had to hurry. Topolev had planned for I-day to coincide with the arrival of a Chinese trade delegation in Los Angeles and a performance of a Chinese pop group in Seattle. The Chinese were slated to arrive on the West Coast in three weeks' time. Exactly when the epidemic would begin.

Topolev would become immensely rich, more than an oligarch, and perhaps the Viceroy of the Pacific States.

CHAPTER
Six

J ake's—Jacob's—apartment was as incredible as she could have imagined. He had the entire top floor of the building and the rooms were huge. Minimally decorated, not as an aesthetic choice, but because she imagined he didn't care. The essentials were there—places to sit, to eat, to work. Nothing superfluous, no personal touches. A place to live and work.

They went up in an elevator of stainless steel and black marble, with only two settings. The floor where his office was and his apartment. The elevator opened onto the apartment itself. She stepped out, blinking at the size of the place.

Space was a luxury. Houses were sold by square feet. Though the place was enormous, it didn't feel like an indulgence, mainly because there were few luxuries. It was just... a space.

"Through here," Jacob said, with a hand to her back.

They turned right and walked through an enormous living room, an enormous study and an enormous kitchen-dining area. There were two doors in a large corridor.

Jacob hooked a thumb to the right. "That's my quarters." To the left. "This is the guest bedroom suite." And opened the left-hand door.

Unsurprisingly, it was huge, sparsely furnished with a big bed, a desk and chair, a couple of acres of hardwood flooring, and way on the other side, another door. Probably the bathroom.

"Guest bedroom suite." Alex looked up at that dark, unsmiling face. "You have guests often?"

A wintry smile. "Never. You're the first." He indicated the desk, which had a laptop on it. "Catherine's email is on a sheet of paper next to the laptop. Go wild with ordering. Send your orders to her and she'll expedite everything. Include cold weather clothes. The bathroom has... stuff."

"I'm assuming stuff includes soap and shampoo?"

He nodded. Clearly, he'd just used his quota of words for the hour.

Alex put her hand on the door. "Okay. I'll see you in a little while."

Jacob just stood there, looking down at her, until finally he nodded, turned on his heel and left.

Alex let out a breath. He was such an overwhelming presence. When he left it was like someone switched off a power source that held her in thrall. But, crazily, when he left, she also felt alone and just a little scared.

This was nuts. Alex had been on her own for a long,

long time. She was used to it, liked her own company. But she stood still for a while, getting used to the feeling of Jacob not distorting reality with his strong force field. It was as if color leached from the world when he walked away.

She shook herself. There were things to do, and not much time to do them. She eyed the bed longingly. What she wouldn't give to be able to just lie down for an hour? But she was sleep-deprived. If she lay down, she'd drop into a deep sleep. She'd barely slept for three nights, she'd flown across the country, and the bed called to her. She placed a hand on the mattress and groaned inwardly. Just as she thought. It was a perfect mattress, with a perfect dark blue comforter. Doubtless made of perfect Danish goose down. If she rested on that bed, she'd go out like a light.

With a sigh, she wrenched her gaze from the huge bed and went to the desk to order clothes. Luckily, she had a couple of go-to sites and knew exactly what to order. The main company specialized in high end sportswear made of natural fibers. Alex ordered elegant track suits in light and dark gray, light and dark blue, green, beige and black. A week's worth and wearing the outfits for two days stretched it to two weeks. Lightweight silk undershirts if it turned cold, as Jacob said it might. Several thick cashmere sweaters. Underwear for two weeks, seven pairs of socks, three pairs of soft boots that she knew were comfortable, two pairs of sneakers. One leather, one canvas. At another site she was familiar with, she bought five sets of pajamas, two pairs of slippers and a knee-length down coat.

On the off chance that an official meeting might occur, she also bought a stylish wool pantsuit with a cream silk blouse.

Lastly, at a well-known drugstore site, she bought a good cleansing cream, day cream, night cream, foundation, eyeliner, lipstick, mascara, a toothbrush and toothpaste.

A Samsonite roll-on.

There. It had taken her fifteen minutes and she knew she could live for a while with what she had bought.

She used the credit card Jake—Jacob!—had given her. The Jake she'd known hadn't had a dime to his name. Her parents, bless them, used to tuck some cash in his backpack —which he'd rescued from the dump—at Christmas and his birthday. But this Jake, Jacob, could certainly afford a couple of weeks' worth of clothes for her. It was a rounding error for him.

She wiped that thought from her mind. Though she'd wanted to make a point of being able to pay her own way, it made sense that orders from a Black Inc. credit card would arrive faster. And she had other things to worry about. Like a possible threat that could wipe out civilization. Next to that, a tussle over who paid for what seemed pointless.

All the sites said to expect deliveries within the hour. But the first packages arrived almost immediately. The power of money.

The bathroom—she wasn't surprised to see—was incredibly sumptuous without being ostentatious. Just acres of space, marble flooring and walls. A shower bigger than her first kitchen, with a billion spouts. She didn't need them all. The overhead rain-forest spout was enough.

She put her head back and breathed in the steamy air. The water was lavender scented.

Of course it was.

She stood under the hot, scented stream for a long time, palms against the sandstone tiles. She needed this, this moment out of time. It felt like she'd been worried forever, couldn't even remember a time when she wasn't scared out of her mind, thoughts racing like lemmings to a dark edge.

And then—Jake! Jacob. The boy who'd filled her heart with sorrow and regret suddenly reappearing as a man before her. And what a man. She'd run through the scenarios over and over in her head these past years, and to her shame, in almost all of them, Jake was beaten down by life. How could she think otherwise?

He wasn't thriving in school and had been held back twice. Already, there was hardly any college in the country that would accept him. Maybe some vocational schools. And everyone knew it was hard, almost impossible, to rise without some form of college education. He'd left Bend without even graduating high school.

He had a temper. She'd seen it on occasion, though never ever directed at her or her folks. If her mom and dad had seen him when he fought a bully, they'd probably have prohibited her from seeing him, he was that adept at violence. He turned cold and efficiently used his strength.

So, a man who hadn't even graduated high school, without a dime to his name, with a temper… how would that man fare in life?

Not well. Or so she'd thought. She'd been so sad thinking of him. Imagining him down on his luck somewhere. Maybe sick. Maybe homeless. Maybe dead.

She was wrong, of course.

The Jake Simpson she knew, the tragically lost boy who'd disappeared from her life, had turned into Jacob Black, one of the richest, most powerful men in the country. In the world.

And not only that. Somehow, the man he had become held her in his thrall.

If you'd held her feet to the fire, Alex would have confessed that she suspected she was asexual. Her few lovers certainly were not happy with her. She'd read descriptions of being 'turned on' and thought they were exaggerated.

They weren't.

Being near Jacob was like being plugged in to some hot and electric source of power. In the midst of anxiety and danger, she'd come alive, shocked and startled.

He was so imposing. Not just his size, though she was astonished at just how big he was. He'd always been tall, but he'd also been painfully thin as a teenager. Now he was filled out, but not muscle bound. A big man, broad in the shoulders and chest, lean in the waist. But over and above his size, it was the pull of power that overwhelmed her. Not the power of his money but of his person.

She'd been around powerful people before, of course. She'd testified at a congressional committee where Senators were as thick as cockroaches in an abandoned kitchen. She'd spoken with CEOs of important pharmaceutical companies. She'd shaken hands with Nobel Prize winners.

None of them that aura that Jacob did, of immense personal power, of a charisma so great it almost bent gravity.

And that aura included... sex. Oh God. Alex had been taken so much by surprise that she hadn't actually acknowledged what being so close to Jacob did to her. It just lit her up. Head to toe.

The water beating down on her was hot, but she remembered that inner heat that shimmered through her at his closeness. Intense and uncontrollable and completely new.

This was going to be so hard, over and above the horror of Elias going AWOL with massively damaging knowledge in his head. She was going to have to keep her cool around Jacob and ignore the heat.

But her body remembered. Oh man, did it ever. As the water beat against her back, Alex could feel her breasts as if they were a separate part of her body and not some tissue hanging from her chest. They felt swollen and warm, the nipples super sensitive. Her groin, too, felt warm. That had never happened to her before.

And Jacob wasn't even handsome. He had harsh, irregular features and a burn scar and a knife scar, both, on the left side of his face.

Didn't make any difference. He had testosterone coming out of his pores and would instantly make any woman forget even the handsomest man.

It occurred to her that he might have a mistress or two. A man like that? Super masculine, incredibly rich and powerful? Of course he did. He even had quarters for them in his home, so he could have a sex life without it interfering in business.

Who knew how many women had used this shower? It was fully stocked with shampoos and conditioners and citrus-scented soap.

He said he'd never had overnight guests using her quarters. But then his women probably slept in the master bedroom. With him.

Alex turned off the shower coming from the ceiling and dried herself off with one of the stack of huge fluffy towels. When she was done, she folded it up neatly and put it on one of the steel stools, since there wasn't a heater in sight. But she wasn't chilly. The room was a perfect temperature.

All her packages had arrived.

She was familiar with the track suits. She had three of them from that company back home. It took her but a moment to dress, put her wet hair up in a scrunchy she had in her purse, and put on socks and sneakers. The sneakers were brand new, of course, but again, it was a brand she knew and they were instantly comfortable. Who knew what they'd find at the other end of the trip, and who knew if she'd have to run.

All the packages had been brought into the bedroom, together with a medium-sized roll-on suitcase.

Alex was used to travelling and she packed quickly. Everything she'd ordered fit into the suitcase. She zipped it up and rolled it over to the door.

Right outside the door, Jacob was waiting. He was dressed all in black and had a black duffel and a roll-on suitcase of his own at his feet.

Her heart gave a little thump at the sight of him. He'd been looking down, frowning, at a watch the size of a dessert plate but straightened at the sight of her. His eyes met hers, black gaze intense, and her heart gave another little thud. She was still mad at him, but apparently her heart wasn't.

It was going to be a long flight.

CHAPTER
Seven

How Alex could be exhausted and stressed and frightened and still look so beautiful was beyond Jacob's comprehension. She was still a little pale, looked tired and was dressed in leisure wear, but she'd still turn heads anywhere she went. Those fine features, witchy pale-blue eyes and delicate bone structure, would last her the rest of her life.

She was wearing a pretty track suit the exact color of her eyes, and leather sneakers, exactly the right kind of outfit for the mission they were going on. But then she knew exactly the kind of situation they could be walking into.

She was smart and not just beautiful.

It was going to be hard not to stare at her, and he had to kick himself in the ass on a regular basis to remind himself to look away once in a while. He didn't want to freak her out. But man, it was hard.

He cleared his throat. "Everything ok? You find everything you need?"

She gave a small smile. "Everything is fine. I'm sure your guests find the guest quarters comfortable. Lavish, actually."

Jacob frowned. "I wouldn't know. I told you, I've never had guests over before."

Alex blinked. "Never? That bedroom suite is awfully elaborate for something that is never used."

He shrugged. "When I was designing my living quarters, I specified guest quarters because I thought it would be easier to have my mission heads staying over when planning, but in the end it was easier just to have everyone stay at a nearby hotel. So you've inaugurated the whole set up. Here, let me have your bag."

"No, you've got your own stuff, you don't have to carry mine."

"That's okay." Jacob hoisted his duffel, which clanked, clearly full of equipment, then took both suitcase handles. "We don't have far to go."

It was only two floors up to the rooftop. The helo's rotors were already spinning. Jacob tried to shield Alex from the wind, but it was impossible. He just tried to get her into the cabin as quickly as possible. One of his men stowed their luggage away as Jacob helped Alex up the stairs. He sat her down, pulled across the seat belt, put a noise cancelling helmet on her, then did the same for himself. The instant he could, he signaled the pilot, who pulled them up and away.

"Airport's only about half an hour away," he said into the mic and she nodded.

"I remember."

He glanced at her sharply, but there was no sarcasm in her tone. She was simply stating a fact. She'd taken the helo trip from the airport and remembered the length of the journey.

For the first time, Jacob looked at her trip cross country from her point of view. She said she felt she'd been 'shanghaied' and he could see that. Usually, he thought things through carefully but from the instant he'd received word that Dr. Alexandra Hethering had stepped into Black Inc. in Atlanta, he'd been in a fever to get her here as fast as possible.

He hadn't been subtle about it, but in the end, here she was.

With him.

She might be a little less pleased at this than he was.

He'd have to work at that.

And take care of her. She'd had a little color in her face after the shower but now she was paper white. She must be exhausted. Days of worry, not sleeping nights. Flown across the country, where she didn't eat or drink anything, and there'd been no time for food.

Jacob had given orders that the plane be stocked with food and drink because it was going to be a long trip across the Pacific. The plane would be fully stocked and the bedroom would have fresh sheets on the bed.

He looked at her, at that tired lovely face, and ejected

that thought right out of his head and out of his dick. She was in trouble and he needed to take care of her. That didn't include necessarily sex, much as he wanted it to. Women needed to be in the mood. He himself would have cheerfully had sex on the helo's seats if she gave even the merest hint she'd be up to it. Which she definitely wasn't doing. She wasn't even looking at him.

"Relax," he murmured into the mic. It was a channel only for them. "Get as much rest as you can."

She looked at him, some effect of the light turning her eyes silver, a flash of it. She nodded and leaned her head back, closing her eyes. Jacob held his hand hovering over hers for a moment, then placed it over hers.

Her hand was cold. He'd been right. She was running out of steam. Behind them was a thermal blanket and he put it over her, tucking it into her sides. She fought it a little, then went out like a light. He watched her for a long moment, caught his pilot watching him in the mirror.

Jacob had told nobody about Alex except for Nick, one evening when he got shit-faced. They'd both been shit-faced and heartbroken over losing teammates in a firefight and Jacob's lifelong rule, broken only for Alex and her parents—*never let anyone know what's going on inside you* —had been broken. But other than Nick, no one knew anything about his private life. He'd never openly been with a partner.

The pilot was going to talk about how the boss was treating this new woman who'd popped up. Let him. Jacob didn't give a shit who knew he cared about Alex. It wasn't anyone's business but his own.

He pulled out his ruggedized tablet and started going over the intel Nick had sent.

The pilot was good—if nosy—and landed them gently on the tarmac at the airfield. Alex was still out. Jacob shook her shoulder gently, but she didn't wake up. He shook her again. "Alex. Wake up. We're here."

She inhaled sharply and opened her eyes, that light-blue gaze meeting his and he saw surprise flare. She looked around in confusion and he saw the exact moment she was oriented. She was with him, they were going to embark on a plane to Vostokova and they might be travelling to stop the end of the world.

It was all there on her face before she shut it all down, gave him a bland smile and a nod.

He nodded. "You must be hungry. There will be food on the plane."

"Oh." Alex looked startled, as if she'd forgotten the concept of food, of hunger. "I am hungry, thanks!"

There it was again, that instinctive politeness. Thanking him for thinking of feeding her. Jesus.

The helo pilot was transferring their stuff to the plane, including his gear. Jacob leaped down to help Alex to the ground and she thanked him again. He had to stop that habit she had, it made him feel awful.

Thanking him for helping her off the helo. The steps were high and hard to navigate, he wasn't about to let a tired Alex, who hadn't eaten all day, come down those steps on her own.

He gave her his hand and the instant they were on the ground, she pulled away. She wasn't subtle about it.

OK.

Jacob motioned for her to go up the stairs to the plane, walking right behind her. He gave a sigh of relief when they were inside the plane, an Embraer Legacy. The pilot met them at the door. Captain Conan McCann. He'd worked for Black Inc. for five years. On the tarmac, the steps were pulled away and McCann pulled the door closed.

Just like that, the outside world was cut off. Inside, the cabin felt calm and orderly and quiet. And private. They were going to be together non-stop for the next fifteen hours, something he'd dreamed of for the past eighteen years.

Jacob stopped by the cockpit to say hello to McCann and the co-pilot. He hadn't asked for any assistants or attendants in the plane. The pilots would stay in the cockpit. He and Alex would be alone.

The plane was outfitted with a full office and a bedroom with a shower in the back. They would be living there for the time it took to get to Vostokova. The closest he'd been to her in years.

There was a small business center, with armchairs around an oval conference table. Alex sat in an armchair and Jacob took a seat next to her. Maybe she wanted him to sit across the table? Tough shit.

"I'll get you some food as soon as we reach cruising altitude."

Alex nodded and clutched the seat arms as the plane started taxiing. Was she a nervous flyer?

"Don't worry." Jacob placed his hand over hers. "Captain McCann flew with the Air Force for twenty years. His copilot has a lot of experience as well. We're in very good hands."

Alex side-eyed him. "You think I'm nervous?"

"No, not at all," he lied. "Just letting you know. It's going to be a long flight. There might be some turbulence. Again, I want you to know both pilots are the best in the business."

Alex sighed. "I do sometimes get a little nervous flying. I can control it, don't worry."

"Not worried. Not at all." He squeezed her hand gently. She said she'd been shanghaied and he'd said no, she hadn't been shanghaied, but the truth was she had been. He knew Dylan, who could act the part of a gentleman perfectly, though he wasn't. It had been made very clear to Dylan that Alex was to be treated with kid gloves, but Dylan was also a rock and would have also made it very clear to Alex that she had no alternative. That she was flying off with him whether she liked it or not.

Jacob hadn't actually been thinking clearly or he would have—have what? Because once Alex entered the doors into Atlanta's Black Inc., she was coming to San Diego, to him. No question. But he hadn't factored in that she might not like flying.

Jacob tapped on a built-in screen on the tabletop and showed it to Alex.

"That's what we have on board to eat. Choose whatever you want. You can have hot food too, of course." Even if he'd dismissed flight attendants, Jacob could operate the microwave just fine.

Alex bent over the screen and studied the menu carefully. Jacob had asked for the plane to be fully stocked, and it was. It wasn't five-star restaurant fare, but there was a good selection of food, and an excellent selection of wine and beer. He knew what he wanted. A hot pastrami and coleslaw and a local artisanal beer called Rickety Bridge. Later, for their second meal when they'd crossed the Pacific, he might have a sliced steak salad with shoestring potatoes. There were also snacks if they wanted them.

"You decided?"

She looked at him. "You have quite a selection here. I've flown first class twice and this beats it."

Damn right. Anyone flying on this plane was working with or for Black Inc. and was either flying into or out of trouble. They deserved the best. "So what will you have?"

"I think the wild mushroom tortellini and the pear and escarole salad."

"Sounds good. You can unbuckle now."

"What?"

"We're in the air."

She glanced, startled, out the window, as they flew over San Diego. There was a faint line of light on the western horizon where a touch of sunlight lingered but you could clearly see where the brightly lit shoreline of the western reaches of San Diego met the black ocean.

"Wow. That was smooth."

"Told you."

"You tempted me with food so I wouldn't be nervous."

He resisted smiling. "Busted. But since I did, let me get it for you."

Jacob knew how the food service worked. He made a point of knowing how all things in his company worked. He could answer the phones, clean the floors, man the canteen if he had to. In the early days he'd been his company's armorer and vehicle mechanic.

The catering was well organized. In a few moments, he had Alex's tortellini, piping hot, in front of her and had his hot pastrami sandwich. Their salads were on the sideboard and drinks right in front of them when he sat down.

Alex sighed. "That's well done. Maybe you missed your calling."

"Mmm," he said as he bit into his sandwich. Delicious. "Black Inc. Catering. Has a certain ring. How are your tortellini?"

"Fabulous. I was really hungry. Maybe I should have eaten on the way over, after all."

Jacob turned to look her in the eye. "Dylan said you wouldn't accept anything. Not even water."

She rolled her eyes. "I was not at all certain I wasn't being kidnapped in a totally non-threatening kind of way. With the best of intentions."

Jacob blew out a breath. He'd really fucked that up. He

could normally game out how to do thing, but he'd dropped the ball. All he could think about was Alex on her way to him and not how Alex would perceive being tossed across the country like a package.

She turned her head to him. "You know, you should apologize."

Jacob didn't do apologies, unless he had fucked up massively, which he never did. But: "Sorry."

She fixed those blue blue eyes on him. "That sounded like it hurt."

It did. "That's okay."

"Why don't you try again?"

He'd forgotten that about Alex. She rarely let go of something until she got what she wanted. Too bad he had always admired that in her.

"Ok. A little out of practice here, but I'll give it a shot. I'm sorry—I'm really sorry I had Dylan accompany you—"

"Drag me."

Deep breath. "Yeah, okay. Drag you across the country. I hadn't given instructions to him on what to tell you so it must have seemed as if you were being strong-armed."

"Politely strong-armed, but yeah. It wasn't fun."

Oh, shit. He'd have shot anyone forcing him onto a plane. Fought with all his strength and he was a strong man.

Alex was not a strong woman. She'd said she didn't do martial arts and anyway she could never have beaten Dylan, who was a black belt and a fourth dan. It would never have come to that, but she couldn't have known that.

She chose not to rebel because it was clear she couldn't win.

Jacob was now sorry he'd put her in that position.

He looked her straight in the eyes and spoke from the heart. Something he never did. Every word out of his mouth was always calculated, but not this time.

"I am so sorry I put you through that. I wasn't thinking at all. All I knew was that you turned to my company and I needed you here as fast as you could come. So I gave instructions I now regret. I am really sorry."

She gave a half smile. "Okay. Does the galley stretch to dessert?"

And just like that, it was over.

He'd apologized, she'd forgiven him, that was that. Alex didn't bear grudges, he remembered that. *He* did. Fuck, yeah. He could hate someone forever. He still bore a grudge against the fuckhead who'd bullied Alex in her freshman year, though she'd probably long ago forgotten him.

She wanted dessert? He'd give her dessert.

"It does. Crème caramel with pear, chocolate cake with rum, raspberry and fig ice cream. I could do a plate with small servings of each, too. A little sampler."

"I don't know if I have room for that. But I would like a small scoop of raspberry and fig ice cream."

Jacob rose. "We'll have another meal before landing and at any rate, everything is available at all times. Just check the galley."

In a moment, he slid a dessert plate with the ice cream

and watched as she tasted it. She closed her eyes for a moment in delight and his heart nearly stopped. No makeup, tired, in a track suit, didn't make any difference. Alex was still the most beautiful woman he'd ever seen. With her eyes closed with pleasure he had a sudden vision of her, stretched out on a bed, eyes closed tight with pleasure from what he was doing to her.

He wanted to do it all, right now. Even his imagination was having trouble keeping up because he wanted to kiss her mouth, her breasts, her belly, her sex. All at the same time.

He wanted to touch her all over, run his hand over all that smooth pale skin. Down over that long neck, down to cup what he could see were perfect breasts, over her belly, down to the area between her legs. He didn't know what she looked like naked—not yet anyway—but he had a really good imagination.

He couldn't have her open her eyes and see him fucking her with his eyes. What he was feeling was plain, and he had a hard-on to show it. He knew enough about women to know that he wasn't even halfway home with Alex. She was good hearted, yes, but in her eyes, he'd avoided her for eighteen years. Let her think he was homeless, or dead. And most of all, he'd abandoned her at her absolute lowest point.

He'd had his reasons but she didn't know them.

He in no way could assume that she was thinking lustful thoughts about him the way he was about her. And he couldn't assume she'd jump into bed with him right now, either, which was what he wanted more than he wanted his next breath.

Wasn't going to happen until they had time to talk, and he wanted to be touching her when they had that talk.

But Jacob Black, a man renowned for his self-control, couldn't seem to control his dick around her. What the fuck?

He turned toward the galley, thinking of weaponized smallpox, millions of people dying a horrible death, evil triumphing, the end of society, until his dick started behaving.

And thank God there was a soft bell tone. Truly saved by the bell. He turned, sat down next to Alex, pressed a button in the arm rest. A big monitor descended from the ceiling.

Three pretty women were sitting in a room with a huge modern painting in the background. Hope Ellis, Emma Holland, Riley Robinson. His magic fairies. The smartest women in the world, right after Alex.

"Hope, Emma, Riley. Good to see you. How's Felicity?"

"Fine," Hope answered. "Mick has a fever and she's staying home. Metal will be taking over when Mick's fever goes down. But we'll brief her and she'll be back online soon. We've got what you asked for."

"Great." Jacob had no doubt that they'd get what he asked for. They'd never failed him yet. "First, let me introduce Dr. Alexandra Hethering. She's a virologist with the CDC and has a problem we're hoping you can help with.

Alex, meet Hope, Emma and Riley. The fourth member of this little brain trust is Felicity, who just had twins. These women know everything and what they don't know they can find out. Unfortunately, they don't work for Black Inc., not for my lack of asking. They work out of Portland, Oregon, for a solid company, ASI, that happens to employ four men who are their partners, so I can't entice them away."

"But we're always available to you, Mr. Black," Emma said.

Jacob touched Alex's hand. "Emma saved my life this year, Riley saved the world, and they have all saved my bacon. They are miracle workers."

Alex was smiling, raised her hand. "Hello ladies, nice to meet you. So, what're your specialties?"

"You name it," Emma said.

"Intel," Jacob said. "They can discover anything about anybody. And Riley can walk up buildings."

Riley smiled and rolled her eyes. "Hardly. I do some low-level rock climbing. So, what's the problem and how can we help?"

Jacob tipped his head to Alex. "You want to brief them?"

Alex, bless her, didn't hesitate. The fact that he trusted them was enough for her.

"Okay." Alex put her elbows on the table and leaned forward. The three women were each in a separate field on the screen and Alex and Jacob were in a small square in the upper right-hand corner. "Here's what we've got. I'm a virologist with the CDC, and at the moment, I am completing a project with a colleague, Dr. Elias Field. Dr. Field is an expert at bioengineering. He is also an expert on smallpox."

Three indrawn breaths could be heard through the mics.

"I will cut to the chase. Dr. Field disappeared three days ago, right in the middle of a project, which is unheard of. He has shown signs of a sudden influx of money and I received a phone call that originated from Zalny in Vostokova. Zalny was a bioweapons lab during the Soviet era. I have no idea what he's doing, why he is missing and I am really worried."

"What's the worst-case scenario?" Riley asked.

"Okay." Alex's lips firmed. "Bottom line. The worst-case scenario would be an aerosolized form of smallpox with enhanced lethality, possibly 100%, and a reduced period of contagion. It could destabilize any country, possibly the world."

Silence.

"How can we help?" Emma finally said and Jacob wanted to kiss her. Wanted to kiss all of them. All they ever wanted to do was help and their help was always massively useful.

Alex glanced at Jacob and he nodded. She was doing just fine. "Well, for starters, I'm wondering what is at Zalny now." She typed numbers into the keyboard in front of her. "Jacob's colleague Nikolai discovered that there has been construction work done there. If, as I suspect, Zalny is an illegal bioweapons lab, it must have been restructured because it had been abandoned after the fall of the Wall. Decommissioned. I just sent you the coordinates. Would you have a way to, I don't know, go over past satellite footage to see how much work has been done on the site. It was left a concrete ruin back in 1989. A lot of work would have to have been done on it to turn it into a modern lab."

"On it." Emma and Hope bent over their keyboard and did what the women always did when tackling a problem—they disappeared into their computers. Jacob doubted whether they'd even notice an air raid siren going off close by.

"Also," Alex said, "would there be a way to see if whatever entity is there ordered a CRISPR-Cas9?"

"A what?" Jacob asked. Alex had mentioned this but he couldn't remember the context.

Now it was Riley's turn to bend over her keyboard. "CRISPR," she answered while pounding on the keys. "It's a technology that allows geneticists to edit parts of the genome. Exactly what someone hoping to alter the smallpox virus would need."

Alex nodded.

Once more, Jacob was astonished at the breadth and depth of the knowledge of these three young women. They were like Alex—super smart and understood the science and technology of the world.

If this thing could be stopped, these women would be the ones doing it. He and his men would be providing the infrastructure and muscle and, if necessary, the violence to stop it. But if this were Star Wars, the women were the heart of The Resistance.

"Thanks so much," Alex said.

"Got it!" Hope shouted, fist pumping the air in triumph. She lifted her head, green eyes blazing, looking about twelve years old. "Up on the other monitor."

Alex and Jacob turned to a big wall mounted monitor to the right. Alex frowned. "What are we looking at?"

And then the image came into focus and it was the Zalny site covered in snow. In fast forward, in jumping segments corresponding to an overhead satellite covering the area, then disappearing over the horizon, they watched as the small, crude, bunker-like building went away and trucks brought in building materials as excavators dug a massive hole. The hole was fortified with struts and a massive roof-like structure was erected, hiding the work underneath. Trucks came and went as the snow built, then melted, then the hills turned pale green and then dark green. And then the small crude building was hoisted back into place.

"How much time—" Jacob began when words appeared at the bottom of the screen. February 20-May 30.

Three months.

The Queens were all numbers women but Riley was the numberest of them all.

"So," she said. "Let's assume the underground lab has four floors. That about right, Alex?"

Alex nodded.

"And let's assume a standard lab size. Let's say, each floor 20 meters by 20 meters and a height of 3 meters."

Again, Alex nodded.

"Walls and ceilings are usually about 20 centimeters thick. And I'm assuming the standard density of concrete, which is about 2,400 kilograms per meter cubed."

"Go on," Jacob urged. He'd have been hard pressed to establish those assumptions without a lot of research even if you had put a gun to his head. Riley had simply pulled them out of her head.

"So about 2,200 tons of concrete would be delivered to build a four floor underground lab." She shook her head. "That's a lot of concrete. And of course, it depends on how much they built laterally."

"Space would not be a major concern for this kind of lab," Alex said.

"They wouldn't need a lot. The bottom story would be the level 4 lab. If there is one."

"Hard to imagine all this effort without a BSL-4 lab," Jacob said.

Alex sighed. "Yeah."

Jacob could tell she was having problems processing everything. She took it for granted that anyone educated enough to build a lab would do it for the common good. It was her default setting—people worked for the good. The sun rose in the east, set in the west and people were basically good.

It had taken her three days to confront the fact that her colleague, Field, had decamped with a ton of knowledge in his head that could be used for terrible purposes. Her mind simply didn't run along those tracks.

His did.

Yeah.

Jacob had seen enough of the world to know that most of mankind was selfish and could turn brutal if their interests were touched. He and his company operated on behalf of the ones who weren't brutal, though they weren't the majority.

"Queens of IT," Jacob said, and sketched a sitting bow. "I thank you and salute you."

"Yeah." Alex shook her head. "You guys are amazing. Thank you so much. We need to know what we're walking into."

"Be careful," Emma warned. "That country is pretty lawless."

"But you have Jacob," Riley said simply.

"And Black Inc.," Hope added.

"Before we sign off," Jacob said, "can you see if any flights have gone from around the Atlanta area to any airport near Zelenograd in the appropriate time frame? Say, from five days ago. It would be a private flight, anything from a Gulfstream on up."

"Gotcha." Emma bent immediately over the keyboard.

"We're on it," Hope said, and shot a two-finger salute off her forehead.

"We'll also find out if a CRISPR-Cas9 was delivered to the site."

The connection switched off.

"Wow." Alex blew out a breath. "I feel better knowing they are on our side. Why aren't they working for you, again?"

That was a sore point. "I wish they were." Jacob could hear the chagrin in his voice. "I've asked often enough. At one time or another I've offered them all jobs with me, really good jobs, but they are engaged or married to ASI guys, and they're happy where they are, and they all like living in Portland. But we cooperate with ASI all the time, it's a very good outfit, and at least one Queen is always available to help us. We call them the Queens and the Queens are always ready to help."

"And you're in the same time zone," Alex said.

"There's that, too. The Queens are really hard workers. They work around the clock if they need to. And have."

"That's good that you have them. That you and ASI can count on each other." She was silent a beat. "The CDC used to be like that. You could absolutely count on help from anyone, day or night. We were all working for the same goal, public health. To protect people."

Jacob could hear the wistfulness in her voice. "But now?"

She sighed. "But now..." She sighed again. "Never mind. We have enough to deal with right now."

Jacob made a mental note to press her on this. Later.

Alex ate the last spoonful of the raspberry and fig ice cream, placed the spoon on the plate and sat back with a sigh. "That was wonderful. If the world is going to end, at least we can go out in style."

Jacob touched her shoulder with his. "I'd very much like for civilization not to end. We can do without culinary delights, but I do like running water and antibiotics."

"Dentistry and Netflix," she sighed.

"Cellphones and air conditioning."

"Yeah." Alex leaned her head back. "We could lose it all. I keep coming back to that. To what could possibly make someone like Elias team up with the bad guys. Bad guys nowadays have immense power. They truly could end the world as we know it. Who would want that?"

Jacob had an answer to that. "People who think civilization could fall but not for them. There are some who actually wouldn't mind if we lost civilization as long as they are at the top of the heap of ashes. They think they can keep all their privileges, even though everyone else has been reduced to starvation."

"And cities reduced to rubble."

"And humanity left with roving gangs of bandits."

"I keep hoping Elias isn't part of this. That he is being kept... I don't know. Against his will."

Jacob kept his mouth shut.

She sighed. "Yeah. I don't think so either. Funny to actually hope that someone has been kidnapped."

"Better than the alternative."

She nodded. Was silent. Finally she turned to him. "Speaking of unpleasant topics..."

"Yeah?"

"I wasn't going to talk about this, but I have to, because I can't wrap my head around it. And, you know. The world might end soon. So. Why did you disappear? Never get in touch? I'm not sure you'd have even contacted me if I hadn't had this problem. But why? You knew where I was. Black Inc. broke ground a month after I was recruited to the CDC. In fact, it broke ground my first week on the job. I remember reading about it in the newspaper. There was even a photograph of you, but from the back as you planted a tree. There wasn't a close up. Everyone made the point that you were publicity shy."

"Publicity averse," Jacob corrected. He wasn't shy about anything. "There are valid reasons for my face to be not well known. Security reasons. I have two people in Black Inc.'s PR office whose job it is to keep my face out of the papers."

"I can sort of understand that. And I can understand that a security company would want to keep individuals anonymous. But you were establishing a branch of your company in Atlanta, presumably since you wanted CDC business. I heard about Black Inc. at the CDC almost immediately. And you said you were familiar with the organization chart. You must have known I was working there. Why didn't you... reach out?"

Horribly, Alex's voice broke and she turned away sharply for a moment. She was hurt.

Fuck. She was right to be hurt.

He didn't have a valid reason. Nothing that made sense.

"I didn't, ah, know how you'd react. Didn't know if I, ah, would mess up your private life. Didn't know what was going on with you. I, ah, didn't want... didn't feel..." His voice trailed off because his throat closed up.

"Whoa." Her eyes widened. "That's ridiculous. All you had to do was ask. Everyone knew I was single. As a matter of fact—" Alex drew in a shocked breath. "Jake Simpson! Or rather Jacob Black! You were *afraid!* You were afraid to approach me. I can't believe this! Big, strong, powerful Jacob Black, *afraid* of contacting an old friend. What did you think? That I'd—I'd hit you? What?"

Jacob's jaw set. He wasn't afraid of Alex. He wasn't afraid of anyone or anything. He'd defeated enemies by the score. He'd been in firefights and kept his cool. He'd built a multi-billion dollar enterprise from nothing. He wasn't afraid.

Yes, he was.

"Yeah," he mumbled.

Alex cocked her head, cupped a hand around her ear. "Speak up, I can't hear you. You were—"

"Afraid." The word came out between his tightly clenched teeth. It hurt. He said three words he'd never said before to a human being. "I was afraid."

Any other person would crow. Jacob Black, brought low. But Alex didn't. She just looked at him and said, softly, "There now. Was that so hard?"

Hard? "Like pulling teeth."

She laughed. "No, really. Tell me why you never came to me when you knew where I was. I didn't know at all

145

where you were. In my most depressed moments, I imagined you hurt. Homeless." She swallowed. "Dead."

Jacob was ashamed. Ashamed that he hadn't come forward. Ashamed that he'd let her think the worst. That he'd made her worry for him.

"I think—I wasn't sure of anything. That you'd want to talk to me. You could be angry. You could have forgotten all about me." That was one that kept him awake at night. As long as he didn't contact her, he could convince himself he would, at some point, contact her. Then she would welcome him, it would all turn out ok. It was truly a coward's way of thinking and that wasn't him. He'd always faced everything head on.

Except for Alex.

She looked at her hands. "I hadn't forgotten about you." Her voice turned husky. "Not for one day."

Oh God. Jacob turned in his seat, wanted to take her in his arms, but she stood up. "You know what? I'm really tired. It's" —she checked her watch—"2 am for me. I've flown across the country and I've had several sleepless nights. I'm really glad at this point that you're dealing with this too. That I have you, the Queens, this guy Nikolai, on my side. But if I'm to be in any way effective when we land, I'm going to have to sleep some."

Jacob didn't want to sleep. He wanted to keep talking to her. To *Alex*, something he'd been dreaming about for eighteen years. And then he wanted to take her in his arms, kiss her, touch her. Fuck her.

No, not that. He had plenty of fuck buddies. This

wasn't that. Wasn't a desire for a roll in the hay to get his ashes hauled. He wanted to make love to her, something he never did. Never wanted to. But he did now.

But—*just look at her*, he thought. She was pale, with purple shadows under those beautiful eyes. She was standing stiffly upright, something he recognized because he did that, too, when he was exhausted. Kept himself upright through will power alone.

He wanted her with every fiber of his being, but she was nearly falling over with exhaustion. So, nope.

"Does this plane stretch to blankets? Normal soft ones, not the crinkly thermal ones."

"Of course. In the closet at the entrance. But maybe you'll just want to go to bed. Bedroom's through there." He indicated with his head.

"I saw it. And saw there's only one bedroom and one bed, so I'll bunk down here." She pressed a button and the back of her seat lowered. "I imagine it's a lie-flat seat, so I'll be fine."

"Whoa." Jacob had to keep his jaw from falling open. "Wait. No way. Are you joking? You're taking the bedroom and I'll bunk down out here. Believe me, I've slept in far worse conditions."

"No." Alex had taken one of the blankets from the closet and had spread it over herself.

No. What the fuck did *no* mean? "What are you doing?"

Her brows came together in a frown. "Jake. Jacob. What does it look like I'm doing?" She pressed the button in the armrest and the seat reclined even further. She closed her eyes. "For a smart man, you're being very dim."

Jacob snatched her blanket away.

"Hey!" Alex's eyes popped open and she sat up. "What are *you* doing? Give me that blanket back."

She reached up, but he held it above his head, where she had no hope of getting it back. "No way. You are going to sleep in a bed. In your pajamas, between sheets. You are *not* going to sleep on an airplane seat."

Alex shot him A Look and pressed the button in the arm rest until the entire seat was flat. Jake knew it did that. It was a plane designed to allow his people to sleep before a mission. But not Alex.

She was sitting up straight. "See? It unfolds into a bed. I'll be perfectly fine."

Jacob ground his back teeth. This was not going to happen. "You. Will. Take. The. Bed." When he took that tone his employees scrambled. He didn't use it often but when he did, it got results.

Not this time.

Her chin lifted.

"Are you ordering me around?"

Of course he was. The idea of her sleeping on a chair when she didn't have to—while he slept in a bed—was something that made his brains scramble. It didn't compute in his head in any way.

"No," he said. "It's just that—"

"Good. Now hand me that blanket. I'm really tired."

He could actually *hear* his teeth grind now. "I can't let

you sleep here." The words felt as if they were being pulled from his mouth by red hot pliers.

"Excuse me?" Alex's cheeks were pink. "You can't *let* me? What does that mean?"

Jacob was losing this, together with his patience. He always won negotiations, always. He never lost his patience.

Except for now.

He dropped into the seat next to her.

"Alex." This was supposed to be his Reasonable Voice, but it came out rough, mumbly. "I can't let you sleep out here while I take the bed. You can't ask that of me. I wouldn't sleep a wink, you wouldn't sleep as well as you could. Please."

That wasn't convincing at all. But the part of his brain that was a born negotiator was offline, unavailable. He didn't have any reasonable arguments, other than the idea horrified him. He knew he should let it go. With anyone else, he would. After trying several times to do the gentlemanly thing, and being rebuffed, he'd just give in because it didn't make that much difference.

Except it did. In this case, it did.

This was Alex and he simply didn't have it in him to have her sleep out here. He should be convincing her, but it felt like his tongue was too big for his mouth. It wasn't a life or death situation. He should just give in. But he couldn't. All he could do was stare at her miserably.

Alex's face suddenly softened. She put her hand on his

forearm and he stared down at it. He could feel the warmth through two layers of fabric.

"Look." Alex's voice was reasonable.

He wasn't ready for reasonable, but he had to listen to her. It wouldn't change his mind, but he'd listen.

"I realize this is some—some misguided sense of chivalry. No—" she held up her hand when he opened his mouth. "Let me speak. So, you don't like the idea of you sleeping more comfortably than I will, and under ordinary circumstances, I wouldn't object. I'm not crazy and like everyone else, I like to be comfortable. But—we don't know what we're walking into, Jacob. Whether Elias is there willingly or under duress, he's with bad actors, there's no doubt about that. I will be your technical advisor, but it's you, your guy Nikolai and your men who will be subject to possible violence. To action. I simply can't let you face possible danger on little rest for no reason at all beyond you being gentlemanly. Just can't do it. And don't ask me to."

Jacob felt his entire body warring with itself. "I can't do it either," he said, voice hoarse.

Alex tipped her head back, rolled her eyes and stood up. Good, she was seeing reason. "Get up," she said.

Jacob stood up. "I'll show you the bedroom and bathroom."

"No need." Alex headed to the bedroom door. "We'll share the bed." She stopped and her head swiveled to him. "This is not an invitation to share anything but the bed. I'm counting on you to behave."

Jacob held his hands up in a gesture of surrender. "Behaving," he said.

Hot damn!

Sharing a bed with Alex was top of his all-time list of things he badly wanted to do. It wouldn't be what he'd envisaged. But it was a pretty good step forward.

"And wipe that smile off your face," she said sternly.

He didn't even know he was smiling. Jacob's default expression was a scowl so he tried to scowl, but it was hard. He followed her, deliberately not smiling, into the airplane's bedroom.

CHAPTER
Eight

ZALNY, NEAR ZELENOGRAD

E lias Field was sorry. Really, *really* sorry.

He was being observed through a two-way mirror, so he shuffled around the underground lab, making sure his movements were slow and awkward. Back home, at the CDC, he and Alex moved like ballet dancers in their suits. But it was the only thing he could think of to slow everything down, because from what he could tell, they were barreling straight to indescribable horror.

And it had started so pleasantly, so easily. A conference in Budapest, where he was a keynote speaker. The invitation had been a surprise, on behalf of a new pharmaceutical company based in Zelenograd he'd never heard of. But the invitation came with a business class ticket, reservations at the Budapest Four Seasons, pickup at the airport in a limo. First class all the way.

And then meeting Dr. Kasich, head of Teknolab, the

pharmaceutical company, who'd been charming and flattering and had taken him to the finest restaurants.

And then the flattering comments on his scientific papers led to an amazing offer of a consultancy with very high fees. It was borderline illegal, certainly unethical, at least according to CDC rules, but the CDC was not making him rich. This gig could make him rich in a couple of years.

The commitment was not onerous. Being available for consultancy work 20 hours a month, which could be done via videoconferencing. Two trips to Budapest a year.

The stipend to be paid into a bank account in the Bahamas, to save on bureaucracy and, incidentally, on taxes.

It was an offer made in heaven and Elias leaped at it. His life took an immediate turn for the better. No longer scrimping and saving because the CDC wasn't paying its top-tier scientists their due.

Alex never seemed to mind. Not in the least. It was really annoying. She not only didn't complain about the hours or the pay, she seemed content in the job.

Well, maybe she didn't have ambitions, but he did. Hell, yes.

The consulting job was easy. A few Zoom calls, a few emails. Once, a CDC report before it was published. Piddling things. And in return, the money and some fully paid conferences in places like Maui, Acapulco, Bali. Business class tickets and amazing hotels.

He'd been very pleased.

Right up to the request to show up at an airfield where he was strong armed onto a private jet and flown to a country he couldn't identify. He'd asked and asked where they were going, but the pilots didn't answer and the two men who were clearly guards weren't talking. The flight had taken around 15 hours. He could have been anywhere in the world.

They'd landed on an airfield with no signs, he didn't even know which language was spoken. He still didn't know where he was, in his fourth, or maybe fifth, day.

At first, he'd been treated with respect, but it had been made very clear that he had no choice in the matter.

That first day he realized that nobody cared that he was going to lose his job. He was sure Alex would cover for him for a few days, but after that he was toast. It frightened him a little that they didn't care at all. They were showing him that after this, his usefulness was zero.

At the airfield he'd been hustled into a SUV and driven for an hour. He gave up trying to communicate with anyone. Maybe nobody spoke English.

Once they arrived at their destination, he was even more puzzled. A hilltop in the middle of nowhere and a shabby concrete bunker. But then he understood. Inside the bunker was a space-age facility. A research lab with absolutely anything a researcher could possibly need.

So they were in some kind of rogue facility.

As soon as he arrived, a tall, thin, very fit man showed up. He was dressed in some kind of uniform, but Elias didn't know anything about military matters. He couldn't tell which country the uniform represented, nor could he tell the rank of the person.

The only thing he knew was that the man spoke perfect English with some kind of faint Eastern European accent. And beyond his rank, he was powerful. He obviously had enormous clout if he could kidnap an American citizen and fly him halfway across the world. But besides that, the man carried himself with authority, the real deal. Elias had met a lot of politicians who thought they were powerful, but this was something else.

The man's light-gray eyes were eerie, almost transparent. And icy.

"What's your name?" Elias had asked with a shaky voice.

The man had given an icy smile that was scary as hell. "You may call me Colonel," he'd said.

God. Colonel. So he had an army or at least a military apparatus behind him.

And then, Elias been basically locked up here in an underground lab which included a BSL-4 lab and given precise instructions.

That was when it was clear to him what this was about, and what the money and paid vacations had bought them. What Dr. Kasich and the Colonel were buying.

Horror. That's what they were buying.

And the end of the world.

* * *

W AS SHE CRAZY?

Sharing a bed with Jacob Black, who'd been Jake Simpson when he'd broken her heart, was dumb. Sharing a bed with who Jacob Black was now, was stupidity on a vast scale. The man he was now was temptation incarnate. Powerful and powerfully attractive.

And she was attracted, and how. So she should be staying far away.

Except she'd spoken the sober truth. He needed to rest. The more she knew about the situation they were flying into, the worse it became. Jacob was going to need to be rested. And he'd been clear that he simply couldn't let her sleep on the perfectly comfortable airplane seat. The thought horrified him. He couldn't hide it.

So Alex, who was pragmatic by nature, opted for the only solution—sharing the bed. She'd taken him by surprise and had to make it very clear that she wasn't inviting him to have sex with her. Just to share the surface area of the bed so he could get a decent night's rest.

But his face...

The bedroom was comfortable, she wasn't surprised to see. Like everything about Black Inc., it was top of the line without being over the top. High quality but no frills.

"You can change in the bathroom," Jacob said. "I'll change out here."

Oh, God. They'd both be naked. At the same time. With only a door separating them. A wave of heat shot through her at the idea. It was totally inappropriate and unstoppable. All her life she'd thought herself essentially indifferent to sex and here her hormones had woken up in a frenzy at the wrongest possible time. With danger on the horizon and with regard to a dangerous man, who'd already broken her heart once.

Why couldn't she have felt this for Mark Childers, that really nice Senator's aide she'd met when testifying before Congress last fall? He'd been smitten, had asked her out several times, and when she finally accepted, had taken her to dinner at the most expensive restaurant in DC. And she'd been bored out of her mind.

Or how about Sam Jagers, the Deputy Director for Policy at the CDC? She'd gone out with him a couple of times and had contemplated going to bed with him, which would have had the added advantage of being a good career move. He was tall, handsome, suave. Well dressed, well spoken, well connected.

Such a pity he gave her the creeps when they kissed.

That was when, since she was a scientist, she examined the hypothesis that she was asexual. Decided she needed more data, but was keeping an open mind.

Well, she wasn't asexual. Right now, she was on the verge of exploding from sexual desire. Her legs were shaky. Her breasts felt super sensitive, the nipples erect from contact with her freaking *bra*. The lower half of her body was on fire and she was actually wet.

She'd studied human anatomy and physiology thoroughly in college and had studied sexual reactions and when she read about women getting wet, she'd rolled her eyes. She remembered the words exactly.

As a woman becomes aroused, blood flow to the genitals increases, which triggers the release of fluid from the cervix and the Bartholin's glands, which provides lubrication during sexual activity. Often, the more aroused you're feeling, the more vaginal lubrication your body will produce.

It had been exactly like reading about the pancreas. Some obscure organ that did its thing on its own. Nothing really to do with her.

Now she could be the poster girl for vaginal wetness. She could feel it, feel moisture trickling down her leg from her red-hot vagina. It was actually embarrassing and she was angry at her body for betraying her.

She looked at herself in the mirror and was astonished at what she saw. Of course, she'd had a nice meal with a glass of excellent wine, but that wasn't it. There was color in her cheeks, her eyes shone, her lips were somehow swollen and red though she wasn't wearing lipstick.

Down girl.

While she put on her cotton pajamas and washed her face and brushed her teeth, she talked herself down. Yes, Jake—Jacob!—was attractive. Yes, he was super sexy, though he was anything but handsome. He did have that Emperor of the World vibe thing going, though. There was that.

But sleeping with him would be a huge mistake. Taking her internal temperature, it was clear that this man could mess with her head in a way no other man could. She'd loved him. He'd left her. Brutally. He could do that again. Probably would, in fact.

Yes, he seemed interested. Well, why not? In the most real sense, she was the one who got away. A missing notch on his bedpost, of which she was sure he had many. He was rich beyond measure, hobnobbed with heads of state. And beyond that, had that uber male thing going that was like catnip to women.

Some kinds of women, of course.

She'd have prided herself on not being like those women, though apparently she was. Who would have thought that cool, collected Alex Hethering was so susceptible to rich beefcake? Just like a million other women.

On that depressing thought, she pushed open the bathroom door and felt her heart give this massive kick. There he was, standing by a small console that doubled as a desk. He was sex on a stick in pajamas. Black silk, of course. Made her light pink cotton pajamas look like a child's.

He was looking at the screen of a laptop, totally absorbed.

"Hey," she said softly.

His head came up as he quietly closed the lid of the laptop. "Hey yourself." He frowned. "You okay?"

"Yeah." She sighed. "Having some depressing thoughts."

"Having a few of those myself," he said. Though honestly? He looked exactly the same.

Jacob walked barefoot over to her and damn him, even his feet were incredibly sexy. Long, perfectly shaped, a few black hairs on the toes.

He held out a huge hand, unexpectedly. And even

more unexpectedly, she put her hand in his, without hesitation. "Which side?" he asked.

"Left."

"Okay."

He led her to the left-hand side, keeping her hand in his. With the other, he turned down the comforter and sheet. The sheet was cream-colored, the comforter was dove gray. Restful. "In you go."

She slid between the sheets, realizing how tired she was. The food and wine had given her a calorie boost, but she was exhausted. They were well out over the Pacific and she'd started her morning in Atlanta.

Jacob opened a door in the bedside table, hand hovering. "Flat or fizzy."

"Fl—" A huge yawn overtook her, nearly unhinging her jaw. "Flat. Sorry."

He placed a small water bottle by her bedside, then touched her hair, briefly.

"Nothing to be sorry about. You're tired."

She nodded.

"Get some sleep," he said gently. Then: "Lights 5%." And the cabin lights dimmed almost to darkness, leaving only a light glow. Enough not to bump into furniture.

With a pang, she realized that he remembered. As a girl, she'd been afraid of the dark, and he had never let her be in the dark. She was better about it as an adult and didn't freak any more. But utter darkness still unsettled her.

"Thanks," she said softly and he nodded.

The room was incredibly quiet, only the faintest hum betraying the fact that they were 35,000 feet in the air. Alex could feel everything—the cool sheets, Jacob's gaze like hands, the black edges of sleep starting to tug at her.

"Sleep," he said quietly. She turned over and fell immediately into a sleep as deep as the night.

"Alex, I did it." Elias's voice held pride and glee. He motioned to the screen of an electron microscope. "Look."

She looked, heart beating wildly. Elias was brilliant but operated according to his own rules and interests. What she saw made every cell of her body recoil in terror. A virus that should have been wiped off the face of the earth decades ago, vibrant and modified and deadly.

Her gaze lifted in shock to Elias's face. He looked delighted.

"How could you?" she asked, horrified.

He recoiled. "How could I? Stupid question. You always think so small, Alex. What's the matter with you? You have to think BIG."

The last word came out as a boom, the sound echoing around the room, taking time to die down. They were in some sort of room with doors in all four walls. The walls were painted black. She shrank back with a gasp at his voice, suddenly loud as a gunshot.

"Big," Elias repeated, his grin growing until it stretched horribly from ear to ear, showing sharp teeth. And he was suddenly big, his head brushing the ceiling, hands huge, opening and closing.

He was terrifying, waves of cold coming off him as if

he'd just been in a freezer. The room was freezing cold, too. Cold and dark. The air heavy, hard to breathe.

The doors—all those doors—suddenly opened with a loud clatter and people spilled out, as if they'd all been leaning against the closed doors like stacked wood. The first few fell to the floor, then others tripped over them, others still shuffling out. Alex could see the corridors and they were all teeming with people, pushing forward, tripping over themselves.

A dank odor accompanied them, a rank smell of decay. A smell of death. Moans rose from their ranks, moans of pain. Someone stumbling in from the closest door to her fell to the ground. A woman. First to her knees then, rolling to her side, face turned to Alex. The woman had pale eyes that stared up at her, beseeching.

Begging for something. For what? What could Alex give her? What did she need?

Her hand reached up, touched Alex's. The hand was cold, clammy, not like human skin. Alex recoiled, then saw that the hand was suddenly covered in pustules. And so was the woman's face. Everyone's face, disfigured with smallpox pustules. Like a scene from the Middle Ages, death and destruction everywhere she looked. People writhing on the ground, claw-like hands reaching out, feet drumming. Everyone in agony.

Everyone dying.

The mass of people, limbs intertwined like some huge monstrous organism, began crawling toward her, scarred hands reaching for her, the moans rising...

One hand grabbed her ankle, pulling it. She was going to fall straight into the mass of dying people. She kicked, hard, but another hand reached out and another...

She screamed.

Something strong held her, she couldn't move, couldn't breathe. She needed to get away, fast, before she drowned in the wave of people. They clawed at her, moaning. Something was holding on to her, something strong. She couldn't move, couldn't breathe. Couldn't scream. All that came out of her mouth was terrified mewling. She shook and shuddered and whatever was holding her tightened its grip. Not painful but unbreakable. She flailed and came awake on a gasp and a smothered scream.

"Whoa!" a deep voice said. "You're having a nightmare, honey. Wake up, that's right. Open those baby blues for me." Jacob tapped her cheek.

She opened her eyes and saw Jacob's dark worried face above hers. He was holding her tightly but let go a little when he saw she was awake.

"Man, you scared the fu—, you scared the shi—, you scared me," he finally said.

Alex sat up, shaken. She wanted to tell him that he could say shit or fuck around her but didn't have the strength. Parts of the nightmare still had her in its grip, and she shuddered.

Jacob tightened his arms around her again, as if he could absorb her shaking. She couldn't control anything her body did.

"Sorry," she gasped. This was horrible. There was no

way to hide herself, conceal what had happened. She felt raw, as if someone had peeled her skin off, leaving only beating organs, completely vulnerable.

"Nothing to be sorry about." Jacob shifted, never letting her go, and she somehow found herself half sitting, leaning on him, completely in his embrace, and ohmygod, that felt good. The black cloud of the nightmare was dissipating by the second, leaving only ashes in her mind. "That was a bad one," Jacob said.

She was lying with the side of her face against his chest, warm, hard, reassuring. His voice rumbled in her ear. A perfect nightmare-killer.

"Yeah. Bad." Her voice was weak still. She felt ashamed, but not enough to pull away. In the dark of the night, being held by him was delicious. Like there was a bulwark against the evils of the world.

For years after her parents died, she'd had nightmares, waking up in the dark, lips pressed together so she wouldn't wake up Great-Aunt Frances, who didn't like her sleep interrupted. Not by crying in the night, not by nightmares, not by her niece sick with a fever.

She'd learned the hard way to hide it all.

She didn't feel she needed to hide it now. Jacob wasn't showing any signs of exasperation with his sleep being cut short. She was lying fully on him. He had one strong arm around her back, one big hand on the back of her head. She rose and fell with his regular breathing.

He wasn't talking, letting his body do his talking for him. He was here for her.

"Do you have nightmares?" she asked his chest. Stupid thing to say. What macho guy would admit to nightmares?

He was silent a beat. "All the time," he replied.

She lifted her head in surprise. The very low light showed his expression. Sober, serious. White brackets around his mouth.

"Yeah?"

He nodded.

Well, yeah. Of course. Every article described him as a 'highly decorated soldier'. The military didn't give out medals for neatness or punctuality. They gave them out for outstanding valor. For bravery in the face of extreme danger. For running toward danger even when people shot at you.

She knew herself. Knew if someone shot at her, she'd run away as fast as her legs could carry her.

He'd shot people, been shot at. Had seen things that would have wrecked her forever. Yes, of course he had nightmares.

"I have a recurring one. I'm mired in mud, can't move my arms or my legs, can't reach my weapon and a haji stands above me and aims his rifle straight at me. So close I can see inside the barrel. His trigger finger moves and I wake up."

Alex thought about that. About what would cause nightmares like that.

Jacob nudged her with his shoulder. "And you?"

"Me what?"

"What was your nightmare about?"

"Don't remember." She frowned.

"Sure you do."

"What?" She swiveled her head to glare up at him. "What did you say? How dare you! You think you know my nightmare better than I do?"

"There was darkness," he said. "Darkness and cold."

Her mouth snapped shut.

"A heavy menace in the air. Someone threatening you."

"Someone threatening all of us," she whispered. "How did you know?"

"Nightmares have structures, and I know all of them."

And Alex looked at him. Really looked. Looked beyond her anger and hurt at his abandonment. Looked beyond his power and wealth, even. And saw him. Jake Simpson, who had somehow morphed into Jacob Black. A dirt-poor rawboned teenager who'd never known love and kindness, except for what he got in the Hethering household. A boy who'd grown up with a monster for a father and who joined the military as soon as it was legally possible.

He'd said that he was immediately recognized as top soldier potential and was fast-tracked into the field. While she was navigating college classes and term papers, he was fighting for his country, a boy who'd known nothing but violence and degradation all his life, except in her home.

There was absolutely nothing left of that boy in Jacob's face. He was hard, battle-scarred, having seen and done things she could scarcely imagine. His face was like a brick wall, unyielding.

"Yeah, I'll bet you know nightmares, inside and out," she said softly. He nodded. "Do you wake up scared?"

He looked like he was scared of nothing on this earth, but the very nature of nightmares was that they were terrifying in a way you can't defend yourself from. Monsters coming up from your subconscious, reminding you of the skull beneath the skin. Reminding you of pain and death waiting around every corner. By definition, in a nightmare you were powerless. Couldn't move, could barely breathe.

The body was flooded with specific neurotransmitters —gamma-aminobutyric acid and glycine. It was the body's way of protecting you from acting out your dreams, paralyzing chemicals the body sent out to keep you still while asleep. You were in danger and couldn't move.

Nightmares were terrifying.

"Oh yeah." His voice was a deep rumble, a bit hesitant, as if the words were dragged out of his very soul.

"But you never tell anyone, right?"

Suddenly, there was a glint of humor, like light glancing off a sword. "God, no. I have a reputation as the Antichrist to uphold."

Alex sputtered out a laugh, realizing how hard it must be to maintain that façade of deep unshakable power, uncrackable and unbreakable.

Jacob smiled and—there he was! All of a sudden, she saw him. Jake. Saw the boy she once knew so well. The boy she had loved, though she'd been too young to recognize it, but it had been love. Everyone had shunned him, mainly because they feared him, but she hadn't been afraid of him, not ever, not for one second. Though she'd felt protected by him, she hadn't realized how deep the feeling went. He was just Jake. Always around, always willing to help.

Her father, bless him, had been a wonderful man but not practical and not muscular. Jake had been both practical and muscular. So whenever there was a need for something heavy to be shifted, or something to be fixed, Jake always volunteered, was always there. He seemed to instinctively have what the Hetherings lacked—an understanding of how the physical world worked. He shoveled their snow, tuned the car, cleaned out the basement and the grouts and even fixed the roof. He did everything fast and well and clearly was more than willing to repay them for having him over so often by doing chores.

She'd been so used to having him around. It had been like having a force field around her. She'd only realized what he meant to her when he left. She'd felt so bereft, alone and scared.

And here she was. Scared again. But not alone.

She had Jake.

They stilled, both of them.

She was still half lying on him, both hands on his pectorals. His chest was so massive. She could feel the hard muscles through the silk, the wiry chest hairs. Feel his heart beat, strong and steady. She'd never felt a male body like this, a sculpture made of marble, but warm and breathing.

He lifted his head, eyes fixed on her. He drew closer, watching her every inch of the way. Maybe wondering whether she'd object to his kiss?

Foolish man.

She wound her arms against his neck and bent down to him. It was awkward, she kissed the side of his mouth, but that was soon rectified. He brought his hands to her head and steadied her and yes, their mouths aligned and it was a real kiss.

Oh, God. Hot and wet, his tongue deep in her mouth, it was the best kiss she'd ever had. Even better than the last one eighteen years ago that had jump started her hormones.

Her mind blanked and she became just skin, feeling his skin. Mouth, tasting his mouth.

Without breaking the kiss, Jacob turned them over together until he was on top of her, kissing her so hard it felt like her mouth would melt into his. His heavy weight pinned her to the mattress and it anchored her. She smoothed her hands over the heavy planes of his back, feeling the muscles working as he shifted to get a better, deeper taste of her.

She dug her fingers into the muscles of his back but could barely find purchase. He was like steel. Hot steel.

The kiss went on and on. She lost all awareness of time, of where she was. All she knew was that she was on a bed, with a low humming in the background and Jacob hovering over her. Her entire horizon was filled with Jacob. All she could see, in the few moments she could open her heavy eyelids, was Jacob. He filled her entire world, the only reality she could perceive.

Her skin was supercharged, one huge erogenous zone from the top of her head to her toes. The entire front of her body was touching Jacob, her nipples tingling and hard. Her stomach was against his and she could feel clearly the cut abs, hard and strong even through the heavy silk of his pajama top.

And she could clearly feel his penis, like a warm steel pipe, against her belly. It—it was alive. Moving and somehow becoming longer and thicker the longer they kissed.

Jacob's mouth left hers, and before she could mourn the loss, he was running his lips and tongue over her jawbone, up to her ear, then back. He ran his mouth over her neck, tongue along the vein. Surely he could feel how hard her blood was pumping? And then he nipped her, just a brief bite that didn't hurt but that marked her as his. It was exactly the nip a stallion would give to his mare.

Mine.

She felt it down to her toes, goose bumps arising along her arms. He nipped again, his breath making a whooshing sound out of his lungs.

And just like that, that dreamy feeling of melting into his kiss became desire, red-hot and sharp. Unlike anything she had ever felt before

And heat, all over. Like an oven had been turned on inside her. Not just her sex was hot, but her entire body, from head to toe.

His mouth roamed over her face and she stretched her neck to give him more access because, *ohmygod,* all those stories about the neck being an erogenous zone were true! Running his tongue over her neck made her break out in goosebumps. She shivered and he whispered, "Alex."

"Right here," she whispered back and then she couldn't say anything else because his mouth found hers again and the kisses became deeper than before. She jolted a little every time his tongue touched hers.

His fingers opened the buttons of her pajama tops and he folded the two parts open. He lifted his head to look at her naked chest and made a noise deep in his throat. A little like a lion purring.

He stared at her breasts, features tight. A big hand came up, cupped her, his thumb circling her nipple. She shivered.

His gaze came up and he looked into her eyes. "I dreamed of this. You have no idea how many times I dreamed of this. This is even better than I imagined."

Alex didn't have any words, all she had was the hot breath that escaped her lungs. She was burning up inside.

Jacob licked the area between her breasts as one hand kept holding her breast, the thumb circling it. Then he took her breast in his hand and offered it to himself. He suckled, hard, using lips and tongue and teeth, devouring her and it was almost overkill. His hot penis was right over her mound and he pressed against her and she lit up. She arched, writhed, breathed out hard. He pressed even more against her. Somehow, even through the pajamas, her sex had opened up and his penis was between the folds. Every time he moved, he seemed as excited as if he were inside her, moving in and out, his breath harsh and loud in her ear.

His hips pressed against her, rubbing against her clitoris and it was so electric she couldn't breathe for a moment. He moved against her again and she started climbing up a mountain, each movement propelling her further up, pleasure so intense she saw spots on the insides of her eye lids.

"Oh!"

He pressed again. And she came.

Just from that. From his mouth at her breast and pressing against her through two sets of clothes.

The most amazing thing. Her whole body was involved in the orgasm, shuddering and clenching. For a moment, she couldn't breathe, it was so intense. Her whole body was aflame, the heat centered in her sex which was clenching.

So unfair. She'd never had anything like that happen to her, not even during sex with other men. Real sex, too. Penis in vagina, grinding away sex. That hadn't done it for her, nope.

The most she might get would be a tight little orgasm, centered in her groin, over almost as soon as it began. Not always pleasurable and always leaving her wanting more, but not with the man she was with.

And here basically all Jacob had to do was touch her and she lit up like a rocket. A man who had left her eighteen years ago and she hadn't had real sex—not the soft pleasurable type—since. Had felt so incredibly alone. Then he showed up and her body betrayed her.

Alex burst into tears. It was so freaking unfair. She was like a lock and only Jacob held the key.

Instead of disturbing him, or wondering what had made the crazy lady cry, he simply rolled until they were on their sides, and held her. She cried in despair, that the world of sex had only been shown to her now, and she was thirty-five years old. She cried at all the long, lonely years before this. She cried because she had truly tried to find a partner and yet every man she'd ever been with, even only dated a time or two, had left her so cold that she'd doubted herself. Doubted whether she'd ever find a man who would turn her on.

Well, she'd found one. It had taken her eighteen years and maybe they were going to die soon. She'd lost eighteen years of love and closeness. And for what?

The tears kept coming, hot and bitter. Her chest ached as she tried to repress the sobs. This was so ridiculous. The only thing she'd had these past years was her dignity and here she'd lost it.

Alex tried to cover her face with her hands, but Jacob held them gently in his. So she buried her face against his shoulder. It was the most primitive instinct—not to be seen as weak. She didn't think he was the kind of man to make fun of her, but she hated this. Hated the tears that were spurting from her eyes, the sobs burning in her chest.

Out of control, when her whole life was nothing but control.

However, like all storms, it died down. Her breathing was less ragged, the tears eventually stopped.

She was lost, as if some outside force had grabbed her and shaken her.

"I had an orgasm," she said, dazed.

"I know, honey." That deep voice, low and lulling. She watched his face carefully but there was no smugness. None of that male pride in bringing the little woman to pleasure. He just looked serious, with a little undertone of tenderness.

Alex rubbed her eyes. "That's never happened to me. Not like that." She thought about it and punched his shoulder, knowing full well she hadn't hurt him at all. It had felt like punching iron.

He was a smart man and simply took it.

"Hush." He kissed her mouth, her cheeks, her closed eyelids.

Her mouth trembled. "It's so unfair! I tried to feel something with other men but it just... it just didn't work. And here you come along, after abandoning me brutally at my darkest moment, then you never get in touch for eighteen years, though you've known where I was all this time, and you drag me across the country and basically all you do is touch me and I explode!"

"Well, let's take a part of that." He took her hand and ran it along the scar on his cheek. It was long and deep. A knife scar. Well, he'd been in battle. When holding him, she'd felt another knife scar along his lower back and what felt a lot like a bullet scar on his shoulder. "You know what this is?" he asked.

"A knife scar. You seem to have a lot of scars." And it occurred to her that she was really lucky he was alive. He could have died at any moment in all those years in the military. He wouldn't have founded Black Inc. She wouldn't have had a place to run to. And, she thought with a sigh, she would never have had that spectacular orgasm.

"I have a lot of scars, yes, but this scar is special." He ran a finger down the side of her face. "My father gave it to me."

Alex's eyes opened wide. "Your father!"

He nodded. "He'd been drinking more than usual and there was something building up in him. Some kind of poison, and it centered on me. He'd always been a cruel father but there was something else brewing. Some kind of sickness. It came to a head and he knocked me out. When I came to, he'd handcuffed me to the table that was attached to the floor. I couldn't get out. And my head hurt. I think I was concussed. I stayed handcuffed on the floor for two days."

Alex listened to him, appalled. Her own parents had been so loving. She simply couldn't imagine a father treating a son that way. But she'd seen him with her own eyes.

"I—I met your father."

Jacob closed his eyes. "Oh, God."

"The day I buried my folks I wanted to see you so

badly. You never came. I knew you lived out at the trailer park so I biked there. I called your name and your father answered. He was drunk, said you'd left. It was... it was pretty horrible."

"Yeah." Jacob kissed her cheek. "I'm sorry you met him. And I'm sorry I didn't know that your folks had died, that you had to deal with everything alone. All I knew was if I stayed, I'd end up killing my father and my life would be over."

That day, that horrible day she buried her parents and Jake abandoned her, had been in her head for eighteen long years. Though she didn't want it, the memories were ever fresh and she relived that day over and over again. But now, all the elements had been put in a kaleidoscope and were jumbled into a new configuration.

"You wouldn't even look at me when you were in the bus," she whispered. "You pretended I didn't exist."

That was the worst of all. The most humiliating memory. Beating her fist against the bus and Jake resolutely ignoring her. Time and again she'd asked herself if she'd someone done something to make him angry at her and could remember nothing. His hostility had seemingly come out of nowhere. It had baffled her and hurt her deeply. In many ways, it had hurt more than her parents' death.

"I couldn't turn my head," Jacob said, deep voice soft. "You'd have seen the knife wound. You'd have wanted to help. I know you. You'd have wanted to go to the police, or maybe have your father talk to my father. It wouldn't have ended well and I just knew you'd somehow get hurt. My father was escalating fast. He would have come after you if he knew I cared for you. I couldn't stay. I knew I had to get out."

She sighed. With each word, some blackness, some of the tangle of despair she'd lived with so long, floated away.

"I missed you so much."

Jacob nodded. "We've lost so much time." He rolled with her in his arms, and in one swipe of his hands, pulled down their pajama pants. Then he was on her with his full weight. "This first time has to be fast."

His legs opened her and he entered her, hard and fast. It wouldn't have worked if she hadn't already had an orgasm. He was huge, hard like a club. He hammered into her but instead of hurting, it was pure flame, pleasure so intense it was almost painful. She disappeared and another person took her place. Not a cool scientist, no. A wild woman, drowning in pleasure. Her hips rose to meet his thrusts, hard, harder until she arched her back and exploded.

Then Jacob gave one last hard thrust, so deep inside her it felt like he could reach her heart, and with a shout started spurting inside her, prolonging her own convulsions.

Oh, God! She'd had no idea sex could be so intense. It took her long minutes to come back to herself. She was shaking and sweating, small explosions going off in her body.

Jacob collapsed onto her, head on her shoulder, lips against her ear.

"We didn't use birth control. I didn't think of it once. I have condoms somewhere but they could be on the back side of the moon for all the good they did us." He didn't sound put out or disturbed.

His words registered slowly because all the synapses in her head were fried. Finally, she put together the words he'd said and reconstructed the sentences.

She sighed and caressed his head, running her fingers through his long black hair. "It's ok. We often go into the field in unsavory places. The CDC strongly encourages the women to go on birth control. I have an implant."

"Good." He hadn't pulled out and she could feel him becoming erect again. Her vagina closed around him once, twice, and he hardened some more. Their bodies were talking to each other, a sort of call and response. "Because we're just beginning."

CHAPTER
Nine

"Wake up, honey."

Alex knew that voice. A male voice telling her to wake up was a rare thing in her world and she should be curious, but she was also on an amazingly comfortable bed, and there was a low hum that was lulling. And she was still half asleep.

Didn't want to wake up, nope. Some deep instinct told her that waking up fully and facing the day would not be as pleasant as lying on this bed, half asleep.

There was a faint aroma of fabric softener and then the sharper aroma of coffee wafted under her nose.

"Wake up and smell the coffee."

Alex opened her eyes and there he was. Jacob. In a black tee shirt that hugged his broad shoulders, black jeans and bare feet.

Jacob. The man she'd had hot sex with for hours. She turned stop-light red.

Oh, God. It had been *years* since she'd blushed. She could barely remember the last time. Maybe on her second day of biochemistry and she flubbed an answer to a question barked out by the prof. Certainly not in response to a man looking at her narrow-eyed, as if he wanted to gobble her up.

No, she couldn't deal with this, the dreaded Day After.

They'd had sex so intense she'd almost passed out, and right now, she was remembering every second of it, while Jacob watched her. He knew what was going through her mind because there was no way she could hide her feelings.

Just *her* feelings.

He didn't look embarrassed or ill at ease at all. And he certainly wasn't blushing, though it would be hard to tell on that dark, weather-beaten face.

She sat up, realized her breasts were bare and snatched up the covers and covered her breasts, pulling the covers up to her neck. If she could have, she'd have pulled them over her head. But that would be childish.

Her face was cherry-red, she could feel it. Damn her fair skin and damn the effect he had on her and while she was at it, damn sex. The sex had turned her entire world upside down.

"Hey." His voice was soft. He was holding an espresso cup in one hand and with the other motioned for her to scoot over in bed to make room for him.

She scooted, feeling like a fool.

Jacob Black had probably had a hundred—a thousand

—lovers. Was probably used to sophisticated women in his bed.

Well, she was sophisticated. Had a PhD and a master's and had a high-level job. So why was she blushing and why was her tongue suddenly this inert thing in her mouth? Why was her mind such a blank?

Gah.

Jacob handed the cup to her and she sipped then gulped. Delicious. Perfect. Of course. She stared down into the cup, hoping that it would tell her something. Make her feel less awkward. An Indian friend in college had told fortunes from tea leaves in the bottom of cups. No fortune to be read here, just a little bit of fragrant brown liquid.

His finger ran down her face, from temple to chin. It felt like a line of fire.

"You're blushing."

Alex closed her eyes and wished intently that she could teleport herself somewhere else. Or press fast forward when they could be in the cabin, calmly discussing strategy. And she'd be fully dressed.

"Alex, don't be uncomfortable with me, please."

She shook her head.

He took her cup and put it on the bedside table. Turned and took her in his arms. "I want you to be happy. Like I am. I haven't been happy in a long time. Maybe not ever, not like this. This is very rare. We should enjoy it. Very few people have what we do." He dropped a kiss on her forehead. "Please."

She let out a great sigh and with it went her discomfort. He was right. Last night had been... amazing. She'd never felt anything like it. Maybe never would again. They'd both been through very hard times and should appreciate when life threw pleasure at them.

It might not last. It probably wouldn't. And they might die today or tomorrow.

He nudged her with his shoulder. "So. Was it good for you?"

Alex laughed, pulled away. He was smiling. It looked so strange on that hard, grim face.

"You're going to have to feed me before I answer that."

"Roger that." Jacob chuckled and stood up, offering his hand. "If you want to take a shower, breakfast will be ready when you come out. Then we'll talk strategy."

"Ok. You cooking breakfast while I shower sounds like a reasonable division of labor."

She took his hand, swung her legs over the edge of the bed, and stood up. She was naked but somehow it didn't bother her. That attack of extreme prudery had passed, some vestige of her past that didn't exist anymore. Jacob had examined her body in all its details last night and that thought finally caught up with her. The prudery train had passed.

It bothered him, though.

He closed his eyes and grimaced. "Please get into the bathroom quick. You're pure temptation."

Delighted at the thought of being temptation, she sashayed to the bathroom. Well, this was a change. Usually she was admired from the neck up, not the neck down.

The shower was small but deluxe, the first shower she'd ever seen in an airplane. It got the job done, though. Sex and a hot shower did her a lot of good. When she caught a glimpse of herself in the bathroom mirror, she looked refreshed, color high, eyes bright. She hadn't slept much, but obviously fabulous sex was a good substitute for sleep.

Jacob stood when she entered the main cabin, checking her out, head to toe. It wasn't sexy. He was checking on her well-being, like you would with a teammate. "Looking good," he said, finally, satisfaction in his voice. "We're going to have another long day, so eat a good breakfast. It'll have to be brunch because we slept in and we'll be landing soon."

Alex side-eyed him. "Whose fault is it we slept in late?"

"Mine." He smiled. "Don't regret a second of it. But do eat, we won't have another meal until we're at the hotel."

There was a pretty decent selection of breakfast food. Croissants, Danish pastries, toast, butter and several jams. A ham quiche. Burrito. Mushroom omelette. Potato and chorizo hash. Smoked salmon, scrambled eggs. A cheese platter and a fresh fruit platter.

"We could go to war with this breakfast," Alex said lightly as she sat down. He didn't answer and she looked up at him, his face suddenly gone grim.

"Yeah." His jaw flexed. "Truth is, we might actually be going to war. So eat up."

That sobered her, but didn't put her off the food. A

surge of energy ran through her. They might be going into battle, but for the best possible cause. She'd dedicated her professional life to keeping people safe from disease and this mission was what she did, on steroids. They might possibly save millions of lives. A just war, if ever there was one.

She ate more than she'd ever eaten for breakfast, had two cups of coffee, and finally pushed the plates away. Jacob put everything on a big tray and carried it into the galley.

He came back and sat across from her, elbows on the table. "So. Your Dr. Field has been gone for four days now. Can you give me an idea of what kind of timing we're talking about? How much damage can he do in four days? How long does it take to—what's the word? Bioengineer?"

"Yeah." She leaned forward. "The answer is—it depends. That's not a copout. It's highly dependent on the circumstances. On the virus he has available to work with, for example. Editing viral genomes is tricky business, highly delicate work. He'd have to design the modifications, test them. He'd—I guess he'd first have to make sure that frontline drugs won't be effective against anything he has engineered."

Jacob frowned. "There are drugs to treat smallpox? I didn't know we had that."

"Not perfect drugs, no. But good enough, maybe. Brincidofovir, for example. It was recently developed and approved by the FDA. But of course its effectiveness hasn't been tested in sizeable populations. It was tested in vitro, using similar orthopoxviruses and not just variola. So, testing to make sure the new virus can resist Brincidofovir would be item number one on the agenda. That would take at least a couple of days. There's also Tecovirimat, but it is of limited use against variola. And, just to be complete, there's Cidofovir, but it's only been tested on animals suffering from a virus similar to smallpox. I don't think he'd waste his time on that."

"So we're talking a timeline of what? Weeks? Months?"

Alex shook her head. "Sorry to keep answering the same way but—it depends. The… people he's working with might have already made some headway and might need him for the final steps in weaponizing smallpox. Or they might be starting from scratch, in which case it'll take months."

"That would be better. Not too happy knowing the apocalypse might be just around the corner. Are we sure it's smallpox we're talking about? Not something else?"

"I just don't know." Alex considered. "I understand what you're saying. But here's the thing. Virologists all have the same base training but then we branch off into specializations. And at that level, knowledge is pretty much stovepiped. We become superspecialized. There aren't many generalist virologists and they tend to rise through the admin ranks and become administrators. Not on the frontlines of research. So really, he could be anywhere on the timeline in the process of designing a synthetic virus. Also, I have no idea how sophisticated his equipment would be."

"There's a lot of money sloshing around in the world, honey. And a lot of it is in the hands of bad guys. If he's been recruited to design a killer virus, count on him having unlimited amounts of money behind him."

She sighed. "And our budgets keep getting cut."

"Yeah?"

"Yeah. As if fighting pandemics weren't important to keep a country safe. You'd think we'd have learned that in the last couple of years. As if studying illness weren't vital to keeping a country healthy. I don't understand it. We had two long-term experiments cut short for lack of funds the same day the government announced the design and production of a new stamp honoring a dead rapper. The amount for both was the same."

He leveled a sharp look at her. "You happy where you are?"

Alex tilted her head back for a second, thinking. "Happy. Define happy."

He reached across and took her hand. "Happy doesn't need defining. It is absolutely unmistakable and you've basically answered my question. What's wrong? The CDC is the gold standard in your field, isn't it? You're at the top of the heap, at the age of thirty-five."

"Yeah," she whispered. "Top of the heap."

Jacob placed her hand between both of his. His hands were warm, hard, strong. The warmth spread up her arm.

"Talk to me. Tell me." He brought her hand to his

mouth. His breath was hot against the back of her hand. Lips soft, short beard crinkly.

She was overwhelmed by the sensory memory of that mouth and beard kissing all down her body. Scratching her breast as he sucked on her nipples. Against the very sensitive flesh of her inner thighs as he kissed her sex exactly as he kissed her mouth.

A flash of molten heat shot through her. He was watching her carefully out of those dark, dark eyes, looking right into the heart of her. Lying to him right now felt not only wrong, but impossible.

"I'm unhappy at the CDC." There. Words she thought she'd never say came just plopping out of her mouth. She nearly looked around her to see who'd said that because it couldn't possibly be her. Could it?

There was complete silence, even the rumble of the airplane engines was muffled.

"I'm listening," he said, that deep voice gentle.

Well, yeah. She was saying something crazy and he had to pacify the lunatic. She was in an elite job anyone with her training would kill to have. He must think she was ungrateful or impossible to please.

Alex's hand curled around his, clinging to him.

"When I was recruited, it was a dream come true. Something I'd been dreaming of, working toward since forever. There's no higher job I could have in my field. No better job. We study life itself. We save lives. We are on the cutting edge of science. We're well paid. Certainly well paid for scientists."

She sounded insane even to herself. Who wouldn't be happy with that?

"But?"

She drew in a deep breath, blew it out. "It's—it's hard to pinpoint. We've had three Directors in as many years, and it seems like each Director is more political than the last. There are also people in middle management more interested in PR than in the actual science. As if talking a good game is the exact same thing as making discoveries. Science is messy. There are a lot of dry holes. A lot of mistakes are made in getting to the established truth and there are some who want easy fixes. Something to announce, particularly at budget time. Sometimes—" she looked away.

"Sometimes?" Jacob prodded.

She gave her head a sharp shake.

He took her chin between thumb and index finger and gently brought her head around. "Finish that sentence. Sometimes..."

"It's silly."

He waited. He didn't look impatient. He also looked like he could wait forever.

"Ok. Sometimes I think about quitting. I have a colleague, Darby Robbins. And a really good friend I met at Harvard who is a materials specialist. May Chou. Really smart. We've been sort of toying with the idea of designing a new type of biohazard suit that would be easier to wear while offering more protection. The idea is to have a gel—"

"Whoa." Jacob jolted. His whole face lit up, dark eyes

wide, as if he'd just received an electric shock. "A better biohazard suit! My God, that is something we really need! I'd finance that, absolutely. Any amount you need, sky's the limit. I lost two good men in a sarin factory in Syria last year. You'd be saving lives. And they would sell. Fuck, how they'd sell. How far along are you?"

"Hmm." Alex took her cell out and scrolled. "Here." She showed him the design of a prototype she, Darby and May were working on. Instead of the bulky space suit-like balloon look, it was sleek. Like something Spiderman would wear.

Jacob put his nose next to the screen. "What's that material?"

"That's May's masterpiece. It's a graphene-based material, you could stab it and it wouldn't tear but it's very thin."

Jacob lifted his eyes to hers. "In the Teams, we lost a medic because the suit caught on a bone spur and tore."

"Never happen with this. We've subjected the material to everything but a nuclear blast. The tensile strength is through the roof." She looked at Jacob, who seemed so excited. Did she trust him with this information? Yes, she did. "As a matter of fact," she said slowly, "the tensile strength is greater than steel. That is privileged information."

"Your May really is a genius." Jacob tapped her screen. "I hope she is planning on patenting it."

"She is." Alex smiled. May was ferociously defensive of her material, which she called 'Smoke'. "It's also lightweight, not bulky as you can see. Very flexible, with articulated joints. The user has full range of movement."

"If it doesn't breathe, are there temperature control issues? MOPPs get insanely hot, as you know."

"There's a memory foam element for comfort and it adjusts to the wearer's body heat and the external environment. And we designed special sealable openings so the wearer can get in and out of the suit quickly. It also has a built-in life support system, supplying oxygen and removing carbon dioxide, with biometric monitors to track vital signs and detect any breaches or contamination."

"Now I have suit envy." Jacob sighed. "I want those suits. As many as you can provide. At whatever price you ask."

Alex smiled. "Not so fast, slick. We're still very much in beta. And though we think we will eventually have a very, very viable product, none of us are businesswomen. We can manage the technology but not the commercial aspects. I've been boning up on business, but I fall asleep on page two of any book on economics." It was true. She'd inherited that from her folks, who could talk about Gone with the Wind and Ulysses and the biology of ants forever. But they hadn't been able to balance their checkbooks.

Jacob tilted his head. "I definitely have a solution for that. Black Inc. has some amazing financial officers, but we've got one who is a genius at managing businesses. Nicole Sorenson. Can plant umbrellas in the ground and make them flower. Can make deserts bloom. You'd like her a lot. She often complains about working in our mostly male environment. Says we bring the average IQ down. She's not wrong. In your brainy female environment, she'd blossom. And she was engaged to one of our guys who died because of a leaky suit in Syria, so she'd be highly motivated." He put his hand on her forearm. "What about it, honey? Oh man, I can just see it. I'd throw money at you, so you can work without financial concerns. You and your partners would be happy, guaranteed."

Hmm. She'd probably already lost her job at the CDC. She'd downplayed how unhappy she was there, too. A whole new influx of middle managers and top managers had arrived with, apparently, one goal. Making the lives of the scientists miserable. What Jacob proposed was amazing and opened up new vistas. She, May and Darby, working together on a project they were passionate about.

And they had other ideas in the pipeline.

They'd batted around another idea—better detection of viruses via sensitive nucleic acid detection assays. Cutting down on antibiotic use, screening of donated organs, knowing fast whether to take isolation precautions... the advantages were enormous.

Not having CDC bean counters constantly poking their noses in... Yeah. She had no doubt Jacob would make good on his promise of generous funding.

But... she'd be tying herself to him on the basis of what?

Probably really good sex, if she was honest with herself.

Probably not a good idea.

"Let me think about it," she hedged. "If we're both alive at the other end of this, we can talk about it."

"I promise you—" Jacob began, and a soft bell rang.

The pilot had the same voice pilots had all over the world. Authoritative, absolutely calm, completely deadpan. They'd have that voice even if the plane were spiraling down in flames. "Prepare for landing in twenty minutes. Weather in Zelenograd is sleeting, current temperature 5°. A storm front is moving in, forecast of a couple of inches of snow. Mr. Black, I've been advised that a car will be waiting for you on the tarmac."

"Buckle back up," Alex said and watched Jacob's frustration with secret glee. He was used to people doing exactly what he said. Let him stew a little. She sat back, picked up her iPad and started reading the *Virology Journal*.

CHAPTER
Ten

J acob bit back his frustration when he saw Alex settle into her seat and start to read a scientific journal on her tablet. For her, the discussion was over.

He thought he'd died and gone to heaven when she said she was unhappy at the CDC. Because in the back of his mind, he'd already been planning his move.

Jacob was a planner. Short term and long term. And already he was making plans to redirect his headquarters from San Diego to Atlanta. It would make things awkward because he'd be pretty far from the military installations he usually worked with and not on a coast, but what the hell. He'd dealt with more difficult problems. He could live and work out of Atlanta if he had to.

And it was clear to him that he'd have to, because he wasn't ever going to leave Alex's side again. Life had tossed her his way when he'd been too much of a fucking coward to go after her before, and now he was going to hold on tight because he wasn't getting a second chance. He'd already fucked up for eighteen years by not having the nerve to approach her. Not going to happen again.

So: Atlanta, much as that was going to be a pain in the ass.

And then it turned out that maybe relocating wouldn't be necessary! Oh man, he'd nearly jumped out of his seat when it was clear Alex wasn't happy at the CDC. With her credentials, there'd be plenty of jobs for her in San Diego. There were a number of pharmaceutical companies, she could teach at the university. No problem.

And then the bombshell. Alex and two brainiac friends were working on better hazmat suits! Every time Jacob had to send a team into harm's way with bioweapons in the mix, he sweated. He still had nightmares about watching Rojas and Zabrinsky die a horrible death after exposure to ricin in Syria. Those suits would protect his guys. One less thing to worry about.

God.

And what he wouldn't give to have Alex's two friends on board. He envied ASI their Queens. Maybe he could have Queens of his own. Brainiac females who solved problems and, incidentally, brought the beauty quotient up.

Yeah.

Jacob slanted a look at Alex, but she was engrossed in whatever she was reading, not paying him any attention at all. Ironic. He'd had a couple of women who'd fixated on him, wanted his complete attention all the time, and it had grown very old very fast. And now he was sitting next to the woman he wanted more than any other on earth and she was ignoring him.

It was genuine. At the moment, she wasn't paying him any attention at all, scrolling through her tablet, looking for something.

Another soft ping that didn't distract her at all. She gave no sign of even hearing it.

He pressed a button in the arm rest and the screen lowered from the ceiling, Nick's face filling the monitor. Jacob had to nudge Alex in the ribs. Her head came up, eyes unfocused. She frowned at him. "What?"

He indicated the screen with his head.

"Oh."

"Talk to me, Nick," he said without taking his eyes off Alex. He turned to the screen. "I assume you have news."

"Yeah. I know you guys are landing soon, but I thought I'd give you a sitrep on the situation on the ground. I spoke with air control at the airport and your flight's details will be erased as soon as your plane touches the ground. There will be a car on the tarmac, and he'll drive to the bottom of the stairs. You shouldn't be exposed for more than a minute and we're blocking the security cameras on that side of the airport until you are in the vehicle. Here's your driver." On the screen appeared an ID, Mikhail Bogdan, 36. US citizen. Hard face, close-cropped black hair.

Jacob nodded. "He was with us in Singapore last year. Good man."

"That's right. He's one of two operators who will be

assigned to the two of you and to Dr. Hethering when we're not with her. Two others will spell them, in 12-hour shifts."

To his side, Alex shifted in her chair. Jacob flashed her a warning look, but she didn't say anything.

Good. This was non-negotiable. He wasn't going to fuck around with her safety.

"Okay." Jacob frowned. "Any leads?"

"One, maybe two. We'll go fishing tomorrow."

"We can't go fishing today?" Alex asked.

"Would love for Jacob to hit the ground running, but it'll be dark soon. I found someone who might be an informant, but he'll only meet in daylight. Very skittish. Not even money could change his mind, which means whoever he's afraid of is beaucoup bad. Fucker's incredibly greedy. Sorry, Doctor."

Alex waved her hand. "I told you it's Alex, and no problem."

The pilot came on. "We've begun our descent. Please stow away loose items and fasten your seat belts."

"Okay, I'll see you soon," Nick said. "I'm at the airport."

"Roger that. See you in a few."

Jacob turned to Alex but she was engrossed in her tablet again. He reached across her gently, pulled the seat belt over. She lifted her arms but was barely paying attention. He got a glimpse of her tablet screen and understood one word in ten.

Well, he'd got himself a brainy woman, so he'd better get used to it.

He settled and waited until the plane's tires gently kissed the tarmac and nudged Alex again.

"Honey?"

She looked up at him blindly.

"We're here."

ALEX HAD TRAVELED WIDELY for the WHO and the CDC but Vostokova was new to her. Stepping out of the plane onto the steps, she took a deep breath and looked around. It looked like an airfield in the middle of nowhere, at dusk. The air smelled of aviation fuel and dust and coming snow. The sky was low and gray, casting no shadows. In the distance was a building that looked like a bunker.

"Honey?" Jacob had preceded her and she understood he wanted to go first in case there was danger. He scanned their surroundings constantly, but it didn't look like there was a living soul in the airfield. Jacob was holding his hand out to her. "We have to be quick."

"Of course," she murmured and followed him quickly down the few stairs and into a waiting SUV with the passenger door open. Jacob motioned that she should get in first. She slid in and as soon as Jacob pulled the door closed, they took off.

"Hey, welcome to beautiful Vostokova," a deep voice rumbled from the shotgun seat.

"Hello Nick," she said and he smiled at her in the rear-view mirror. As with Jacob, it looked like smiling hurt that hard face. "Doctor."

"Alex," she gently corrected.

"Alex." He shifted his gaze in the mirror. "So I've checked you into the Stella Hotel. It's what passes for a five star in this place, but don't get excited."

Jacob slanted a glance at her. "Don't worry about me," Alex said. "On mission, we sometimes sleep in tents. If it has clean beds with mattresses and running water and no cockroaches, I'm fine."

Nick dipped his head. "Yeah, I think I can guarantee a cockroach-free experience. Jacob, I have eight men and they are on a rotating roster. We have—"

And he and Jacob launched into a highly technical discussion of their security arrangements, including the alarming term 'lines of fire'. She didn't want to know. She'd learned early in her long scientific training that trying to follow technical experts when she didn't know the basics was pointless. If she followed closely, she understood one word in five. If she paid less attention, one word in ten. They knew what they were doing. After a couple of minutes, she just let go and looked out the window at the passing scenery.

It was a typical third-world country that wasn't doing well. The airfield was surrounded by fields, with low rolling hills. Dotting the hills were stone huts which elsewhere would be shepherd's huts, but here were probably homes. The land was divided up by low drystone walls, most of which needed fixing.

It started to sleet. Not pretty postcard snow, but wet slivers of ice that made everything look hard and abandoned, like an alien planet. Inside the vehicle it was toasty warm and completely insulated. They drove through the terrible weather as if it were nothing. The driver had complete control of the vehicle, whereas she would have freaked. Jacob and Nick continued speaking as if they were driving in the Bahamas.

She was sure they didn't even notice the weather.

Many stone houses looked abandoned, but still had lights in them. Soon there were more houses and what, if you were charitable, could be called towns. A few stone buildings with tin signs over the doors, but still no one to buy what the signs were advertising. The landscape eventually turned into one continuous town and she could actually see some people, bundled up against the cold, huddled against the sleet.

No one looked happy.

And then they were in the city, a mix of recent construction and Soviet-era cement brutalism architecture. They passed by a church with an onion dome, a local market with all the produce carts covered up by tarps, a small park with a few leafless trees. They were following a tram line now and a narrow street opened up into a large cobblestone plaza with, smack in the middle, the statue of a medieval monk.

Across the square was a huge stone building with an elaborate façade and *Hotel Stella* written in huge red letters across the top of the building.

"We're here," Nick said unnecessarily and they swerved into the parking area in front of the hotel. A valet came rushing out from the lobby and picked up the keys. He motioned to another valet for the bags but both Nick and Jacob said no.

They picked up their bags from the back of the SUV and carried them in. The only thing Alex could carry was her backpack. They headed straight for the elevators.

"Don't we have to check in?" she asked.

"Already done," Nick said absently, watching the floor numbers. They stopped at the last floor, the 12th. The elevator doors swooshed open and they were in an elaborate foyer with huge bouquets of fresh flowers. "So, you guys have the entire top floor to yourselves. Two of my guys will be stationed out here at all times, in shifts. If you order room service—and it's not bad here—the food will be delivered to your guards and they will deliver to you. Jacob, at every shift change, you'll get notification on your phone together with the ID of the men standing guard."

That sounded really thorough to Alex. She and two colleagues had been assigned guards on a mission to a Malaysian island known for both pirates and terrorists and they hadn't known who the guards were until they showed up.

Jacob's phone pinged and he ushered her to a couch.

"The Queens," he said. "They've got something." He put the video up on a big flat screen on the wall over the bar.

It was Riley, the blonde. "Hey Jacob, hey Alex." She smiled. "Hey Nikolai, good to see you!"

Nick settled in an armchair with a sigh and a glass of brown liquid in his hand. "Riley! Run up any buildings lately?"

She rolled her eyes. "Not lately, no. But we *do* have some intel on what Alex asked for. So—it looks like a company called Teknolab has ordered several of the following." Riley checked another screen. "Here we go. Two CRISPR-Cas9s, thermal cyclers, DNA sequencers, fume hoods, flow cytometers, spectrophotometers. That sound about right?"

Alex's heart dropped. "Sounds perfect—especially if you're planning on creating a bio monster. If what I'm dreading is true, they will also have live samples of small-pox, though that wouldn't be on any register and will not be recorded."

"How big would the sample have to be?" Jacob asked. "Carried in a truck?"

"It could be carried in a purse or a small backpack," Alex answered grimly.

Silence.

"There's more," Emma said, in a new popup window.

Alex sighed. "More?"

"Yeah. We tracked traffic between this lab and the former Soviet site and there's been a lot of traffic. Several trucks a day. But not in the past week. Not too sure I get that."

Alex did. "It took a while for the Zalny biolab to come online. In the meantime, they were using the labs at Teknolab. But there might have been a breakthrough and they might not need Teknolab anymore. Or else they have built up the former Soviet lab to the point they don't need Teknolab anymore. Whichever, it's bad news."

Silence again, until Emma broke it.

"Jacob, Nikolai, we're sending you as much information as we could find on the lab. They've got two addresses. One is the administrative headquarters and the other is the research lab itself. Sending you the schematics of the lab. Someone wiped it from the internet, but Felicity, who is sneaky and understands that part of the world, found it again in the original building permits, which they forgot to wipe out because they clearly thought that the government security—which was for shit—was enough."

Schematics of a laboratory complex came online and Alex leaned forward to study them. She flipped through the pages on the screen, very familiar with how labs were structured.

"Everything seems normal here, except..."

Jacob put a hand on her shoulder. "Except what, honey?"

She quickly glanced around, but no one so much as blinked. She was so unused to this. To being considered part of a couple. For a moment she flashed on the fact that her life had changed in the blink of an eye, it seemed. She'd had a few affairs, but had never been paired up in other people's eyes. This was completely new.

Well, she'd think of that afterward, when this mess was over. Hoping that she and Jacob wouldn't be living in a dying world.

Alex sat back. "The lab is sort of... primitive. Good enough for basic research, more than adequate, but not for much more. This would not be a lab that Elias would find suitable for the work he's used to doing. But maybe there's another lab, say underground? Though there isn't an underground lab in the schematics, it could be a secret lab? I don't know. You guys will have to figure that out. All I know is that what I see here is a very ordinary research lab without the resources, or even the space, to carry out advanced bioengineering."

Jacob turned to Nick. "Can you find out if there's more than one lab at the site. We have to feel our way here. And ladies—" he addressed the Queens. "Can you find out the ownership structure of this company?"

"Sure thing," Emma said, nodding, her rich red curls bobbing. "We'll get a full report to you as soon as we can."

Alex was beginning to understand the Queens. She was sure they'd get a copy of the ownership structure as fast as humanly possible.

"Thanks." Jacob nodded at the screen and the Queens winked off.

"Right." Nick slapped his knees. "My men and I are going to do some recon tonight, report to you in the morning." He slid over a leather covered menu. "Order from room service, you won't be unhappy. See you in the morning." He nodded at Alex and Jacob and left.

Alex sat back and tilted her head until she was looking at the ceiling. It was ornate, with stuccoed embellishments and looked a little like she imagined a French bordello would look.

Jacob took her hand. She felt that touch throughout her body, warmth shooting through her. "Tired?"

"Yeah," she sighed. "But not tired like after a long walk. More like tired after taking ten biochemistry exams. Wrung out and anxious."

"Well, I wouldn't know about that. Never took a biochemistry exam. But I do know about being wrung out and anxious and I imagine some good food and wine—or maybe a beer—are in order. Apparently, the country is known for its Pilsners. Maybe a decent meal will help."

"And a good night's sleep."

Alex looked up, feeling Jacob's stillness.

"Uh-uh." His face was drawn, nostrils white, voice husky. "You're not spending all night sleeping. I have plans for a chunk of the night. The way I'm feeling now, we'd be having sex for eight hours straight, but I'll try to restrain myself. Let you get *some* sleep."

She blushed crimson red. She could feel the blood rush to her head and heat course through her body. Oh my God. What was the matter with her? She was a grown woman, pushing middle age. How could she blush at the mention of sex with Jacob?

Well. Probably because sex with Jacob was something

completely new. Something she'd never had before and which should have a different name, because the sex everyone else understood was something completely different.

He was looking at her intently, heat deep in those dark, dark eyes.

She should say something sophisticated. Witty, even.

"Gah," was the only thing that came out of her mouth.

"What are you going to have?" he asked and she blanked, completely. Was he asking her to suggest new sex positions? They hadn't swung from the chandeliers yet, since there'd been no chandeliers in the plane. There were definitely chandeliers here. She looked up, wondering whether they'd support his weight.

"I'm going to try the baked cabbage with caviar."

Her eyes widened. Was that code for something? Some highly complex sex position. *With caviar.* Maybe requiring unusually lithe limbs, something available only to few people?

He tapped the menu and reality whooshed in. The menu. Food. He was asking her what she wanted for dinner.

This was terrible. Alex had always been all business when travelling for work. Now she had had what felt like 50 IQ points surgically removed from her brain, and was going to be good for nobody if she was unable to keep her head around him.

Particularly if they were supposed to save the world.

She cleared her throat, glanced at the menu and chose the first thing she saw.

"Baked farm beetroot with roasted greens and goat cheese."

"Sounds good. Do you want to unpack and maybe put on pajamas while I order?"

God. Jacob was doing his best to make her comfortable, to please her. She needed to stuff her brains back into her head. And dampen down her hormones.

"Yeah. Um, thanks. I think I'll take a shower, too." She fled as he picked up the hotel phone. She had herself more in hand by the time she came back into the living room part of the suite. The bedroom was nice, bland and comfortable. The shower was fine. She'd unpacked and put her things away. Those mundane things had helped calm her down, make her feel more at ease.

Jacob stood when she entered the room. He'd set up dinner on an occasional table, having even found a table-cloth somewhere. He seated her and seated himself and pulled the silver domes off their two plates. Everything looked good and smelled good.

She closed her eyes as she put the first forkful in her mouth. There was an explosion of fresh flavors. "Whoa. This is good stuff."

His mouth quirked. "Yeah. Wait until you try the beer."

Her amber beer was in a tall glass that sweated. She tried a sip and her eyes opened.

"Told you."

"Can we have alcohol? If we're on a mission?"

He sipped his dark ale. "Yeah. Nothing's going to happen tonight. Nick went to look at the lab, but it's dark and empty. And there's a snowstorm going on. We're better off tomorrow, when Nick has an appointment with an informant early in the morning. Plus, Nick has some more men arriving tomorrow morning. We need to plan things, not go off half-cocked."

"Makes sense. I'm just scared Elias might be hurt, or—"

"Or?"

"Or... making progress," she finished, miserable. It still hurt to think of her colleague, a man she thought she knew well, helping to *design* a dangerous virus instead of working to defeat it. Nature herself was pretty good at creating lethal viruses without the help of scientists creating brand new ones. It went against their grain, against their training, against everything the CDC stood for.

"Yeah."

"Have you ever had a colleague—I guess you'd call them teammates—who betrayed you?"

Jacob took a moment to wipe his mouth. "No. I've had a few teammates make mistakes—I've made a few myself— but nothing that would equal betrayal. We have a very long and careful selection process."

"So do we," Alex said sadly. "We have years and years of academic training, on the job training, every second of it dedicated to fighting disease. I thought—I thought it would be ingrained to fight disease and not create it."

"Greed seems to be a powerful motivator," he said, dark face tight and grim.

"I don't think it is for you," Alex said, realizing suddenly that it was the truth. He was immensely rich, but there was nothing of the rich man about him. At the moment he was dressed for work. Everything he had on was suitable for field ops. Good quality but certainly not fashionable. Even the watch he was wearing wasn't an expensive piece of jewelry, like the watch he'd had on back at headquarters. He could certainly afford an expensive watch if he wanted. It had some extra dials on it and doubtless it doubled as a radiation detector and phone and radio transmitter, and probably could make coffee, but it looked pretty ordinary. Not gold, not silver. Stainless steel.

Everything of his she had seen was top quality, but not ostentatious. And he hadn't once talked about money, about how much this was costing him, though it was clearly costing him a lot. He seemed genuinely alarmed about the threat, but nothing else.

"No." He sat back. "I'm not money motivated. As a matter of fact, the money I'm earning astounds me. It's useful because I can get my guys the best gear on the market, but that's about it. We do well because... well, because we're good at what we do. Not because the company squeezes every ounce of profit it can, like some security companies do."

She sighed. "It's a truism, but money can't buy happiness. I know that firsthand. It's why I can't understand Elias at all. To endanger people for—for what? A new car?

Expensive vacations? Fancy clothes? We earn more than enough for our needs. How could he do this?"

Jacob took her hand, studying it. He linked his hand with hers and as always, at his touch she felt warmth and strength infusing her. "Money definitely can't buy happiness," he said softly. "Right now, I'm happier than I've ever been and I've had money for a long time. There is no way I could buy what I'm feeling now, the happiness you make me feel."

He was stealing her breath from her. His dark eyes were so intense she felt she was going to fall into him. His words affected her deeply and she knew he felt the same way. There wasn't any amount of money in the world that could make her feel this intense bond, this connection. When he took her hand, it was as if something slotted into place. Forces aligning, her destiny taking shape. For the first time in her life, she felt like she was exactly where she was supposed to be, with the man she was supposed to be with. She'd stepped into a future that held Jacob and it was meant to be.

Her throat was too tight to say the words. All she could do was look him in the eyes and nod.

Jacob rose, tugging her hand. He bent his head to her, nose nudging her hair away from her face, mouth to ear so that she heard the words but felt them, too.

"Come to bed with me, Alex."

CHAPTER

Eleven

ZALNY

A glitch.

One of Topolev's spies at the airport showed him the photos of two men and a woman who had just entered the country. Ilya recognized two of them. Jacob Black, who ran a famous security company, so powerful it was a real threat. The kind of company that was more powerful than many countries.

He did not recognize the other man but he did recognize the woman—Dr. Alexandra Hethering. Elias Field's colleague at the CDC—and insurance. This might not be a glitch. It might be an opportunity. Perfect. If Dr. Field refused to cooperate then he would have Dr. Hethering hurt and if that didn't work, he would shoot Field in a place guaranteed to cause maximum pain without killing him and coerce Dr. Hethering into cooperating.

Because time was running short.

The outbreak was scheduled to occur in three months'

time, on May 4th. I-Day. He'd also invested a huge amount of money, shorting airlines and health insurance companies and the tourism industry.

A huge Chinese delegation was scheduled to arrive in Los Angeles for bilateral talks for an historic trade pact. The largest Chinese delegation ever to set foot in the United States, a harbinger of much stronger ties, or so the American newspapers said. At the same time, a Chinese pop group would hold a concert in Lumen Field in Seattle. The concert was sold out. Sixty-eight thousand tickets. Which meant sixty-eight thousand infected in one go. Many more thousands in Los Angeles. When a mutated virus was suspected, the suspicion would fall on the Chinese. The mutated virus would spread like wildfire along the West Coast, spreading inland. When the virulence subsided, Topolev would send in troops to California, Oregon and Washington in the guise of aid and solidarity. Within a year, the entire Western seaboard would be a Russian protectorate.

And the Rodina would rise once again, with a new empire.

* * *

"Honey, I have to go."

Alex blinked and sat up in bed, feeling groggy. Had she overslept? No, the sky was dark outside, part of the sky a slightly lighter shade of gray. It was still dawn. She felt energized and exhausted, both. But Jacob looked like he always did. Tireless, like he could work all day and all night and never show the effects.

Jacob left and returned almost immediately bearing a small cup of what smelled like excellent coffee. "They have an espresso machine. I left breakfast for you on the table. You can heat up the croissants in the microwave. I'll probably be gone all day, so order lunch whenever you please. A maid will come in to clean, and I'll ask you to stay in the foyer with one of the guards and the other will be with the woman at all times. The Queens will give you a situation report around noon our time. They are making progress with the ownership chart of Teknolab, together with the bios of the owners, and they are putting together a complete list of equipment the company has and any patents they have applied for.

"You'll be safe. There will be two men outside in the foyer at all times. I left a sheet of paper with their names, their shifts and a photocopy of their IDs so you'll know what they look like. Please don't leave the suite today. I know that's asking a lot but we're stretched very thin and I'd hate to have to ask Nick to provide more manpower because he's overstretched as it is."

Jacob's eyes creased a little with stress. He felt he was asking her for a lot. But he wasn't.

Alex sat up and placed her hand on his chest. "Of course. I don't want to be a source of stress for anyone. I have plenty on my plate because I've begun going back over all of Elias's reports, dating from a year ago. I downloaded everything before coming to Black Inc. Plus, I'll be

going over the information the Queens will be giving me."
She glanced outside the window. The sky was a slightly
lighter shade of gray now, but the clouds were low and
sleet pinged against the windows. "Not to mention the fact
that the weather is terrible. I'll stay put, promise."

"And... a favor?" Jacob asked.

"Of course." Alex meant it. Anything she could do for
him, she would.

Jacob brought out a flexible plastic rectangle from his
pocket. He peeled it apart and extracted what looked like a
small band aid. "Okay here's the deal. We all wear these on
the backs of our watches. They are transponders, transmit-
ting GPS coordinates, and are unjammable. It's saved lives
and it just might save my sanity. Would you—would you be
willing to wear one?"

Alex didn't answer. Just undid the buckle of her watch
and held the watch out to him, face down.

Jacob let out a breath. "Thanks. I think I'd go crazy if I
couldn't know where you were, even though you are going
to stay put. Right? And I left a Black Inc. ruggedized cell
on the table."

He pulled back, hands on her shoulders. She nodded.
Of course. It made sense to her. When on field trips,
everyone could be tracked by their phones. Viruses and
bacteria couldn't mess with cellphones but bad guys could.

Jacob let out a breath.

"We have no idea what the situation is, if someone has
clued in to our presence here." He took her hand and
brought it to his mouth. "Go back to sleep if you want to, I

just wanted to tell you I'm heading out. Didn't want you to wake up to an empty bed."

Going back to sleep. No way. Jacob was going out on a mission. Walking into possible danger. She felt little flutters of panic in her stomach.

Rising, Alex put on the hotel bathrobe and followed Jacob to the door.

"Honey, you don't have to see me off. I'd just as soon you grab another hour or two of sleep."

"I—I couldn't sleep," Alex said starkly. "Not knowing whether you are in danger or not." She grabbed the collar of his parka, suddenly terrified. She'd just found him and here he was, walking into possible danger. Life couldn't take him away just as they'd found each other again, could it? Life couldn't be that cruel, could it?

Of course it could. Life was cruel. Life killed her parents when she was sixteen. They'd been young, healthy, their whole lives ahead of them and their lives had been snuffed out like a candle in the wind. There were no guarantees.

She clutched his parka, pulling his head down. "You'll be careful, won't you? Promise me you'll be careful."

She was being foolish, but she couldn't help it. Couldn't help this leaden feeling in the pit of her stomach, the dread.

Something in her face must have told him she was truly frightened. He didn't make fun of her. He just placed his big hands over hers, warm and hard.

"I'll be careful," he promised, deep voice serious. "I am

the most careful man you've ever met. Nick, too. I'll come back to you. Promise."

She gulped, suddenly choking, unable to pull in air. *Ohmygod.* Was it going to be like this every time? For the first time, she realized what she was getting into, being with a man like Jacob, who lived with danger every day. Was she going to be terrified every time he walked out the door?

"What if—" she began but he bent further and kissed her. Hard and deep, a kiss she felt down to her toes. He held her tightly against him, so she could feel how strong he was, how steady.

"I'll be back," he said again when he lifted his mouth.

Alex gave a shaky smile. "That's what Schwarzenegger said."

"And did he come back?"

She nodded her head. "Yeah, he did."

"There you go. So will I. I'll definitely be back."

He turned and an instant later was out the door.

* * *

ALEX's bare feet hit the floor. She'd been on tiptoe to kiss him. The marble floor felt cold. She felt cold. What to do?

What she always did.

Work.

Shower first. Breakfast, then to work. There were Elias's files to go over. She hadn't finished. There might be some clue to what he was planning, what he'd been working on, but she doubted it. Still, going over his files was necessary, if only to cross that off the list. As she'd said to Jacob, a lot of dry holes in science.

She was showered and dressed and on her second cup of coffee when her laptop pinged. ASI. The company of the Queens of IT.

Good.

"Hey, lady." Emma beamed at her. She looked fresh as a rose, though it was 2 am in Oregon. "Hey. Hey." Hope and Riley chimed in.

"Hi guys. It's late where you are."

"Yep." Hope grinned. "We've just finished a report on the ownership and governance structure of Teknolab. It's pretty complete and has a few surprises. We've sent it to you and Jacob. You guys receive it?"

She checked her email. Sure enough, she had an email from ASIQUEENS, with a big attachment. "Yeah. Got it. I imagine Jacob got his, too. He's not here at the moment, he's out with Nikolai doing what they call recon."

"Good," Hope said. "Because we want to talk to you, not him."

Alex put down her pen and looked at the screen where the three women, each in her own window, were looking at her expectantly.

"So... do you need some information from me?" she asked when no one said anything.

"Absolutely," Riley said.

"Yep," Hope said.

"You betcha." Emma nodded her head enthusiastically.

"What do you want to know?" Alex imagined they'd want more information on the nature of viruses or on bioengineering and started ordering info in her head. Biology often confounded non biologists. It was tricky and slippery and she wanted to be clear.

"So... Jacob." Emma rested her chin in her hand as she bent her head toward the screen.

"Yeah. Tell all." Hope leaned forward, too.

"Don't leave out any details." Riley shook her head. "I had dealings with him in DC and man, that dude is scary. But super hot."

Emma shook her head. "I think all our guys had more or less given up on him meeting someone. There was talk of a girl in his youth. Sort of like the one who got away..." her voice petered off and her eyes widened.

"You!" Emma practically bounced in her chair as she pointed at her screen. "You're the Mystery Woman, Alex! The one who got away! I'd bet anything!"

By now, Alex was getting used to feeling her face going traffic-light red. She sighed and willed the blood back down. It was too late, of course, because the three women were super smart. Their voices became a babble.

"So, when did you get away?"

"And why?"

"When did you get back together?"

"Who took the first step?"

"What's he like in bed?"

That last question, asked by Hope, came in during a little lull and she looked around. "What? We all want to know, right? I mean we all have our guys and no one's complaining, but... Jacob Black. Need I say more?"

"On a scale of one to ten, how is he in bed?" Emma wanted to know.

Well, Alex knew the answer to that one. "A hundred."

Three happy sighs.

After a moment, the questions started up again.

"Who made the first move?"

"Do you guys go back a long way? How far back?"

"Is he as hard-headed as our guys? We have a theory that SEAL training makes them impervious to reason."

"Ladies, ladies!" Alex held up her hands in a time out gesture. "If I tell you the whole story, can we then get down to business?"

Three heads nodded assent. Hope: "But don't leave out details."

There were a lot of details that Alex wasn't willing to share, but she could give them the barebones story, and she did.

Silence, as they digested things.

Hope frowned. "He actually said those words? 'I was afraid.' Those very words?"

Riley's eyes were wide. "That doesn't sound like Jacob Black. That doesn't sound like anything our guys would say."

Emma nodded. "If he actually said he was afraid, this

is serious stuff. You are really under his skin. So—that's how you guys are together?"

"And that's how we're together," Alex said. "Sort of. But I don't know how long it will last or even if it will last beyond this mission."

The three women looked at each other. "Oh, it'll last," Riley said. "I don't think he's ever been paired up with anyone. He's made it clear he's with you. This is Jacob Black we're talking about. He invented serious. Last night I asked Pierce and Raul, who know him fairly well, if he had a reputation as a ladies' man, and they looked at me as if I'd grown another head. So if he's never been seen with a woman on his arm and all of a sudden, there you are—" she lifted her shoulders in a shrug. "This thing has legs."

"I want to be invited to the wedding," Hope said seriously, and Alex broke out in a laugh. After a moment, the three women joined in.

"I want to be invited, too," Emma said. "Riley and Felicity, as well."

"Yeah." Riley nodded sharply. "You have to promise. Pleeeeze?"

Alex was amused and exasperated at the same time. She threw up her hands. "All right! If we ever get married, you three—and Felicity—will be the first to know. But it's not going to happen."

"We don't just want to know," Emma specified. "We want to be invited to the wedding. I bet it'll be a blow out. Jacob doesn't do anything halfway."

Alex blew out a breath of exasperation. This had taken

on a life of its own. She was like a branch caught in a flooded river, barreling down to the sea. "Okay, okay!"

"Promise?" Riley cocked her head, waiting for a reply. "Nail it down. Be specific."

"Okay." Alex bit her back teeth, but there was only one way out of this. "I promise you all will be invited to the wedding," she gritted. "Which is imaginary."

"No, it's not. And you need to promise to invite our plus-ones." Emma pursed her lips, frowning in concentration as if it were a big business negotiation.

"Done," Alex promised on a sigh.

"We didn't record this," Hope said, "But we have really good memories, all of us. So we're going to hold you to your promise. If there's a meat or fish option, I opt for the fish. Riley's vegetarian. Emma is sometimes lactose-intolerant and Felicity isn't picky. Our guys will eat anything not nailed down. Don't forget."

Alex gave up all resistance. "I won't forget. I have a really good memory, too. Emma, no cheese. Felicity has no preferences, Riley's vegetarian, you want the fish. The men will eat anything."

"Excellent. Now, do you want to hear what we've found out about this company?"

Finally, back to business. She blew out a breath of relief. "I really do, yes."

"Emma's our finance genius. She used to work for a big bad bank making money for people who don't need any more, and sure as hell didn't deserve anymore, so I'll have her report."

"It's true." Emma didn't blink at that description. "Currently I work on the side of the angels, but I did spend a couple of years working for Satan. Now, Teknolab. It was founded by a biochemist, Dr. Georg Lazlo, in 2005. In Vostokova. Lazlo was born in 1956 so he spent most of his early career working during the Cold War. Lazlo worked for a state research lab under the Soviets. I was quite literally unable to find what his specialty was. I couldn't find any papers he'd written or co-written. All I could find was that he had worked at a research institute in Leningrad, now St. Petersburg, and believe me when I say I had to dig very deep to find that."

"That's not reassuring news." That was putting it mildly. Alex felt a slight shiver run through her body. "Soviet scientists didn't really have careers the way we think of them. They worked for the state, whatever research they produced belonged to the state, and if they were working on anything that ran counter to the various treaties we had with the Soviets concerning bioweapons, then they just disappeared underground. So him not being well known is not good news at all."

"Yeah," Emma said, frowning. "We suspected something like that. He still kept a really low profile even after the Soviet Union collapsed. We couldn't find a trace of him until he opened Teknolab in Zelenograd ten years ago. But here's the thing. Teknolab was a run of the mill pharmaceutical company, producing knock offs of popular drugs when the patents ran out, until about five years ago. Then it was bought by a company called

Viralogics, which bought 54% of the company shares, effectively becoming the owner. Lazlo didn't have a significant number of shares but... oddly enough, he went on a spending spree. I found four deluxe apartments in his name in Montecarlo, Rome, London and Moscow, for a total of twelve million dollars. He has a fleet of four S-class Mercedes Benzes and has just shy of five million dollars in Credit Suisse."

"Wait." Alex blinked. "You found out how much money he has in a Swiss bank? How did you do that? Switzerland has bank secrecy it takes very seriously."

Emma gave a mysterious smile and said nothing. Alex gave an internal sigh. Clearly Emma had used unorthodox —if not illegal—means. But given what they suspected was going on, that was nothing.

"Sorry," she said sheepishly. "Forget I said that."

Emma nodded briskly. "So, we've established that, as of five years ago, Dr. Georg Lazlo has become extremely rich. Even though he doesn't have controlling ownership of the company he runs."

"Who does? Who is the owner?"

The three women looked at each other, but it was Emma who answered. "A Russian. And trust me when I say I had to dig deep—practically to the earth's core—to get this name."

"Okay."

A dramatic pause. "Ilya Topolev. Colonel Ilya Topolev."

Silence.

Alex was baffled. "Should that name mean something to me?"

The three women looked at each other again. "Clearly you don't work for a security company."

"No, I work for a research institute. So who is this Colonel Ilya Topolev?"

"He is head of the Russian Federation's FSB."

Alex still looked blank.

"It used to be known as the KGB. And Felicity says it is still almost as dangerous as the KGB used to be."

Alex sat back, the breath whooshing out of her lungs. "Oh, my God."

"Yep." Hope nodded briskly. "This is bad news. Very bad news."

"Did you tell Jacob?"

"Just now sent the message. He's going to be pissed."

"The informant didn't show." Nick's voice was grim. "And I'd offered him enough money to salivate. No way he was giving that up." Nick met his eyes.

Jacob knew exactly what that meant. Someone had gotten to the informant first. The informant was no doubt six feet underground, or in the river, or cut up for parts. Maybe on a meat hook somewhere.

There was silence in the vehicle as they chewed over that thought.

"What?" Nikolai asked, as they parked the vehicle two

blocks away from Teknolab. They'd both heard the ping of an incoming text. Jacob's eyes widened and Nick stared at him. Jacob never showed emotion on the job. This was the second time today. The first time was leaving Alex.

Nick said he'd looked as spooked as a wild pony. Nick had had to go over the security arrangements twice, reminding Jacob there were two of their best men on guard duty. Plus, Alex had promised not to leave the suite and Jacob admitted that Alex could be trusted. She was a serious woman and would keep her word.

But—he was leaving her alone, unarmed. Jacob squelched that thought as soon as it popped in his head. He had been about to go back up to hand her a spare Glock 19 he had when Nick had gently pushed it away and asked whether Alex had ever held a gun in her hand.

He'd asked Alex before and she'd said no, she'd never even touched a gun. Nick just gave him A Look. There was no way Alex could defend herself with a gun if she'd never even held one before. Nick knew that, just as he knew that there were two men outside her hotel suite who had probably shot over a million rounds between them, and definitely knew how to use a gun.

Jacob had never gone on a mission with his attention split. In the field, he was like a laser beam, tightly focused on what needed to be done. And now he was completely poleaxed by Alex and the thought of her vulnerability. The thought of leaving her behind, which upset him. Though taking her with him was out of the question. But he was *leaving her behind*. She had two bodyguards, but they weren't him. He'd just found her and he was terrified at the thought of losing her.

And now this.

"What?" Nick asked again. Jacob turned his cell around so Nick could see it. It was from the Queens and short and to the point.

Teknolab is owned by Colonel Ilya Topolev, of the FSB.

Jacob felt his anxiety notch up a thousand degrees, which was insane. He was never anxious. Ever. He was a binary man. Either something was or wasn't.

Either it would work or not.

Whatever the outcome, he would live with it, because he was a realist.

But now, with Alex in a hotel suite on a mission with a fucking FSB officer in the mix, not to mention a deadly disease, he could feel waves of anxiety swirling around him.

He could keep himself safe. He'd spent the past eighteen years doing just that under harrowing conditions.

Could he keep Alex safe? He had moves, knew how to keep himself alive in even desperate situations. Alex didn't have those instincts. To keep her safe, he should be by her side, 24/7, and he wasn't. He couldn't be. He and Nick and his men had to get to the bottom of this and he couldn't have Alex around. The need to operate without having Alex around warred with his need to make sure she was safe.

Jacob wasn't used to warring with himself. It was dangerous.

"Stop that." Nick's voice was hard. "Just fucking stop."

"Stop what?"

"Stop worrying. I can see into your fucking head, the waves of anxiety are that thick. What's the matter with you? You know better than this. Alex is fine. You know my men, they're your men, too. They're not going to let anything happen to her, you *know* that."

Jacob breathed out through his nose, like a bull. "This is hell, worrying about someone else. Not used to it. I don't worry about you."

"I don't worry about you, either. We're both tough sons of bitches to kill."

"But Alex isn't." Jacob shut his eyes. "She'd be real easy to kill."

Nick's voice was hard. "Then why the fuck did you bring her if you're going to worry like this? She should be back home. In Atlanta or San Diego, or wherever. Not here on the front lines."

"That's what I told her!" Jacob smacked the dashboard. "It's madness, her being here."

"What?" Nick's head slowly swung around. "You didn't want her here and she's here anyway? What the fuck?"

Jacob was immediately sorry he'd said those words, because it was like having his beating heart nailed to the wall for everyone to see.

He sighed. "She insisted on coming. Said she could be useful."

Nick just stared.

Jacob shrugged. "I wasn't willing to tie her up. What else could I do?"

"Apparently, nothing. I never thought I'd say these words, but... you love her."

Jacob hung his head. A deep strangled noise escaped from his throat.

This was so terrifying. He realized now he'd loved Alex what felt like all his life, but he'd never actually said the words to himself. Never fully acknowledged it.

Now it permeated his existence. He wasn't the free agent he'd been up until now. Now there was Alex to factor in. To think of, to care for, to protect. Her wishes had to be taken into account. His life wasn't entirely his own anymore.

It was unsettling.

"Stop it," Nick said again, this time punching him in the arm. Hard. Nick knew how to punch and it got Jacob's attention. "Get your head back in the game and let's go see what this is all about. You're no good to anyone, let alone Alex, in this condition."

Jacob nodded and they exited the vehicle.

Teknolab looked abandoned, empty. They approached carefully, helped by the miserable weather. Gray, sleety, foggy. They donned stealth coveralls and wore balaclavas, all of which reduced their IR footprint to nearly zero. Any infrared cameras would register a slight temperature anomaly but certainly not enough to identify a human intruder.

There were security cameras everywhere but they didn't look turned on.

Tekno was in the middle of a concrete plot with little to no plants to soften the look. Along one side was a hedge of some plant that had not only lost its leaves to the winter but the branches looked gray and dead. Clearly Teknolab's budget didn't run to gardening services.

The building was isolated, with no way to approach stealthily. Jacob and Nick were crouched behind a low wall some fifty meters away and studied the terrain. There wasn't much to study—it was barren, stark, exposed.

They looked at each other and communicated in hand gestures. *Do we make a run for it?*

If there's someone in the security office we're fucked.

It was Saturday. Maybe the company wasn't open on weekends. There were no cars parked in the vast parking lot. No lights on. No signs of life.

They looked at each other again.

Jacob was torn. Rushing a building with no cover at all was insane. But they didn't have many leads and there was always something to learn, even if you paid for it. This was where bioengineering equipment had been delivered, and if the trucks making it to Zalny were any indicator, that equipment had been delivered to a rogue lab. Teknolab could give them intel on what to expect at Zalny. There would be documents. Nick could read them and they could send scans to the Queens who would use AI to translate them.

There were risks, of course.

If the signs of abandonment were a ruse, they'd be caught. Interrogated, probably. The element of surprise would be lost. Neither of them had any identifying marks on them or their clothes. Jacob would shut up and Nick would do the talking. His Russian was excellent, he could pass for Russian. They would draw out the interrogation. It would give them some time to notify their team, who knew where they were. The team would come.

The risks were great. The risk of not doing anything, not learning anything, was greater.

Nick was looking to him for instructions. Jacob was team leader. He was the one to decide. Go/no go?

Go—it could be an ambush. They could be killed.

No go—they'd be left with no intel, which might be available inside.

Go/no go?

Go.

He pointed with his fingers forward and Nick nodded. Jacob knew that if it turned out to be a bad call, Nick would never blame him. You made the call. You went with the intel you had. They had none and needed some.

Nothing was ever easy.

They looked at each other and Jacob nodded—go.

They sprinted across the concrete apron to a side door. They took up stations against the side door, weapons up, Jacob to the right, Nick to the left.

Jacob brought out his IR scanner and pointed it to the wall. The screen showed no heat spots. Not even a mouse.

Certainly not a human. He stood back, aiming his gun at the lock when Nick held up a finger. Kneeling, Nick took out his lockpick kit and in a few moments the door was open.

Lockpick? He mouthed and Nick shrugged. Jacob hadn't carried a lockpick in ten years. And how crazy that the door to a pharmaceutical lab only had a regular lock? He hadn't seen one of those in ten years, either.

The door swung open to a dark, cavernous space. They both put on a set of night vision goggles, only they looked like glasses. Not the unwieldy goggles attached to helmets that most soldiers still used, but an experimental set that could pass for normal glasses in public.

The room was milky, not green, in the enhanced light from the doorway. It was the lobby of a company. A curved reception desk, old fashioned phones, benches around the perimeter. Nothing fancy, nothing that stood out.

Walking quietly, ready for anything, they walked the perimeter of the lobby area, which was bland and old fashioned. There was a set of double doors in the back wall and they doubled up again. Used the scanner again. Nothing, again.

It wasn't locked. The doors opened onto a long corridor with doors either side, clearly the heart of the building.

Nick was studying the signs next to the doors. "Admin, accounting, human resources, public relations... ah, here we are. Doesn't even need translating. Labs. So I guess this leads to the wing where the labs are."

They opened the door and walked in. This far into the building there were no sources of light. Nick placed on the ground a special light source invisible to the naked eye, but which lit up the space as if it were noon on a sunny summer day when seen through the goggles.

It was a series of interconnected rooms, spacious, empty. They passed from room to room and saw nothing but empty space with machinery. Nothing on the walls, not even a duty roster or sheet of paper.

"Okay," Jacob said, "time to call in the expert." He pulled out his cell and called the cell he'd given to Alex. When he heard her voice, calm and low, something in him, something that had been tight ever since he'd left her back at the hotel, relaxed. She was safe.

"Hi," he said. "You okay?"

To her credit, Alex didn't sound exasperated. "Yes, thanks. I'm going over some info The Queens have sent. Quite interesting. The ultimate owner seems to be—"

"One Colonel Ilya Topolev," Jacob said. "Of the FSB."

"Uh-huh. You had a chance to read it." She sighed. "I didn't even know what that was until they told me. Sorry. Scientists lead a sheltered life."

"No reason for you to know. So, honey, I'm going to show you the labs. Can you tell me if you see something out of place? If they seem like normal research labs to you? We're not turning on the regular lights, my phone is filtering LED stealth light. Let me know if there is something unclear or out of place or just wrong. I'll start from the perimeter and work in."

"All right."

Jacob started from the west wall, slowly recording everything there was to see, lingering over equipment. He was prepared to do this for all the labs, if necessary, but was hoping one lab would be indicative of all of them. It took twenty minutes, but finally he finished with the final countertop in the center of the room. There were stainless steel doors below the countertop, but when he opened them, they were empty. Nonetheless, he showed them, too, to Alex. Sometimes absence was as important as presence.

"Okay." Jacob brought the phone closer. He was looking at Alex's beautiful face. It anchored him, made him feel better. "Thoughts?"

Alex was frowning in concentration. "Well, it's hard to think of what you have shown me as a working lab. It has primitive and old-fashioned equipment. Almost all the equipment is at least ten years old. I didn't see any obvious holes, as it were, otherwise I might have suspected that they emptied the lab of the modern equipment, but it doesn't look like that. It looks like a lab that hasn't kept up with the times. Wait a minute. There's something I couldn't tell in that weird light. Can you run your finger along a surface?"

Jacob scowled. "What?"

"Run your finger along that countertop, for example. And along all the surfaces."

Well, she was the expert. Jacob ran his finger over every surface he could and understood when his fingers left a streak.

"Dusty. That doesn't show up under stealth light."

"Dusty," she agreed. "Jacob, that is most definitely not a working lab. Labs are kept meticulously clean. Sterile, in fact. Dust on surfaces would interfere with results. This lab hasn't been used in a while. It's abandoned. I'd say some time ago. I don't think you're going to learn too much from it, unless they left behind paperwork. I'd advise you to look for paperwork and records and then leave."

Jacob nodded at Nick. "Okay. We'll look for docs then we'll come back to the hotel and make a plan to approach the hidden lab at Zalny. How are you doing?"

"Fine." Her face softened. "I'm on my second coffee. This is a comfortable suite, and in an hour, I'll order lunch. Looking at the weather, I am much more comfortable than you. Please don't worry about me. By the time you guys arrive I think I'll have some info for you."

"Make sure you order lunch. You need to eat lunch."

"Yes, mom." Alex rolled her eyes. "You want me to order something for you guys?"

Jacob looked over at Nick, who nodded. "Yeah. Don't know when we'll get there so in about an hour, order a couple of club sandwiches and a couple of—"

He looked over at Nick again, who said, "Cokes."

"Couple of Cokes. See you later."

Alex smiled at him on the screen and he thumbed it closed.

"There now," Nick said soothingly. "Feel better?"

"Actually," Jacob said, feeling sheepish, "I do. We don't

know what we're facing and I feel better that I know where she is and that she's safe."

"Let's finish up in here and we can get back to the hotel. You'll feel even better when you see her."

CHAPTER
Twelve

Topolev followed everything via his men's bodycams. It went down smoothly. They rappelled down onto the rooftop of the hotel from a specially built baffled helo that made a fraction of the noise a normal helo did. His men were in body armor and well armed but they also carried a gas mask with well over an hour's autonomy. Topolev was sure the entire thing would be over in five minutes, but to be well prepared was to be well armed.

It was the Dubrovka Theater crisis in miniature. He'd been right there, in Moscow, during the whole thing. On the 23rd of October, 2002, he'd been training recruits in psy-ops, a weeklong course in the fine art of fucking with the enemy's head. The FSB had subtly started training recruits in electronic surveillance, economic sabotage, false flag interventions. He remembered thinking that his own kind of training—poison pills and grenades and rifles—was starting to be old fashioned.

He was preparing a new generation of recruits in the subtleties of modern warfare when word came that a handful of Chechen terrorists had taken an entire theater hostage. Almost nine hundred theater-goers imprisoned under the watchful eyes and guns of the most backward, ferocious soldiers he'd ever encountered. They were positively primitive, savages.

He'd rushed to the Dubrovka theater, where officers of the FSB, including the Alpha Group and Vympel Special Forces, had taken the lead in responding to the terrorists, troops from the Ministry of the Interior, emergency services, and local Moscow police officers. It was an utter stalemate with a thousand elements of law and order milling around, helpless because the terrorists held assault rifles on almost a thousand hostages.

There was no rushing the theater, no rappelling in from helicopters, no sniping at the terrorists. The terrorists made sure they were embedded among the theater-goers. No one wanted a massacre and every idea put forward involved a probable massacre.

Gas them, the head of the FSB said, and it was the smartest possible move. The only possible move. Using a new drug called fentanyl, a hundred times more potent than morphine.

He excluded the use of carfentanil on Dr. Hethering, one thousand times more potent than morphine. It could tranquillize an elephant and with the wrong dosage would fry the doctor's brains.

No, fentanyl it was.

And it was the only possible move here because he needed Dr. Alexandra Hethering alive and unwounded. Going in with guns drawn would be dangerous. Not to mention loud, guaranteed to draw attention.

At Dubrovka they hadn't known what a lethal dose was, but now they knew better. Topolev knew exactly what the dosages should be. He had a lab full of pharmacologists and scientists able to get the doses carefully calculated and a lot of Narcan available should something go wrong.

He had three canisters made. High, but not lethal, dosages for the two guards outside the hotel suite and a lower dosage for the good doctor. It would put the two guards out for at least four hours and Dr. Hethering out for an hour, tops. She would be functional again by the time they got to Zalny.

First, they had to grab her. In and out in five minutes, nobody the wiser.

The helo hovered over the hotel rooftop, not even settling on the surface. His men—five of them—leaped out with air-purifying respirators, protective goggles and nitrile gloves. Their combat suits covered their skin, though the exposure to fentanyl was going to be brief.

The door to the stairwell wasn't locked. Their contact at the Stella Hotel had unlocked it that morning. There were no security cameras. The contact had taken care of that, too. It had only cost Topolev one thousand dollars. Vostokova was a poor country.

The men entered the stairwell and quietly descended

to the top floor, given over to power panels and supply storage. They got into the elevator and pushed the 12th floor, one floor down.

They deployed on either side of the elevator doors. The two guards would hear the elevator coming and would be waiting as the doors opened. And yes, sure enough, there they were, guns in a two-handed stance, knees slightly bent, weight on the balls of their feet.

Textbook.

They were well-trained, but they were biological entities, as susceptible to poison as anyone. The instant the doors started opening, his men tossed two canisters into the lobby. Fentanyl was released in a stream so strong he could hear it through the webcam on his soldier's chests.

The two guards fell immediately, dropping where they stood, in a boneless heap. His men stepped out of the elevator and over to the door to the suite. One man bent to feel for a pulse in the neck of both men through the nitrile gloves. He nodded to the webcam on his teammates' chest.

The men were alive.

Good.

They would have no idea who or what had attacked them. The elevator doors started opening and they lost consciousness. Even if they had seen his men, they wouldn't be able to remember.

Topolev didn't really care if they lived or died, but finding two unconscious men would definitely create fewer problems than finding two corpses. Corpses gummed up the works, even in a state as weak as Vostokova. He didn't care about these men, what was important was bagging the woman.

As per instructions, they moved fast. They didn't even try to pick the lock or ring the bell. They shot out the lock, tossed in a canister and rushed the room. Topolev saw the woman look up from her computer, startled, then fall to the floor. The woman was tossed over the shoulder of Andrei, still feebly kicking but by the time they got to the elevator, she was completely still.

A minute later, they were on the roof, ducking to avoid the grit raised by the rotors. They tossed in the woman, then followed her into the cabin. The helo lifted off as soon as they were in the cabin. They wouldn't bother tying the woman up, restraining her. She would be out for at least an hour.

More than enough time for the helo to make it back to base.

Topolev sat back. That went well. He now had an ace card in his hand. He thought with distaste of Elias Field, how difficult he was proving to be. He'd wasted his time and money cultivating him.

This Hethering woman was just what he needed.

* * *

NICK DROVE. He'd been to Zelenograd before and anyway understood the street signs. Jacob had no problem relinquishing the wheel, though he usually liked to be the one driving. The one in control.

Well, one of many things that seemed to be changing. Alex was changing him with every passing moment.

The thing was, he was... happy. It was hard to admit, even to himself. Hard even to recognize, but a human understood happiness when it appeared. This mission was hard, potentially extremely dangerous, which usually put him on red alert, a state he'd been in for most of his life. Muscles tense, ready for trouble. Laser focused on getting the job done, whatever the job was. More or less closed off to anything else.

Not now. Now, all his senses were blasted wide open. It was foggy and sleety, but the fog came in snaking tendrils, creating a pearly light and covering up the pocks and bullet holes left over from the last war. Made the buildings look almost... beautiful. The vehicle was really comfortable, a Mercedes Benz SUV with soft leather seats and with that new-car smell.

He was hungry. Jacob basically shut down most bodily functions when on mission. He was rarely hungry, thirsty or sleepy when working and certainly not horny. But here he was, wondering whether it would be unprofessional to slip in a quick little nooner with Alex after lunch.

Man, this was so not him.

Next to him, Nick made a noise.

"What?"

"So weird to see you smiling. I think I've seen that maybe twice in all the years I've known you. The last time I saw you smile was when that asshole government contractor shot himself in the foot trying out the new Rossi Rifle."

Yeah, that had been really satisfying. But Nick was right, Jacob didn't smile on mission. "Not smiling."

"Oh man. Ear to ear." Nick grinned. "Looks very strange on your face, which is definitely not made for smiling. Though I guess I'll have to get used to it."

Jacob punched him in the arm. Hard. Unfortunately, Nick was muscle-bound and didn't flinch. Didn't even move.

Nick pulled out his cell while whistling 'Get Me to the Church on Time'. Jacob's eyes were rolling in his head. Nick thumbed a number on speed dial and touched the comms in his ear.

Jacob didn't say anything. Nick was perfectly capable of driving and talking on the phone at the same time. There was very little traffic and anyway, the police here were not exactly sticklers. Who knew if the country had gotten around to drafting laws on texting and driving. He didn't even know if they had laws against drinking and driving. The country was pretty new, pretty raw.

He'd been looking out his window, recognizing a few landmarks, thanks to having studied maps of the city intensely on the way over. *Study the terrain* was ingrained in him. Going into a situation blind was a nightmare and could cost you your life.

Some snow was sticking to the ground in a park that was two blocks from the hotel. It wasn't a very well-kept park, but the snow covered the bald patches and covered the garbage that had been dumped around the base of a bronze statue of some Vostokovan who'd done something pretty painful, judging from the puckered expression on his face.

The silence next to him made him look over. Nick was tense, thumbing again at his phone. "What's wrong."

Nick met his eyes. "O'Keefe and Dusan aren't answering."

A bolt of horror lanced through Jacob's body. The men who worked for them always picked up on the first ring, unless they physically couldn't. There was only one explanation for them not answering and it was too awful to contemplate.

"Try—" Nick said, but Jacob was already calling Alex. His hand trembled as he thumbed the number on speed dial. His hand never trembled, but now it was as if he were affected by some kind of terrible palsy. Alex's phone started ringing. He felt his heart contracting in his chest as the phone rang and rang and rang. Even if Alex were in the shower, she knew enough to keep the cell with her at all times. Jacob couldn't imagine any scenario where she wasn't answering, unless—

Not going there. But his body was going there anyway. He was pumping out fear sweat in great surges, something that had never happened to him before.

He swayed as Nick took a corner almost on two wheels. Thank God there weren't any local cops around because if they tried to stop them, Jacob would start shooting. They were going to get to the hotel and up to the suite just as fast as humanly possible and nothing was going to stop them.

Nick pulled up to the entrance of the hotel and braked to a rocking stop. Jacob exited running, not bothering to close the door. There was a drumbeat of terror and panic in his head which he was trying to quell by imagining various scenarios.

Alex wasn't answering because she was in the shower and couldn't hear. Her phone was out of juice—though that didn't square with her meticulous scientist brain. Still, it could happen. The phone had fallen and broken. Though that would be hard because his company cellphones were all ruggedized. They cost more, but he had never heard of one of Black Inc.'s phones becoming inoperable, unless it took a bullet.

As he was running through various possibilities, while running to the bank of elevators, he kept coming up against the hard fact that the guards weren't answering. There wasn't any scenario he could think of where that would happen.

Unless...

Nick made it into the elevator cabin just as he stabbed the button for 12 and as the elevator rose—horribly slowly it felt like—they pulled out their weapons and moved into shooting stances. Somehow, Nick had taken the time to grab ballistic vests in the back seat and they both fit them over their torsos.

By the time the elevator doors opened, they were ready for bear.

The doors opened onto... nothing. Both of them had been prepared for a firefight, ready to fight their way into the hotel suite, but there was nothing. Jacob stepped forward warily, weapon up and out, but saw nothing. Nick nudged him, pointing downward, and Jacob saw.

If he hadn't been so panicked, so consumed by tunnel-vision, he'd have seen it immediately too. A couple of canisters. Two downed men.

He pointed his gun at the floor, crouching on his haunches next to the canister. He sniffed the air. "Fentanyl," he said. "There's that ammonia scent. Has to be. They've been out at least an hour. I called Alex at 11:15 and everything was fine. Check them."

Nick bent and put a finger to the side of the neck of both men, looked up and nodded. They were alive.

Heart pounding so hard it felt like it would pound its way out of his chest, Jacob approached the door into the suite. He rapped with his knuckles. "Honey? Honey, it's me. Can you open the door?"

He had his hotel card in his hand and signaled to Nick that he'd go high and left and Nick should go low and right. They'd done this a thousand times before, but never before had he been terrified of what might be on the other side of the door.

He'd had ISIS members, drug cartel sicarios, Albanian traffickers on the other side of the door and all he'd felt was cold determination. Not this gut-wrenching horror at the thought of finding a wounded or—God!—dead Alex on the other side.

He opened the door and they rushed into the room. The empty room. "Clear," Jacob croaked. Nick came back in from the bedroom and bathroom. "Clear. She's not here."

Jacob met Nick's eyes. "She's been taken. She's in the hands of terrorists."

CHAPTER
Thirteen

Her head hurt. Her hands hurt. Her shoulder hurt. Her left biceps hurt. Everything hurt. A deep pain that had come from nowhere.

She lifted her head, and blinding pain lanced through her head like a lightning bolt. For a horrible second, she thought she was going to throw up, as her insides rebelled against the pain.

But she would throw up in her lap, which would be horrible, because she couldn't move. Swallowing back the bile, she looked down at herself. In an upholstered armchair but tied with cloth around the chest to the back of the chair, so she couldn't stand up. Her hands were bound, too, with cloth. Even if she wanted to stand up, she couldn't. And she didn't want to. There was no strength in her body to stand up, to do anything. She could barely keep her head up. All her muscles were lax but hurt.

What had happened? She'd been working at her

computer in the hotel room, she'd heard a sound and then... her mind blanked. And then she'd woken up here without any idea how she'd gotten here.

Where was here? It hurt to move her head and even her eyes, but she tried to take stock of the room she was in.

A... lab. She was in a lab, the kind of lab she was familiar with. A very advanced lab, every instrument the latest version. There was at least ten million dollars of equipment in this room, maybe more.

It was chilled, as labs had to be, and it even had that lab smell. Of electronics and fixing agents and ozone and, underlying that, disinfectants. She was starting to panic, but the familiar smell calmed her a little.

A clock on the wall said 12 though she had no idea whether that meant noon or midnight. The room was without windows. The last thing she remembered was checking her watch at 11:15 am, thinking she might have an apple. Would that be today? Yesterday?

Her watch! Ohmygod! Her watch had a tracker! Bless Jacob for thinking of it. She still had her watch, no one had taken it. She couldn't lift her arm to look at it, but she still had it.

She didn't know where she was, but Jacob would find out. He would find out and come get her.

But... something about the quality of the air hinted at being underground. Or at least encased in concrete. Could the tracker's signal be picked up if she were underground or in a room with thick concrete walls?

What did she know about tracking signals? Was it like a car's transponder? Could Jacob...

"Alex?"

She whipped her head around and instantly regretted it. The pain was so intense she blacked out for a moment. Her hand wanted to rise to her head but it couldn't. She could only sit and suffer through it.

"Alex?"

That voice again. Familiar?

She slid her eyes to the right and gasped. "Elias!"

She almost didn't recognize him. He'd lost weight and had a cadaveric look—skin gray, lips blue. He didn't look injured but there were bloodstains on his lab coat.

He started sobbing. "I'm so sorry, Alex! My life is ruined! What have I done?"

The stabbing pain in her head had scaled down to a throbbing pain. Her mind felt dull and unresponsive but she could think again. A little.

"Elias, are you hurt?"

He lifted his hands. They were handcuffed, not bound by soft material like hers. His ankles were tied together. He seemed to forget that, and stood up and tried to walk to her, but he had to sit down again, hard.

"It's been so horrible, Alex!"

The clouds in her head were dissipating. She was still in pain, but at least her head was starting to function.

Elias hung his head. "So awful. It's been so awful."

Well, Elias, bless him, was a scientific genius but he was also a narcissist and a bit of a prick. So far all he'd said concerned himself and what was clearly remorse at having been such a moron.

Finally, he made the connection. Alex, his colleague. Here, in Vostokova, if that's where they were. And tied up, a prisoner. He frowned at her. "What are you doing here, Alex?"

Yeah. She'd worried herself to death over him, had moved heaven and earth, had moved *Black Inc.*, to come to his rescue and had been—what? gassed?—for her troubles. What was she doing here? Oh, yes, stopping him from maybe infecting the world.

She took in a very deep breath. "Your call came from here, Elias. And I knew that Zalny had a lab researching bioweapons when it was part of the Soviet Union. Even though it was supposedly decommissioned after the Soviet Union fell." She took a chance and moved her head to take as much of the lab in as possible. "Doesn't look decommissioned to me. It even has an HPLC system and those go for—"

"About two million dollars," a deep voice said behind her. "But worth every cent."

She and Elias turned as a tall man walked into her field of vision. He was very erect, fit. Steel-gray hair and a military bearing. Thin face, cold light-gray eyes, almost transparent.

"Who are you?" she asked as she watched Elias shrink back. Elias knew who he was. "Wait." She remembered the information the Queens provided. "Colonel Topolev, I presume."

"Yes indeed. Brava. How clever of you. I am Colonel Ilya Topolev," he said, head cocked. "I'd say at your service but actually, Doctor Hethering, I want you to be at my service. We need your expertise as Doctor Field, here, has been noticeably lacking. He has been stringing us along and we're on a bit of a timeline here."

"Timeline?" Oh, God. Did that mean he was ready to move? In which direction?

"Indeed. As the song says, places to go and things to do. But we are behind and we are going to need you to help pick up the slack."

She felt bile come back up her throat but refused to vomit. This man looked like he would enjoy seeing that. He was tall, whippet-lean with the coldest gray eyes she had ever seen. There was no discernable human emotion in his face.

"Pick up the slack. That's a euphemism if I ever heard one." She drew in a deep breath. "You want to create a weaponized smallpox virus." Her voice was flat, monotone, working hard to keep emotion out of it.

He nodded. "Yes. A very powerful weapon, I think you'll agree."

Alex drew in another deep breath. She wanted nothing more than to rush at him and claw his eyes out. But she couldn't move. And he looked really fit and strong. He could fell her with one blow.

But he needed her. That was a weapon in her favor. It was like having a gun. Something she could wield.

"Weaponized smallpox could kill off humanity, you

know that, don't you, Colonel? Certainly end civilization. Why would anyone want that? It's insane. We spent years and billions of dollars and millions of man hours eradicating smallpox. Bringing it back is..." She couldn't finish the sentence. "It would be as bad as sparking off a nuclear war."

The Colonel shook his head. "Ah, ah, Dr. Hethering. That is where you are wrong. A nuclear war would indeed be a disaster. Complete destruction of the industrial base and the housing stock and agricultural land. Radioactivity for generations. Unthinkable. We'd probably have to live underground for generations.

"However, deadly disease is like the neutron bomb. It kills off people leaving everything else intact."

She stared at him. Who talked like that? Who thought like that?

"I see you are surprised. Have you never heard of the concept of a bioweapon? And yet you are a virologist. One of the best, from what I understand. As good as Dr. Field here, who has proved to be very disappointing. He was... recruited... for a very specific reason and has been unable to fulfill his function."

Alex risked a slanting glance at Elias, who was staring in fury at the Colonel. Elias was indeed a very good scientist, one of the best. If he didn't do what the Colonel wanted, it wasn't out of incompetence. No, he refused.

The Colonel hitched a pant leg up and perched on the corner of a table.

"I see you are not showing any curiosity about what

Dr. Field was recruited to do. And what, I imagine you are starting to understand, we want you to do in his stead."

She kept her voice steady. "Whatever it is, I won't do it."

The man gave a chilling half smile. "I suspect you will. We can be very persuasive." He pulled a gun from a holster she hadn't even noticed before. "I could, for example, shoot Dr. Field in the knee. This would cause excruciating pain. It would shatter the kneecap, turning the solid bone into fragments, leading to severe swelling and bleeding. As you know, since you had to study human anatomy for your degree, the knee is a complex joint which is absolutely critical for walking. The knee would be irreparably damaged, severing tendons and ligaments. If lucky, the result is a permanent limp. If unlucky, amputation.

During the exposition, his voice was steady and emotionless, as if discussing the weather. Elias had gone gray, sweat dripping off his face.

"This is craziness." Alex raised her voice and grimaced at the pain in her head. "If you've done any research at all, you know that smallpox is a massive killer. You would start an epidemic that could kill billions. What would you possibly have to gain? You could kill off your own people. You're Russian, aren't you? Russia stopped vaccinating in the mid-seventies. Russians, like everywhere else, do not have immunity. Any epidemic you set off will fly around the world, certainly to Russia. You'd perhaps die yourself, your family would die. And for what?"

He idly swung his leg and regarded her with cold gray

eyes. "To take things in order, no, I would not die. For that matter, neither would you. I have been inoculated and so have you."

Startled, Alex looked at her left arm. It was sore, and a small band aid had been applied to the biceps. She hadn't noticed it until now. The spot hurt, but she hadn't really focused on it until now since more or less everything hurt.

"And so has Dr. Field."

"That is not how vaccinations work. It takes weeks..." She stopped when he lifted his hand to strike. No one was immune to a disease when they'd just been inoculated. The immune system had to be activated. It could take weeks. At least a week. Certainly not hours. But the Colonel was not listening.

"You are still not seeing the big picture," Alex said. She had no hope of changing the man's mind. He was clearly a psychopath. But she was trying to gain time, hoping Jacob could somehow find her. There was no guarantee she was in the refurbished Zalny lab, but she suspected she was. Even if he knew where she was, how could he find her? She could be a thousand feet underground. But Jacob would find her. She was sure of it. She only had to give him time. As fast as a man could come to her, that was how fast he was coming. "What you're trying to do will slip from your hands and become a worldwide epidemic. With horrible consequences."

The Colonel tipped his head to one side, looking at her curiously, as if she were an unusual specimen. "What do you think I am trying to do?"

She blinked. "Well, it's obvious. You're going to try a terrorist attack somewhere using smallpox. But it will get completely out of hand. Millions will die, it will make Covid look like a picnic in the park. The world economy will come to a grinding halt..."

He put his hand up, stopping her.

"No," he said with a faint smile. "There will be terrible consequences for a limited geographic area. Then the epidemic will stop."

"How do you make an epidemic stop?" she began heatedly, then her mouth snapped shut. *Ohmygod*, she thought. She hadn't thought it through. What had merely been theory was now reality.

"What is Dr. Field an expert in?"

Her head pulsed with pain and dismay. "A—a kill switch," she said reluctantly. Which would change the equations, make the unthinkable possible.

He gave a chilling smile. "Exactly, Dr. Hethering. A kill switch. So you have a deadly virus, made even more deadly and fast acting by bioengineering and which has a built-in kill switch. Why, it would be like a precision tool. Slashing and cutting exactly when you want, stopping exactly when you want.

"Biology doesn't work that way. It won't be as precise as you think. There will be slip ups."

"Of course. But they won't be that important. The important thing is to spread the disease where we want for the length of time we want. And we are almost there. We have the virus we want. We just need an active and precise kill switch. Which your colleague Dr. Field is refusing to give us."

She glanced over at Elias, whose eyes were closed in pain. For the first time, she noticed the bruises on his neck, a swelling along his jaw. Painful movements. Signs of distress everywhere except his hands. He'd resisted.

Good for him. She honestly didn't think he had it in him.

She turned back to the monster. "I'm sorry, you have the wrong person. I couldn't possibly replace Elias. He is an expert on kill switches, though he hasn't perfected one. No one has. Genetically engineered microbes or viruses programmed to self-destruct when certain parameters are met. It's a rewriting of genetic code utilizing a lethal effect, and it's dangerous and incredibly difficult. Almost impossible, in fact. The scientific community has almost given up on the idea of a kill switch until we get better tools."

It wasn't impossible. She knew of several instances in which kill switches had been successfully created to shut down certain expressions of cell reproduction. But not in contagious diseases. And certainly not in genetically engineered cells.

The Colonel tipped his head back and examined the ceiling, then brought his head back down. "We were almost there, thanks to the work of a talented scientist, Dr. Dima Obolensky. All you or Dr. Field would have to do is complete his work. Perfect and replicate in a lab what Obolensky has done."

She gasped. "Dr. Obolensky is alive? I thought he died in 2011. He was a pioneer in bioengineering."

"Indeed, he was. Very talented. And no, he did not die in 2011. That was a useful lie because it was an open secret what Dr. Obolensky was working on. The news of his death stopped the speculation. But he unfortunately— how is this notion expressed in your comic books? Crossed the rainbow bridge. Yes. He crossed the rainbow bridge before his work was completed. He continued working for me and was very close to a breakthrough when he chose to end his own life. Very annoying and inconvenient. I had to find another scientist who could finish Obolensky's work."

"Elias." Alex shot her colleague a poisonous look. He hung his head, longish greasy hair falling around his face.

"Exactly so. We courted him in Budapest and he showed great interest in being courted. But then he has proven to be remarkably stubborn and useless."

His head swiveled to her like a gun on a turret. "Thus, you. We used Dr. Field's phone to scatter breadcrumbs leading here. We didn't think you'd come with a security team."

Her heart knocked against her chest, though she kept all emotion from her face. They knew about the guards and Jacob and Nick. He couldn't be allowed to know what Jacob meant to her.

"Did you kill the guards outside my room?"

"No." The Colonel yawned. "That would not be cost effective. But we did put them out of commission for a couple of hours. They will have a lot to answer for to their employer. They conspicuously failed at the first task of a bodyguard—keeping you safe."

"What did you use?"

"Fentanyl."

Oh, God. Fentanyl was so dangerous. "Is that what you used on me? Because I felt like hell when I woke up. Still do."

"I used a lower dose on you. Your guards will still be out."

Alex sent up a prayer to the god of soldiers that her two guards would indeed wake up and that there wouldn't be permanent damage.

"Fentanyl is extremely dangerous."

"You should be very grateful that we didn't use carfentanil. It's very easy to administer a lethal dose. Requires a careful hand. Now." He clapped his hands on his knees, clearly bored with the conversation. "Let us get back to what we need from you. The insertion of the kill switch gene using CRISPR-Cas9, into a new formulation of the smallpox virus. Dr. Field is refusing. So either we hurt you, Dr. Hetherington, to get Dr. Field to do what we ask of him, and for which we have paid him well over a million dollars, or if hurting you isn't a lever that moves him, we will hurt him to get you to engineer the gene. I suspect you have a softer heart than Dr. Field does. Either way, the work will get done. The work must get done."

As they were talking, the affable affect slowly crumbled and she could see the dangerous psychopath emerge. The skull beneath the skin. It was so frightening because she knew, beyond a shadow of a doubt, that he would use whatever tools at his disposal to get what he wanted. Psychological coercion. Physical coercion. Torture. Even death.

It sounded like he was on a timeline, on a schedule. Things had to happen by a certain date. That could be dangerous, in that he could get desperate if he didn't get what he wanted by that date. Alex needed to walk him up to that line without going over it. All she needed was to give Jacob time to get to her, however long that took. And he would come for her. Like the sun rose in the east, he would come. She knew he would move heaven and earth to get to her.

"So." The Colonel reached down to the ground and brought up a briefcase. There was a keypad lock and biometric pad. He entered in five digits, pressed his thumb to the pad and the briefcase clicked open. Dry ice fog rose up. He picked up a vial and held it up to the light. It was three quarters filled with a light powder. He pulled out another vial with liquid inside. "Here we have it. Mankind's scourge. Rendered even more dangerous but also tamed once one of you two insert the kill switch. The liquid is reconstituted DNA of variola."

He waggled the second vial back and forth, liquid sloshing up the walls.

Alex could barely breathe. Her eyes followed the sloshing liquid, throat gone completely dry. Inside that vial was the death of millions of people. Possibly billions, if it was true that the smallpox had been bioengineered to be faster-acting and more lethal. Death and destruction on a vast scale, unimaginable suffering. Perhaps even the end of humanity.

She lifted her eyes to the Colonel's. His were bright, mocking. Almost as if expecting praise for being so clever.

Her stomach suddenly rebelled, her entire system rejecting what was happening. How she wished her hands were free so she could hold them over her mouth. As it was, she avoided vomiting by sheer will power.

She was looking at pure evil, something she'd never encountered before. This was someone who had no human emotions she could connect to. Someone she could never understand, not in a million years.

Someone who, for gain, could and would slaughter millions without a second thought. There was absolutely no remorse in those glittering light-grey eyes. If anything, he looked very pleased with himself. Someone who'd successfully pulled off something difficult.

She glanced at Elias, but he refused to meet her eyes, keeping his head down. Whatever happened, his life was over. He could die in here, maybe after being tortured. The Colonel looked as if he could torture Elias out of pure pleasure. Or if they escaped and got back to the States, he'd be tried for treason. She'd testify against him, no question. He wasn't evil, like the Colonel. But he'd collaborated with a terrorist, for money. There were no other outcomes. Maybe he could escape, live the life of a man on the run. He wouldn't last five minutes. Elias had no street smarts and had zero ability to live under the radar. He'd always liked to live large. That would never happen. His entire body language spoke of defeat. Head down, shoulders slumped. He'd clearly given up.

But she hadn't.

Alex had no idea what to do, except take everything minute by minute, keeping an eye out for a moment in which she could maybe break away. Or attack the Colonel, crazy as that sounded.

Were there soldiers here, wherever she was? Would she be gunned down? Probably not, since the crazy man needed her. But after?

The Colonel had put the vials back into the briefcase, in their foam cutouts. He stood up. "Enough. Time to go."

Alex was taken aback. "Go where?"

"To the BSL-4 lab where you are to commence working on inserting the kill switch. I don't want to waste any more time."

"No."

Alex was so proud of herself. Her voice didn't tremble and her body language didn't change. She wasn't hunched in on herself or shaking. She was just angry, through and through.

"No?" The Colonel echoed her. "Hmm. We'll see about that." Swift as a snake striking, he whipped out a small rod and put it to Elias's neck. Immediately a buzzing sound filled the room and, horribly, Elias shook in a frenzied, palsied way. All his muscles, from his feet to his head, contracted. His eyes rolled up in his head until only the whites showed. An inhuman sound, the sound of an animal in pain, came from between his lips. He trembled, muscles jumping, tendons standing out. The smell of charred flesh filled the air. A wild keening sound, high-pitched and rasping, filled the air. Elias lost all semblance of a human being and become something else—something that bore no likeness to a human.

"Stop!" Alex screamed and the Colonel immediately withdrew the prod. "You'll kill him!"

The Colonel considered that, head cocked. "No, I don't think so. I think he might wish that it would kill him, but he is a healthy man. In a great deal of pain, to be sure. But this is not life threatening. Not when used for a moment or two. However, using this—" he held the prod up like a chef displaying his favorite knife, "for a very prolonged period of time will create permanent damage to his brain and, eventually, death. A very nasty death, too."

Elias was slumped over, breathing heavily. Paper-white skin drenched in sweat. He moaned, half conscious.

"Dr. Hethering?" The Colonel's voice held mild curiosity. "Are you ready to start working? Because I can keep this up with no difficulty at all. For hours. Eventually, Dr. Field will die in a great deal of pain, as I said. His heart will give out or he will have a fatal stroke. Such a pity. He is a man of lax morals, but there is no doubt he is a gifted scientist. Such a pity to lose a mind such as his. And for what? A little pride on your part?"

Alex saw that the moral horror of what he was proposing was not a factor for him.

She shook her head. "I can't do the work. Elias has

been involved in the finer aspects of gene splicing and bioengineering, but I've been involved more in the research aspect. So I can't replicate what he was doing."

"Nonsense." The Colonel's voice was cold and sharp. "Dr. Field told me that you were as good as he was, if not better. His words." He walked toward her, electric prod in his hand. He held it close to her neck. She tried to back away but had no room to maneuver. Just a few inches more and the prod would be against her neck. "Now come on, Dr. Hethering. Unless you need a little encouragement."

He closed the distance and stabbed her in the neck.

The pain was intense, more intense than anything she'd ever felt in her life. Every nerve in her body was afire. She couldn't move, couldn't breathe, ceased being a person and became a bundle of excruciating, unbearable pain.

The taser was withdrawn immediately, but it had been enough to realize there was no resisting that pain. It overwhelmed her, took over her body. There was no resisting it, not in any way. You couldn't be brave, be stoic, because it wiped out who you were. You lost yourself and became unrelenting pain.

He took out a knife and she instinctively drew back. But all he did was cut the bonds holding her hands and legs together and the strip tying her to the chair.

His cold voice was like a whip.

"Get up now and follow me."

She hesitated, then got up on trembling legs, willing herself not to fall down.

CHAPTER
Fourteen

"Lost her." Jacob wanted to hit something. Hard. Break something. Howl at the moon. "She's lost."

"No, she's not," Nick said sharply. "Goddammit, Jacob, stop fucking around. She's not lost. She's somewhere, waiting for you to go get her. That's what's holding her together, the thought that you are coming after her. So get your fucking act together. Follow the tracker."

Jacob heard the words as if from a great distance. They didn't make sense until he rolled the words around in his head.

And it was that picture—the picture of a captive Alex waiting for him to come—that snapped him out of the fog of grief.

Alex wasn't dead. He'd have sensed it if she were. No doubt about that. It would have been like a tear in the universe. He'd have felt it. They were connected. Always had been, always would be. She wasn't dead but she could be in pain, being hurt, right this minute.

The thought of that was like being knifed in the gut, but he couldn't deal with that right now. Whatever was happening was happening. He couldn't stop anything until he got to her, as fast as humanly possible.

He straightened.

"Glad to have you back," Nick said sourly. "Now see if you can keep your head in the game instead of freaking."

Jacob didn't answer. He'd pressed a button on the side of his watch and opened his tablet on a sideboard. "Fucking transponder only has a range of about a hundred miles. If she's been loaded onto a plane or a helo, we're in trouble. If she's on a vehicle, there hasn't been time to drive a hundred miles. Let's see."

He'd been trembling, but not anymore. If there was any hope for Alex, he needed to keep his head and his nerves. He couldn't waste any time panicking. His entire future—his *life*—depended on him figuring out where she was and moving like an arrow to her.

He zeroed in on a teardrop and the blue dot that was her location, then enlarged the map. "There." His finger traced a path from the hotel, along main roads, then secondary roads, to an out-of-town spot in the middle of nowhere on the maps.

Zalny.

"Fucker's taken her to Crime Central."

"Fucker?" Nick asked.

"The KGB Colonel. It's got to be. Send out the coordinates to all the men you have here. How many?"

"Originally I had ten, but two are down," Nick said, features tight. "If the fentanyl had been stronger, they'd be dead. As it is, they are out of commission."

Jacob nodded, hoping the fucker had used a lighter dose on Alex. She was much smaller than the two operators, who were still out cold.

"Pointless going over security cameras and I have a horrible suspicion there was someone in-house providing help."

Nick's mouth tightened. "Not the owner or management. But yes, it is possible that someone in the cleaning staff or a porter could have been bribed. It's a poor country. We can go over everything later, when—"

"When I get Alex back," Jacob growled, "we're going straight to the airport and straight home. I'll leave it to you to figure out the mechanics of it. Right now, the important thing is to get Alex out alive and, if possible, secure whatever bioweapons might be there."

"Leave that to me." Nick was filling their duffel bags with what would be necessary to infil into a hostile area. "This is a hopelessly corrupt country except for the Minister of Defense, who is a friend. He won't be Minister for very long because he is not corrupt and that's made him enemies. I just hope they don't assassinate him. But in the meantime, he'd be horrified to know what was going on in his country. I'll contact him for backup."

Jacob froze. "No crossfire." Horrifying thought. A shootout, with Alex caught in the middle.

Nick was busy with gear. "Not our first rodeo."

He was throwing body armor and gas masks, breaching charges, jammers, flashbangs. And weapons: UMP45s, several Benelli M4s with high rates of fire in case of intense close combat, a couple of Remington 870s for breaching. The rest of the operators would arrive fully armed.

While Nick was quickly assembling their gear for what might turn out to be an assault on an underground complex, Jacob programmed ten drones with the coordinates of Zalny, opened the window and flew them out.

Then he sent a text message to the Queens asking them to take over the drones and provide real time intel on the area. By the time they arrived, they should have a complete mapping including any guards posted.

Nick was done. Jacob, usually a control freak, would have checked the gear but there was no time. And really no need. Nick knew what he was doing. There were two big heavy duffels on the floor. Jacob shouldered one, Nick shouldered the other and they headed out to the service elevator.

Ready for war.

* * *

ALEX PRETENDED to be weaker than she was, though her

legs still felt unsteady. She was feeling stronger but didn't let that show.

"Come," the Colonel commanded and she looked up, blinking.

A touch of the taser, just a touch, was enough to shock her with pain.

"Come," he repeated impatiently and gripped her elbow. She was on shaking legs. He lifted her almost bodily, steadying her when she risked falling to the floor. "With me."

Still holding her elbow in a painful grip, he started walking to the door.

Alex tripped over her own feet and he shook her, hard. With his other hand, he grasped her shoulder painfully, fingers digging into the muscle. The Colonel stuck his face close to hers, cold eyes boring into hers.

"You will now follow me and you will not waste my time, am I clear?"

The hand, digging into her shoulder so painfully, clenched harder, then lifted and he brandished the prod. When he pressed a button, it emitted that crackling sound which she knew was connected to blinding pain. "I can reduce you to a whimpering heap on the floor, after which I will have one of my men drag you, not carry you. Is that clear?"

Her mouth trembled. She couldn't pull in enough air to talk.

"Is that clear?" he roared, and she nodded frantically.

"Say it!"

"I—I will follow you," she stammered.

He grabbed her elbow again and started walking fast. Alex had to scramble to keep up and had to work hard not to stumble. It took everything she had as she tried to coordinate her limbs.

They exited the room and two guards came to attention. The Colonel snarled something in Russian and they walked down a corridor to an elevator. Alex stumbled and one of the guards took her other arm in a painful grip and they entered the elevator practically carrying her. At one point her toes were dragging on tiles. The elevator took them down three floors and when they exited, she realized that they had reached the BSL-4 level.

Instinctively, Alex looked around. The lab was a room inside a room, like a separate fortress. They were in the outer room, which would be secure even without the massive safeguards of the inner lab.

It was freezing cold. She shivered and instinctively tried to hug herself for warmth, but her arms were held securely.

The men's steps echoed off the concrete walls.

The BSL-4 lab had security cameras posted under the ceiling, but there was no light indicating they were turned on. She had no way of knowing if they were activated or not.

They moved toward the entrance of the inner lab. A series of monitors with warning signs in red flashed, detailing the risks and compulsory safety protocols.

The Colonel and the guard holding her showed no

interest in the warning signs. She imagined that the signs were automated. She also imagined that the Colonel was aware that there was only one risk, and he and his men were inoculated against it.

No matter what he said, she wasn't.

She was being force marched past the airlock into a room with weaponized variola. And she wasn't wearing protection.

They entered the lab without protective gear, which alarmed her at the deepest possible level. She'd never entered a BSL-4 lab without being protected from head to toe. A BSL-4 lab is brimming with danger, an environment totally hostile to humans. Entering basically naked, without any protection, felt like walking off a cliff without a parachute. Unthinkable. Her feet dug into the floor in instinctive protest, but she was carried forward against her will by the two soldiers.

It felt like being marched to her death.

The Colonel's vise-like hold on her upper arm tightened painfully. "Stop wriggling," he commanded coldly.

It was like stepping into a minefield. She didn't know this lab, she didn't know who ran it. She had no idea how careful they were. If smallpox were here, the least movement could shatter a vial.

Even worse, they weren't closing the airlock. It was such an important part of her working day, passing through the airlock, hearing the hiss of pressurized air, knowing that every precaution was being taken. If anything happened in this room, the virus would definitely escape.

A warning signal, red lights flashing. Entrance into a BSL-4 lab without proper gear. But the Colonel wasn't paying any attention to the warning signs. Alex had no way of knowing whether this was because he knew there was no danger, or whether he didn't know any better.

Inside was fanatical order, which made her feel just a little better. Order always made her feel better. Though the people creating the order here were working to destroy the world.

The two men suddenly released her arms and Alex staggered, but kept on her feet. The Colonel had taken out the prod and turned it on briefly. The buzzing electric sound made her heart beat wildly, then he turned it back off.

The point had been made. *I can use this whenever I want, for as long as I want to.*

"Walk around," he ordered. "See if there's everything you need. But if you lie, I will know. And there will be consequences." He'd taken out a cell and was consulting a page. Probably a fellow scientist had made a list of the things that were necessary. She had to delay things but had to be subtle.

Because Jacob was coming for her. She had no idea how, but she knew that for a fact. He was coming and all she had to do was stay strong.

She made the rounds of the big lab slowly, carefully examining every piece of equipment. Everything was top of the line, machines she was intimately familiar with. She stopped at every single one, examining it minutely.

It was a well-equipped lab, more or less similar to the one at the CDC. Someone had spent a lot of money on it. Well, it looked like this was a well-funded terrorist group. Ending the world didn't come cheap.

She had finished minutely examining the ELISA reader when the Colonel suddenly stood straight, tapping his ear. She'd seen both Jacob and Nick do that. Some in-ear comms equipment.

The Colonel's face hardened, features drawn tight.

Without warning, he stepped quickly to her, whipped his closed fist around and punched her in the face. She had no warning, could do nothing to brace herself. It came out of nowhere. The blow was hard and her head bounced off the wall. She would have fallen to the ground, but he held her up by the arm in a brutal grip.

"We have visitors," he growled. "You're going to make them go away."

Her ears rang and she barely heard the words. *Visitors,* he said. Could it possibly be Jacob?

He lifted the lid of a cryo container, cold ice bubbling up, and pulled out a vial. Alex could barely think, her instinct told her the vial was dangerous. With his other hand, he grabbed her upper arm and started walking fast. She was marched right out of the lab, setting off the alarms again. Her legs could barely hold her up. There was a dull pain on the side of her face and she couldn't coordinate her limbs.

The Colonel and the other soldier held her upright as they entered the elevator. They were discussing something in Russian, and the other soldier unholstered his gun. Two years of living in Geneva had given her very good French and decent German but she didn't know Russian at all. The Colonel was giving instructions in a furious voice and the soldier was nodding.

They reached the ground floor and the doors opened and there was a little forest of rifles pointed right at them.

CHAPTER
Fifteen

There had been relatively weak resistance at the facility. Nick's men had arrived and they were fast and efficient, cutting through the guards.

Nick had given orders to use stun guns while inserting into the lab. To use deadly force only when necessary. Jacob wanted to kill all the fuckers, but Nick had stopped that. As long as there was the possibility of KGB operators on the premises, killing them could become an international incident.

Jacob knew he was thinking of his friend, the Minister of Defense, but he still wanted to kill all the fuckers.

They agreed that as soon as they had proof that they were preparing a bioterrorism attack, they could use deadly force.

Jacob didn't need that. They'd kidnapped Alex. Reason enough to kill all the fuckers. But Nick insisted.

So they had stun guns and the real deal. And flashbangs and grenades and rifles and handguns. And combat knives. And door breacher guns. And for most of them, their bodies could be considered lethal weapons.

They put down ten guards before breaching the main doors, but once inside, the building was empty.

Nick tapped his ear, spoke in Russian, then turned to him. "Yuri's men should be here in ten," he said quietly.

The Defense Minister had promised a team of operators, but had to scramble them.

Jacob nodded. They were in a large lobby. It had a modern design, without being over the top luxe. He pointed at the four corners of the lobby and Nick nodded. Security cams, with a little red light. If there was anyone in the building, they now knew they were being invaded.

Jacob's internal DEFCON system went to one, fueled by rage and paranoia. Alex was somewhere in this building, he was sure of it. There might even be her colleague here, Elias Field, though Jacob didn't give a shit about him. Fucking traitor. If he was here, he'd let Nick take him into custody.

But Alex was *here*, in a monster's hands.

The instant Alex was safe, they were racing to his plane and getting the hell out of here as fast as he could make it. And he didn't ever want to feel this terror, ever again. For the first time in his life, emotions were getting the best of him. The ice-cold operator was gone. Twenty years of combat experience gone up in smoke the instant he discovered Alex had been taken.

He knew, because Nick had told him, that he was no

use to Alex in an emotional state. Combat was psychology, gymnastics, geometry all together. Requiring a calm mind and steel nerves and detachment. And he would go back to that... just as soon as Alex was safe.

He and Nick and their men cleared the rooms on the ground floor and were regrouping in the lobby when they heard the elevator start up. It was coming up from sub level 4, which was probably the BSL-4 lab. They were mainly underground, as a precaution.

He didn't need to give orders. Nick and his men quickly formed a semi-circle around the doors, weapons up and shouldered.

It felt like it took the elevator forever to come up, but finally, a *ping!* and the doors opened, onto horror.

The Queens had sent them photographs of Colonel Ilya Topolev. There he was, together with another soldier. And... there was Alex. Bone white, looking terrified. She had two burn marks on her neck which he recognized as either a taser or an electric prod. And one side of her face was turning red and was slightly swollen. She'd been punched.

Jacob's eyes slid to Topolev, who was a dead man walking.

Alex's eyes lit up when she saw him. She made an instinctive move toward him, but Topolev just tightened his hold around her neck. Jacob kept his eyes on Topolev and the other man. Topolev clenched his hand around Alex's neck. The hand around her neck was holding a vial. Jacob stared at the vial. Inside that small glass receptacle were a hundred thousand horrific deaths, maybe more. The stuff of absolute horror, held against Alex's cheek. The other hand held a Makarov pistol against her temple.

The two men took a couple of steps forward, outside the elevator, dragging Alex with them. She was moving awkwardly. She'd been drugged, it was a miracle she was upright at all.

Topolev spoke, voice low and hard. His English was excellent with only a slight accent. "You will all leave now or I shoot her in the head and throw this vial on the floor. You know what is in it, yes? A modified version of variola, the smallpox virus. It has been modified to be almost 100% lethal, much more contagious. I and all my men have been vaccinated against this particular virus so it makes no difference to me, but you will all die a horrible death, yes? Oh, and Dr. Hethering, too, has been inoculated because we need her to put the finishing touches on my little beast."

His fingers tapped on the vial.

Alex drew in a breath, tried to talk, and the hand gripping her neck shook her, like shaking a dog. "Shut up," he growled.

Alex gulped.

"So this is clear," Topolev said. "You will all leave and not come back. I will put sensors further out and if I catch anyone trying to get in, you can assume that I will hurt Dr. Hethering. Maybe not shooting her knee out, not right away. But I am well versed in inflicting pain that is not incapacitating and I will not hesitate. You *will* leave us alone."

Jacob's muscles were locked, warring with himself. He wanted nothing more than to leap on this man, who was holding Alex, *hurting* Alex. He didn't deserve to live a moment more. But a movement of Topolev's finger, four pounds of pressure, like lifting a beer tab, and Alex would fall to the ground, a pink mist at head level the only sign that something living had once been there.

Jacob had seen a lot of heads explode. It was not going to happen to Alex.

He didn't know yet how—wait. Something was happening. Alex was staring at him, then dropping her gaze. Lifting her gaze to his, dropping it.

What was she trying—?

Oh, God, no.

Nick rubbed his head, hiding him opening comms. They had in-ear buds, almost completely invisible. And the hidden mic could pick up the smallest whisper.

"Now, we will retire to the lab," the Colonel said. He looked over at Jacob and at the rest of the team. "I trust you will all behave, otherwise I will shoot the beautiful doctor. But I won't kill her right away. I will shoot her in one knee, then the other. And if you persist in bothering me, I will shoot her in the hip. She will keep the function in her hands but will never walk again and will be in great pain.

"We are going to lock ourselves in the BSL-4 lab, closing the air lock door. Nothing short of an atomic bomb could make it through that door."

He took a step backwards, dragging Alex with him. She stumbled over her own feet.

"Get ready," Nick subvocalized, and before Jacob could object—*God no, it's too dangerous, we can't let her do this*—Alex wrenched the vial from the Colonel's fingers and instantly dropped to the ground. She curled around the vial, cradling it.

Ten rifles sounded, the shots so close together it almost sounded like one loud shot. The Colonel and the guard crumbled lifeless to the ground. Before the sound of the shots finished echoing around the room, Jacob was gently picking Alex up, angling her head away from the dead bodies. It looked like a slaughterhouse, blood everywhere. She held the vial out carefully, and Nick, just as carefully took it.

"Careful, Nick," Alex whispered.

"Better believe it," he answered. "We're susceptible even if you aren't."

"He inoculated me, yes." She shuddered. "But immunity doesn't set in for a few weeks. I'd be as dead as you."

Jacob felt like his mind was about to explode. "You don't have immunity?" he asked, careful to keep his voice even. She grabbed that vial though she, too, could have died?

She leaned into him and he held her tightly. She shook her head.

"Then why the fuck did you pull that stunt?" he asked, his voice becoming louder with every word. He had to stop himself from shouting. One second's miscalculation and

284

he'd be holding a beautiful corpse, her head blown off. And then infected with a monster virus. They'd both be corpses, actually.

Nick side-eyed him.

"Had to," she mumbled, shaking. "Couldn't go back down there. Just couldn't."

He had to stop himself from shaking, too. Alex on the floor with her head blown off was playing in his mind, on a loop.

They stood there, clutching each other, backs to the bodies.

"Hey." Nick put a hand on his shoulder. "We'll take care of this, take out the garbage, secure the place. Yuri's men are at the entrance. Why don't you take one of the vehicles and take Alex back to the hotel?"

"We're going straight to the plane and straight back stateside."

"Yeah." Nick nodded. "But we have a biohazard. A big one. I'm going to bring in my pal the Minister."

"Blow the place to hell, Nick."

Nick nodded. "Actually I was thinking of ordering up a MOAB from the air base at Vicenza. With the Minister's permission and notifying DOD. Blast that motherfucker to molecules. Sorry, Alex. But would that work?"

Alex sighed into his chest. "What's a MOAB?"

"Massive Ordinance Air Blast. Also known as the Mother of All Bombs. The equivalent of 18,000 pounds of TNT. Destroy the entire complex. Designed to annihilate underground bunkers and buildings."

Alex straightened. Looked at Nick. "Yes. That. Bomb it to hell, including the research. It should disappear off the face of the earth."

Nick nodded. "Yeah."

"Oh, and Elias Field is in the building. On this floor. He's probably still unconscious. He was tortured with an electric prod."

"So were you." Jacob's dark eyes were cold as he gently touched burn marks on her neck.

"Yes. But not as badly as Elias. Though he probably deserves it."

"And will spend the rest of his days in prison," Jacob growled. "No question." That motherfucker was the origin of all of this.

"He will," Alex sighed. "But alive. I don't want him to die."

"If he were in the military he'd be tried for treason and put to death. But he's not." Jacob's mouth tightened. "More's the pity."

Alex clearly read what was going on in Jacob's mind and she turned to Nick as the reasonable one. "Nikolai Garin. You will rescue Dr. Elias Field, who is in this building. I do not want to read later that he somehow died. Oops. His head fell on a bullet. That's an order."

Jacob opened his mouth but Nick answered quickly, "Aye aye. Field is in the building, and we'll get him out. Yes, ma'am. Understood."

Jacob was getting impatient. He held a wounded and exhausted Alex in his arms. This had gone on long enough.

For the first time in his life, he yielded executive power. He had other priorities. "Nick, take care of this. Contact who you need to, do what you have to do to get rid of this devil virus and erase all signs of it."

Nick raised his eyebrows. He knew that Jacob was yielding power, knew how unusual it was. He gave an ironic two finger salute off his forehead. "You got it. I'll work with my friend the Minister. He has no desire to have this monster virus in his country. We'll take care of it."

And he would. Jacob trusted Nick to take care of it, exactly as if he were the one doing it. Nick was offended by this as much as he was. This was what they'd been born to do, what they'd been forged to do. But for the first time in his life, there was something besides duty in his head.

He nodded at Nick and his men. "So we're going straight to the airfield, and then straight back home. Bomb the shit out of this place."

"After getting Elias out," Alex said.

"Yeah, that." Jacob ground the words out. "We're leaving now."

"I'll get your stuff to the plane before you take off," Nick called after him and Jacob lifted his hand in acknowledgement. He didn't care about their stuff. He just wanted to get Alex away.

He had plans.

CHAPTER
Sixteen

A lex fell asleep right away in the SUV that was taking them to the airport. Jacob bundled her in the backseat, put his arm around her and settled a blanket on her lap. Though she tried to stay awake to talk over what had just happened, she leaned into Jacob's broad chest, pulled the blanket up and fell into a deep sleep that was more like a coma.

"Honey, wake up."

Alex blinked awake, completely disoriented. She was in a vehicle which had just come to a stop. It was evening, the sky pewter-gray, sleet falling sideways.

Where were they? She looked around, and nothing made sense. They weren't on a road though it was a paved surface that stretched to the horizon cut off by a thick fog.

The only thing she recognized was Jacob. He ran a hand over her hair.

Alex could remember a feeling of danger, a deep menace threatening them. "Are we safe?" she whispered.

"Yes, we are. And soon we'll be back home."

Home. Where was home? For the moment, she couldn't even remember where she lived, could barely remember who she was.

The loud sound of engines started up and a big plane rolled out of the fog toward them, coming to a stop on the driver's side of the car. Jacob leaned forward to tap the driver on the shoulder. "Thanks."

The driver turned around and nodded. "Of course, sir."

He looked exactly like all the other men of Jacob's company that she'd seen. Fit, competent, unsmiling. The only differences she'd been able to discern had been skin and hair color. Otherwise they were interchangeable.

Jacob opened the car door. Freezing cold air swirled in and Alex shivered. He draped the blanket around her shoulders and hurried her up the steps of the plane. By the time the cold started to penetrate, they were inside the plane and the pilot had pulled the door closed with a hydraulic whump.

The pilot disappeared into the cockpit and Jacob rushed her into the plane's bedroom. When the door closed behind them, she found herself with her back to the door and his hands spread on either side of her head.

"Fucking hell." The words came out in a hoarse whisper. His jaw muscles flexed. "Thought I'd lost you."

Alex leaned forward and rested her forehead on his

shoulder. "I thought you had, too. That maniac was going to lock us in the lab behind the air lock. You could never have blasted your way through. Not without killing all of us."

Jacob shuddered. He leaned forward, placing his head next to hers. She could see his fingers turning white as he held onto the door. "Scared to touch you," he whispered. "I want to hold you, but I'm scared of hurting you."

Alex remembered the terror she'd felt in the Colonel's grip. Remembered how that grip had hurt, how he had wanted to hurt her. She could feel—she could almost *smell* —the cruelty, the madness. Jacob would be incapable of that. She'd yearned for Jacob while being held by the Colonel. Yearned for him from the bottom of her heart.

She slipped her arms around his broad torso and hugged. Oh, God, he felt so *good*.

"You won't hurt me," she whispered back. "You can't. You love me."

Jacob stilled, that big body suddenly frozen. She wasn't offended by his silence. He was letting her words settle in him.

Jacob lifted his head, looked her in the eyes. His eyes were so fascinating. So dark that they looked black and yet there was always a light in them.

"I do," he said starkly. "I do love you. Haven't said the words yet."

She reached her hand up to cup his cheek, the one with the scars. "You didn't need to."

"Yes, I did. Because I've never said them to anyone, in

my life." Jacob huffed out a breath, nudged her with his shoulder. "You haven't said the words yet, either."

"Don't need to," she answered.

His eyes lit up. "Yes, you do. You definitely need to say the words. I want to hear them."

He wanted this, wanted it badly. She could feel it in his body, see it on his face. It occurred to her that perhaps no one had ever said *I love you* to him. Her parents had told her they loved her every day of her life. But who would have said that to Jacob? It was possible some woman might have said it, but somehow she doubted that. He didn't let anyone get close to him.

Except her.

He needed to hear those words from her. And she wanted to say them.

Alex straightened a little, looked him right in the eyes. Into his dark, shining eyes. This was important to him, and therefore important to her. "Jake Simpson, and Jacob Black, both of you. I love you."

His big body jolted, and he kissed her, hard, holding her head as he kissed her. Deeply, endlessly. She held onto his wrists because it was as if a great wind had picked them up and tossed them. She lost the ground under her feet and realized only a few seconds later that Jacob had picked her up and laid her on the ground, hands feverishly working.

He continued kissing her as he stripped her. Tracksuit jacket unzipped and off with a swipe of his hands. Her bra off. Did she hear a ripping sound? *La Perla* she thought to herself with a sigh and then thought nothing at all, as she was drowning in sensations.

He somehow lifted her slightly and pulled her pants and panties down and off. She had no idea how he did it, but he also took her boots and socks off. How did he do that? Like magic. Was it all that training with guns? Made him incredibly dexterous? How did he do it so fast? At the same time, somehow, he stripped himself. Some deft movements she didn't see and there he was, naked. Wiry chest hairs tickled her breasts and that same sense of holding something incredibly powerful in her arms.

They'd almost died. Had things gone slightly differently, they'd both be dead or dying horribly. But they weren't dead. They were alive, oh so alive. Life pulsed in her veins, she could feel it. Feel the blood pumping, the breath in her lungs, her skin hot where he touched it. They weren't cold and inert but filled with life and they had the rest of their lives to look forward to.

"Can't wait," he muttered. She barely heard, was about to ask him *what did you say?* when his knees pushed her legs apart and he thrust into her. Hard, so very hard. If she hadn't been ready, it would have hurt. But it didn't hurt, not at all, she welcomed him with every cell of her being, legs open, sex warm and already wet, arms tight around his chest, her entire body telling him that she was his, and he was hers.

He wasn't careful with her. This was a celebration of life and it was with their entire beings that they made love. It was hard and fast. Jacob pounded into her and she held him tightly, his body completely a part of hers, as it should be. He was part of her now.

It was too furious to last. One last powerful thrust and she came, clenching around him as he held himself inside her, pumping his seed into her. When it ended, she was slippery with his sweat and hers. Her legs and arms fell from him and she tried to breathe even though he was sprawled on her, heavy as a horse.

They lay on the floor, gasping and wheezing.

Jacob slowly pulled out of her, his penis touching super sensitive skin. Her breath came out on a huff.

"Yeah," he whispered, bringing his forehead against hers. He turned over so that she wasn't with her back against the floor. She could feel the rumble of the engines against her back, but when Jacob rolled, she was plastered against him, and could only feel the beat of his heart.

Out the small oval window it was night. They were above the clouds, the stars shining brightly, cold diamonds in the sky.

Jacob ran his hand up and down her back and she shivered. Oh God, was this in her future? Her shivering every time he touched her bare skin? It wasn't a bad future but how was she expected to get anything done if she dissolved at his touch?

Still, as a problem, it wasn't a bad one to have. Better than a madman holding a gun to her head, together with a vial of bioengineered variola.

Jacob kissed her forehead, her cheek, her neck. His

mouth found that erogenous zone on her neck and he nipped her. She shivered. Just like Pavlov's dogs.

"Did you know that pilots are like ships' captains?"

Alex barely understood the words. Pilots like captains? What did that mean? And what did she care?

"Mmm," she answered.

He shook her gently. "No, don't zone out on me, honey. Listen."

Well, listening to him talking about captains and pilots was hard when her body was still humming with pleasure. But she made an effort.

"Okay."

"Do you know what a ship's captain is empowered to do?"

"Sail? Or whatever the term is."

"Besides that."

Alex tried to pull a clever answer out of her head, but she couldn't. The riddle was too hard.

"Ok. I give up. What can a ship's captain do?"

"He can marry people. And so can a pilot."

Everything in her stilled, shocked.

He lifted her torso up a little so he could look her in the eyes. He was both smiling and deadly serious.

He slipped a Coke can tab on her left ring finger.

"Marry me, Alex. Make an honest man out of me. Right here and right now."

"There she is!"

Jacob whipped around and, yes, there she was! Descending the massive circular staircase in the three-story atrium of headquarters. The architects had somehow made the stairs almost invisible, so it looked like she was wafting down from heaven.

She sure looked like an angel, with a column of ivory satin, and a lace veil. Jacob hadn't seen the dress, and he was glad because it was a blow to the heart. In a good way. Like a vision coming down the staircase, towards him.

His wife.

The ceremony in the plane was legal. They'd been married for a year and he'd replaced the Coke tab with a massive solitaire, which she had to take off and wear on a chain around her neck when she was in the lab.

Whoever said marriage was work wasn't married to Alex. She was easy going and affectionate and made each day a delight. He was now used to the sensation of being happy and it astounded him. Astounded his colleagues too.

He'd wanted a big blowout wedding as soon as they came back but she was giving birth to her company, Shield, that she founded with Darby and May. Jacob gave her his financial genius, Nicole, who ran the business side superbly well. It turned a profit almost immediately and the profits just went up and up and up. Emma Holland of ASI, who understood money, insisted on being a part of it, too, and had a 10% share, which was making her rich.

Alex and her partners were already rich, the company made ten million dollars in the first quarter. They could have increased that amount if they cut corners in production but they all adamantly refused. Every suit that was sold was absolutely perfect and safe.

Shield was her baby. She threw herself heart and soul into its creation and it was growing, healthy and strong. She also taught twice a week at the University of California San Diego. Alex was happy and busy and brushed him off each time he mentioned a wedding date.

Finally, Jacob put his foot down. He wanted that ceremony. Wanted everyone to *see* them get married. In the end, Alex agreed simply to stop him whining about it.

But she was happy too. It was on her face. She was radiant. Her eyes locked with his as she descended the monumental staircase.

The huge atrium was filled with flowers and behind the staircase an elaborate banquet was waiting.

At the bottom of the staircase was a flower strewn

podium he had had built. Standing to the side, he had his two groomsmen, Nick and Dylan. Alex had the Queens of IT and her two partners, dressed in light-blue silk dresses. They were all beautiful women, but they couldn't hold a candle to Alex, whose shining beauty nearly burned his eyes.

And here she was. His wife. Walking toward him. They had decided to forego an officiant. They were going to speak their vows, she was going to toss her bouquet and then they were all going to party all night.

But first, the vows, in front of everybody. Jacob had spent a sweaty week writing his, two pages long. It had been like being strangled by barbed wire, but in the end, he'd sort of managed to express a little of what Alex meant to him.

The world.

Words didn't come easily to him, but he'd finally managed. The crumpled pages were in his pocket and felt like a ballast of a million pounds.

Here she was. His incredible wife, standing right in front of him, smiling at him. She waited, the two hundred guests waited, as he pulled out the sweaty, crumpled pages from his pocket.

Sudden silence in the huge hall. Not a sound. Two hundred sets of eyes turned their way. His hand shook.

He took a deep breath. Another.

"Alexandra," he said, his voice suddenly hoarse. "I've loved you all my life, and I will love you till the day I die."

And he stopped.

He had other words, excellent words, even poetic words, but they wouldn't come out because his throat simply seized up. He could barely breathe, let alone speak around the boulder that had suddenly lodged in his chest.

Everyone waited for him to continue but he simply couldn't. He stood there like a moron, the words locked in his quivering throat. Looking down at the piece of paper in his hand, the squiggles meant nothing. Could have been alien script.

Alex leaned forward, kissed him on the cheek, whispered in his ear, "It's all right, darling."

Then she said her vows, her voice ringing in the huge space. "Jacob. You are the best, most honorable man I've ever known. I've known you since you were a boy and know you inside out. Every day I spend with you is a joy. You are my rock, even when life gets hard, and I know that every day of my life you will be with me, by my side. Our spirits are intertwined, and even when we are apart, I can feel you in my heart. I love you. You have made me the happiest woman in the world."

She leaned forward again and whispered in his ear, "Plus you are super hot."

They turned and stood, facing their guests, and the cheers and shouts filled the atrium, together with whistles and applause. The glass walls were bulletproof, otherwise the noise was so strong it might have shattered them.

Alex looked serene and happy and that weird moment, that block, had passed. Jacob's spirit soared and he looked out over his friends and colleagues, his wife by his side, where she would remain as long as they lived.

Then Alex moved to the front of the podium, preparing to toss her bouquet to the crowd of excited women below.

Suddenly, she turned, marched to Nikolai and thrust the bouquet into his astonished face. He nearly let it drop, standing there holding the frilly bouquet, trailing what Jacob had learned yesterday was called 'baby's breath'.

"You're next," she said.

Women of Midnight

Midnight Kiss

Midnight Embrace

Midnight Caress

Her Billionaire Series

Charade

Masquerade

Escapade

Dangerous Passions

Reckless Night

Hot Secrets

Dangerous

Dangerous Lover

Dangerous Secret

Dangerous Passion

Small Town Romance

Don't Think Twice

Woman on the Run

Fatal Heat

A Fine Specimen

Runaway

Lisa Marie Rice is eternally 30 years old and will never age. She is tall and willowy and beautiful. Men drop at her feet like ripe pears. She has won every major book prize in the world. She is a black belt with advanced degrees in archaeology, nuclear physics, and Tibetan literature. She is a concert pianist. Did I mention her Nobel Prize?

Of course, Lisa Marie Rice is a virtual woman and exists only at the keyboard when writing romantic suspense. She disappears when the monitor winks off.